Uncommon Places

W. H. Pugmire and S. T. Joshi at the Lovecraft Memorial
Plaque, 22 Prospect Street, Providence, Rhode Island

W. H. Pugmire

Uncommon Places

a collection of exquisites

Hippocampus Press

New York

Cover art and interior illustrations by Gwabryel.
Photo of W. H. Pugmire and S. T. Joshi © 2007
by Greg Lowney.
Cover design by Barbara Briggs Silbert.
Hippocampus Press logo designed by Anastasia Damianakos.

First Edition
1 3 5 7 9 8 6 4 2
ISBN 978-1-61498-023-0

This book is dedicated to my buddy, DERRICK HUSSEY.

.

Contents

An Identity in Dream

I wandered a ruined city that had been under the sea. My sense of gravity was timid, and I walked charily lest I awaken the attention of the star-strown abyss above me. I did not like the red ignition of those dead points of light, which I could feel so weirdly on those spools, my eyes. And so I stumbled up the sand-heaped streets until I came to the Museum of Forgotten Things, the queer underground place of which I had dreamt in my awakened state. I stepped down the crude rough-hewn flight to the obscure level and saw the door ajar. Squeezing through the narrow aperture, I entered into the chamber that was pregnant with an iconography of nightmare, in which I felt at home. I waltzed past the shapes furtively whispered of in cycles of subterranean legend, daemons pent in lore of lunacy by diseased visionaries. Ah, the poignant terror conjured by the suggestive silhouettes that bent to me as if in supplication! "Remember us," they seemed to whisper, "and speak our names." I was tempted to open my mouth in that vaulted museum chamber, yet some aspect of the hungry shadow surrounding me kept my lips from parting.

I came to a wall and its antediluvian ten-panelled door, which proved unlocked. It would not open smoothly, and I sensed that there was something weighty behind it that moved sluggishly as I pushed the worm-eaten wood. I entered what looked to be a workroom, a place of tools and tables. The place was lit by the red illumination that oozed through the dusty window-slits that had been hewn into the ancient brick wall. This crimson light fell onto the heap of disjointed things that had been behind the door and slithered across the floor at my forceful entry, leaving as trail a dark thick stain. I supposed that the mound was damaged and discarded limbs of wax, for they were certainly incomplete. What strange appetite they aroused. How evocative was the stench that emanated from them.

I moved past the tables and their tools, to the circular brick curb of a well set in the stony floor. Bending to that well, I placed my appendages on its cool brick and bent over the circular rim, so as to peer into a pool of liquid shadow, wherein was revealed the ultimate horror in the museum. I did not understand the dark form revealed within that well, the formless face with its eyes that were like unto the crimson stars of some haunted heaven. I was confused by that void, its mouth, the lips of which parted so that a sound rose as bubbles that broke and spoke my name. It was the sound of that name that reawakened memory. Smiling, I dove into the well, sank beneath the swirling surface of the liquid void, and fell homeward.

Artifice

I breathe into the artificial air, where pseudo-stars blink at me from above, their false light trapped into these spools, my eyes. Within my eyes I hold a fractured world, where toys of blood and bone engage in play. I see it all within these spools, my eyes, and breathe into the artificial air. My breath, escaping, makes a little sound that eddies in the manufactured sky in which I watch the frolic of false stars that catch the lifeless light of one dead moon. That lunar husk—so gross and gray and grim—engages the mechanics of my eyes, these viscid spools that blink into false light, the dimming light of imitation stars.

I weave my paper hands into thin air and aid degeneration in its task as quality is quashed and Time is mocked within a realm where progress is denied. The pseudo-stars die in the sickly sky. The ruined moon eclipses into dust. The toys of blood and bone, extinguished gargoyles, lie forgotten on the frozen ground. I linger for one moment in this place and smile upon the product of my play, this stratagem with which I've worked my task, my gimmick of destruction absolute. Content, I shut these spools that are my eyes and breathe into the artificial air as dust and darkness cloak my paper hands.

Cesare

You are lithe and sheathed in shadow. You come to me like some thing from a diabolic ballet, full of grace and danger. How deftly you reach into my dreaming and yank, and how swiftly I am tugged from that somnial plane to your rude wakefulness. Those twigs, your fingers, twine into my hair as you pull me to your silhouette on my floor. I crash onto the cold dark place and am dragged through violent obscurity. I cannot see you except as some lean threat, a thing that taints the aura of whatever you pass through so that everything slants toward you—houses, trees, the sky. My febrile eyes penetrate that welkin, my nails sink into it, so that I rip my name into its texture, crookedly. My white gown flows, more sentient than you, thing of pantomime. My white teeth gleam against those pits, your eyes. What is this thing that spills onto my teeth from your black orbs? Tears? Memory? Oh, I'll share with you my mortal moan, because your white white face is dry. My name is lonely, ripped in skyey solitude. And thus my nails find that pale palette, your visage, and there I rip your name, that name I will not utter. I watch your red name trickle down your puppet countenance, as you carry me over streets of mortal debris. We move, together, out of frame.

The Host of Haunted Air

Empty your heart of its mortal dream.
The winds awaken . . .
        —*William Butler Yeats*

I.

I sat at my shop counter, inhaling the heady scent of olden books, my thoughts drifting and transforming into nebulous dream, when the bell sounded at the door. Chilly evening wind moved the brittle pages of the book that lay before me. A figure entered and quietly shut the door. I took in the male attire, clothes that hung askew on so lithe a feminine frame. I smiled at the green carnation in its buttonhole, at the tall black hat that was shiny with age. Beneath the hat's rim dark eyes peered from a wan and worried face.

"Have you see Jonathan since his return from Thailand?"

"No," I answered, closing the book before me. "I've been rather preoccupied with a new shipment. But I expect to see him at your Black and Red party, which is . . ."

"Three weeks away." She sighed and leaned against a tall and sturdy shelf, looked at her black silk gloves as if she couldn't decide whether to remove them or not. Again, the deep sigh. "Perhaps I'm being foolish." The pause was pregnant with implication.

"Do tell me everything," I coaxed.

"That's just it. I don't know what's up with him. He's been distant, mentally preoccupied. Usually when he comes home from some far-off place he's excited to tell me of his adventures. Now all he does is sit in his pagoda and whistle to himself."

"Hmm. You don't think he's heading for another breakdown or any such thing?"

"I don't know, that seems unlikely. There's something secretive about the way he's acting. That's what really bugs me, I hate being left out. Jonathan's been my intimate companion since father's death, you know. We have a bond. In the past, when something's troubled him, he would always confide in me. I've tried bullying him, you know how he enjoys a bit of brutality; but when I castigate and question he just dismisses me as though I were a clueless child. It's pissing me off. I know he likes his little secrets, his naughty little pleasures or whatever."

"Perhaps he's caught the clap. There is, so I believe, an internationally famous bordello in Bangkok. Or is it Saigon?"

"A case of the clap wouldn't induce him to spend the night in his stupid so-called pagoda." Inquisitively, I arched a brow. "Yeah, I got up to go pee at three in the morning and saw him from my window. He was sitting in the cold wind and rocking back and forth. When I called to him he totally ignored me. Fucking weird."

"Indeed, most curious. And what is it you want from me?"

"Talk to him."

14

"Well, of course . . ."

"Tonight."

"But, my dear!" Helplessly, I held up my hands in a gesture to indicate how frightfully busy I was, as I sat there doing nothing.

"Please, Henry. There's no one else. He listens to you."

"But, my dear, *listen* to that brutal wind. Surely this can wait." But I saw from her expression that it could not. With melodramatic sigh I heaved off my stool, wrapped myself in heavy coat, and escorted her to her car. The house in which they lived, in a well-to-do lakeside residence, was almost a mansion. This had always been their home. After the death of their father, the two siblings had made few changes inside the house, comfortable with the furnishings they had known since childhood. Their personal lives, however, altered absolutely. Alisha often held gala gatherings for her enclave of bohemian mutants. Jonathan began his series of journeys across the globe, often sending me fabulous old books from far-off lands.

I watched the nighted lake as we drove along the boulevard, until as last we came to the graveled driveway that took us to a high metal fence. Alisha pressed a gizmo and the gate began to move. Their property was so densely populated with towering firs and evergreens that it always had an air of seclusion, despite the constant traffic on the nearby lakeside road. The trees grew so close together that even on the brightest days the house stood in lush shadow.

The gate closed behind us as she stopped the car. "He's in his pagoda," she said, as if dismissing both her brother and myself. Haughtily, I stepped out of the car and slammed its door behind me. The wind was chill, and so I pulled my coat's collar tightly around my neck. A line of swaying Japanese lanterns dimly lit the stone path that led across the lawn to the structure that Jonathan called his pagoda, although it but faintly resembled anything found in the Far East. It was like an open garden pavilion with roofing in Oriental fashion. Inside could be found a gigantic Buddhist bell, a fake waterfall, and an amazing assortment of wind chimes. The young man sat on a mat, his legs crossed in what I took to be one of his yoga positions. It made my old knees ache to look at him. His long brown hair was tied in a ponytail. He wore sandals, khaki cut-offs, and some kind of fleece vest. With eyes closed he could not see me as I examined his handsome profile, the lean face with prominent cheekbones and goatee. Even in the dim lighting from the single lantern beneath which he sat I could tell that he was darkly tanned, perhaps from his time in Thailand, to which he had journeyed with some Hindu theist. He looked so remarkably composed that I began to question his sister's histrionics.

Chill evening wind died a little; the music of the wind chimes softened. "Henry." I crinkled my brow in confusion. He had not moved, nor had his eyes opened. How then . . . ? "I can smell you on the wind. You reek of dust and old books. I suppose that Ally has asked you to talk to me."

I spoke as I strolled to him. "Yes, but also to ask my aesthetic advice regarding décor for the upcoming festivities. But she does seem just a tad bit worried. Are you behaving beastly? In one of your tiresome moods?"

"No. I've merely been preoccupied. She simply wants something to fret about, you know how she is. She wants this party to be a fabulous success."

16

"Ah, that might be it. And you're being childish because she is so focused on her party that she is ignoring you. You're both such spoiled children, clamoring for center stage."

"You're stupid if that's what you think."

"Pardon my benightedness," came my bitchy reply. The wind buffeted us once more, and at the sound of clanging I looked at the swaying chimes and saw the new addition. But exactly what it was I could not ascertain. At first I thought it some freakish papier-mâché head, but as I drew nearer it looked more like a metal object encrusted with blue dusting of granulated steel. It had a kind of face; where the mouth would have been it wore an oval aperture the size of a small egg. Two lesser holes suggested nostrils. Where a face would have had eyes were two shallow indentations, but these were solid, sans orifices. Above these, on what might have been a forehead, was a grouping of tiny pea-sized holes that numbered seven.

"Mmm, something new."

"Oh. Yes." I sensed a change in his demeanor, a sudden frigidity. Turning, I peered at him and saw his face filled with wonder, and in the eyes a tinge of terror. He moved his eyes from the thing of metal and noticed my expression. Hurriedly, a torrent of language spilled from his babbling mouth. "I found it in Bangkok, in a curious little shop. There was a main room filled with the most god-awful American junk. But I found this little alcove near the back, dimly lit and cluttered, just the kind of place where I find those old books that so delight you. And there it was, sitting among a disarray of jumble. I thought it was some kind of weird wind chime, so of course I bought it."

17

"It looks rather unearthly."

How nervously he cackled. "Indeed."

I touched a hand to its rough surface. How frightfully cold it was. With what an unnatural—nay—a *disquieting* texture it had been composed. Frowning, I took my hand away. My fingers almost burned with chilliness; and with something else, some kind of nasty residue that adhered to my numbing flesh. Disgusted, I rubbed my fingers on my trousers. A noise caught my attention. I leaned closer to— the thing—and fancied that I could hear wind moving through it. Stepping around so as to examine the back of it, I was startled to see a solid surface with no opening of any kind. But surely it was the mitigating wind that moaned through it, its sound somehow distorted as it sailed through the thing's apertures.

I looked at the length of chain from which it hung, from a small yet sturdy hook that had been soldered to its top. Moving, I faced its front. Had the night grown nippier, or was it creepiness that tickled my flesh? I sensed the night wind fade away. The chimes around us stopped their insistent movement. All was dead quiet, except for the faint suggestion of sound that issued from the thing before me—and Jonathan's faint whistling. I looked at him, with his wide eyes oddly glazed and his moving mouth askew. The mingling of sounds seemed seductive, so beguiling that I leaned closer to the egg-shaped opening so as to hear the better. Yes, I yearned to listen, to press against the coarse uncanny surface and listen to the air that moved within. Perhaps if I were to press my lips together I too could whistle in imitation of its eerie sound. Perhaps if I touched my mouth to the small opening . . .

A hand tightened at my shoulder and pulled me away. I shouted in protest, and then saw Jonathan's panicky eyes peering into my own. Something in their troubled expression filled me with fear, and together we fled the haunted place.

II.

I fidgeted in a chair before a fire. Jonathan had taken me to the expansive library room, and after having prepared coffee for me had fixed himself a large martini. I held the cup of scalding liquid tightly in my hand, grateful for its warmth. Now and then I glanced into the fireplace; but I quickly looked away, troubled at the things I saw, or thought I saw, within the flames.

"Now, Jonathan, explain to me, please, that which has just occurred."

"What?"

"No, do not suddenly play ignorant. You will explain to me this—thing—in your pagoda and its unnatural affect. What it is?"

He paced the floor, refusing to sit; nor would he look at me. "It's what I told you it is." He saw that I was growing agitated and angry. "It's obviously some weird kind of wind device."

"It's 'obviously' like nothing we've either of us seen before."

Sighing in frustration, he finally sat. "Okay. Yes, it's unusual, and has its eerie effect." I snorted. "I can't explain it. But, Henry, we are susceptible to such effects because of our senses. Sounds, music, can either soothe or disturb us. Look at what happened when Stravinsky premiered *Le Sacre du Printemps*. People went mad, the performance ended in riot.

19

Or take thunderstorms, of which you are so partial. Some people run and hide, while you rush to the nearest window. We are creatures of our senses, rational or not."

I pouted. "You are trying to placate me with calm tone and soothing language. Yet not twenty minutes ago you *hurled* me from that place with terror flashing in your troubled eyes."

"I thought you were going to kiss the damn thing! You had the oddest expression on your face. Of course I dragged you away, I haven't cleaned it yet. God knows where it's been or by what it has been pawed."

"I am not placated."

"Then fuck you. " Jonathan rose and fixed himself another drink. My pouting deepened when I saw that he would offer me no refill of the bad coffee. Muttering obscenities of my own, I placed the cup on a nearby table. "Look," he continued, "I agree that the thing is kind of creepy—stop snorting! The thing is, I like it, whatever the hell it is, and that's the beginning and end of it. Tut all you like. I found it, I liked it, I bought it." He glared at me with defiant eyes.

"Very well. I wish to speak with Alisha."

"She'll be asleep. It's late. You're tired yourself." I wanted to protest, but my yawns spoke otherwise. "Come on, I'll drive you home. Just let me change into some trousers."

"I'll meet you out at the car," I told him, yawning again. Wearily, I rose and went outside, into wind and darkness. I felt distraught, emotionally drained. I did not understand the events that had just passed, but was suddenly too tired to care. Turning my eyes to the wretched pagoda, I saw its single lantern move in wind. I saw the shadows that swayed on the figure that stood beneath it, facing—the thing. Standing very close. I was momentarily distracted when Jonathan came out of the house, slamming the door behind him. The echo of sound reverberated in the aether. When again I looked to the pagoda, it was vacant of human occupant.

III.

Days passed. I had received a wee note from Alisha, apologizing for the 'nonsense' of the previous evening and formally inviting me to her ball. I decided to go as the Red Death. An obvious choice, perhaps. My other idea was Little Red Riding Hood, but there are limits even to my perversity. A flowing crimson robe would conceal my girth and look superb. As time passed, I oft reflected on that strange evening. I dwelt on that thing of encrusted blue metal and saw it in deepest dreaming. Betimes I caught myself listening attentively to the wind, fancying that it hummed a variation of the weird tune that Jonathan had whistled when I had been captivated by—the thing. I knew not what else to call it, and so it was—the thing. Yet the more I pondered on it, the more mysterious a thing it seemed, something alien and bad. Yet beguiling. I burned to look at it once more, to touch it—perhaps to kiss it.

At last the festive night arrived. I taxied to the mansion and was let in through the gate by an awaiting knight. I wandered below high swaying trees, moved through oscillating shadow and playful wind. My eyes followed the line of Japanese lanterns to the pagoda, and I hesitantly stepped toward the structure. Its hanging chimes danced in the air. The sphere of blue metal was nowhere to be seen.

"Henry." Jonathan stood a few yards away, holding to me his long pale hands. I walked to him, took his hand, allowed myself to be escorted into the house.

"Your strange new thing . . ."

"Missing," he said, shrugging. That was all; he offered no explanation or conjecture. I felt a peculiar sadness, and a kind of panic that I did my best to conceal. We stood in the hallway, examining each other. He looked resplendent in black tux and cloak. The only red was in the contact lenses placed over his eyes. He grinned at my ghoulish makeup, showing two sharp fangs. Together, we entered the ballroom.

And an alternative world, a diabolic one. The crowd was much as I had expected, beautiful boys in scarlet gowns, masculine women in coat and tails. Somber music was piped in the room from unseen speakers, and bowls of incense filled the place with fragrance. From one darkened corner I espied Alisha, who smiled and slightly bowed. She was magnificent and original as the Lamanite king, Amalickiah. My eyes feasted on her indigenous beauty as I stepped to her. With masculine courtesy she offered me her hand to kiss.

The room was like some fantastic phantasm. The walls had been elegantly covered with drapery of ebony and maroon velvet. Cushions of similar shade littered the floor, upon which groups of youngsters sexually explored each other. I watched as from one of these groupings a young figure arose. Despite the wild orange wig I recognized him as a lad who oft frequented my bookshop and who had a fascination for the yellow decadence of the late Victorian age. I was charmed to see him dressed after Beardsley's splendid work of ink and color wash, "The Slippers of Cinderella." He took from his apron one of the disintegrating roses that had been

22

pinned thereon, and this he offered me with benedictional bow. "To the Great Lord Thanatos, the only god before whom I grovel," he declaimed. I took his flower, cupped my hand below his chin, and pulled him to me. His breath reeked of champagne. Bending to him, I kissed him hard.

"Well," Jonathan muttered, "how swiftly you get into the swing of things. Come, I've a special concoction just for you." He led me to a serving station at which a manservant poured dark liquid from a sparkling silver coffee pot. I took the delicate cup proffered me and brought it to my nostrils, breathing in the brandy with which the coffee had been laced. Normally I had no stomach for liqueurs, but on this night I refused to be a prude. I sipped, and smooth delicious nectar spilled into my mouth, warming my face.

Time passed. After a number of coffees I fell upon a cushion and smiled idiotically at the surrounding sexual frolic. Finally, Alisha clapped her hands and the music ceased.

"Mesdames et Messieurs, the Dance of the Seven Veils."

True decadence crept into the room. What they were, I could not fathom. I had read somewhere of a race of cannibalistic semi-human dwarves who dwelt in some plateau somewhere in Central Asia. These creatures could have hailed from such a tribe. The twisted features of the hateful faces had a sobering effect. They profoundly repulsed. I watched as the ones who carried flute instruments sat in semicircle and placed their pipes to misshapen mouths. The room was filled with discordant piping. A diminutive figure wound in flowing veils danced into the room. Its gyrations moved in rhythm to the esoteric music, and one by one the veils gradually fell from its stunted torso. I saw the small dry breasts and the twin genitalia both male and female.

People began to hoot and applaud as Alisha slowly danced toward the nude monstrosity, holding a silver platter on upturned palms. A sheet of black silk covered the object that tilted on the platter. Ally knelt before the bestial gnome and I watched as the creature removed with knobby fingers the covering of silk. I had, of course, read Wilde's play, and thus I expected to see a grisly replica of the head of Iokanaan. Instead, I beheld a sphere of blue metal.

Shrieking pierced the room. Rushing wildly to his sister, Jonathan took the sphere, clutched it to his heaving breast and dashed madly from the place, into night. Trembling, I arose from my cushion. Figures surged around me, shouting cries of drunken confusion. Blindly, I ran from the scene, seeking silence and solitude. Instinct led me to the lonesome library, with its soothing and familiar world of books. Ah, the wondrous scent of ancient paper bound in leather. And there was the large leather sofa, where on more than one occasion I had slept when allowed to spend late nights poring over Jonathan's volumes. Moaning with aching pleasure, I staggered to the sofa and fell upon it. Happily, I succumbed to dreamless slumber.

A delicate hand smoothed my hair and pulled me out of sleep. Alisha sat beside me on the edge of the sofa. "What time is it?" I asked.

"Almost dawn. Everyone's gone."

Swiftly, I sat up. "Jonathan!" She shrugged. "What on earth do you mean by that absurd motion?"

"He's vanished." Her face was pale, but her eyes very dry.

"Then we must find him! He has—that thing!"

"It can wait. You need more rest." Her voice was soothing, calming, hypnotic. I tried to protest, but her hand—so smooth and white—pressed against my lips. "Hush." Groaning in suitable demurral, I allowed myself to sink again into the depths of delicious somnolence. Alisha hummed a haunting melody, one that would have disturbed me were I not so fatigued.

When again I awakened, I was alone. I felt rested, yet worried. Something, some unwelcome sensation, had shaken me from slumber. And then I heard it, from outside, the sound of whistling. And my blood froze, for the dissonant din was identical to the horrid music that had been played by that gang of goblins on their evil flutes, played to the sphere of blue metal. I pushed out of the sofa, stumbled over my long scarlet robe and hurried to the library door. All was hushed. The dull light of early dawn was skulking through the high windows. Fearfully, I found my way outside. The air was cold and very still. I saw the figure who knelt within the pagoda. I went to her. How strangely she smiled as I approached. I wanted to speak to her, but some unspeakable horror kept me numb and silent. I bent my knees and joined her on the ground. Leaning toward me, she pressed her cool mouth to mine. She puckered and exhaled. Both she and Jonathan were skilled at whistling, with a tone that was sharp and forceful.

"Please," I begged her. "Stop."

She did not heed me, but rather gazed into the early light, her eyes suddenly rapt with wonder. The chimes above us began to sway. I turned. The thing stood just outside the pagoda. I took in the dark torn garments. It had lost its splendid cloak. The long dark hair was too caked with blood to stream in the growing gale; some of it was crudely wound around the metal hook that pushed out of the top of the human head. One crimson contact lens still covered a wide dead eyeball. The open mouth was imbued with gore, and from that orifice there came a low unearthly sound of moaning air. Here and there the flesh of the face was torn, showing the blue metal beneath the skin, the damnable blue metal that had somehow conjoined with once-living tissue.

Alisha's lips pressed against my ear. "It hungers for our hot mortal air." Like a thing possessed she rose. I was too deadened with terror to try and stop her as she walked to that which had once been her brother. My blood was icy sludge, my limbs heavy with immeasurable horror. I watched as the young woman pressed her mouth to the mutation's outrageous visage. How oddly her frail body jerked; what ghastly noise rattled from her pretty mouth. At last she fell before me. I wept to see that she was a lifeless shell, her once-lovely mouth bruised and blue.

The thing towered above me, not moving; yet somehow I felt it beckon me. I heard from beneath the dead face a noise of ravenous air, air not of this earth. Sobbing, I shut my eyes, trying to exorcise the nightmare before me. On my eyelids I could see the tendril shadows of swaying chimes, and my ears took in the music of wood on wood, metal on metal, glass on glass. Most horrible of all, I could feel the hunger of the thing that summoned.

I opened mine eyes. I stretched my sensitive limbs and rose. I lurched to that shell of dilapidated humanity that had once been my friend, but was now my awful, my inescapable doom.

Hempen Rope

I awakened in the alley with a rope around my neck. With blisters on my fingers. With nothing in my heart. I got to my knees, but no higher, for I did not want to breathe the upper air, in which I could see microscopic specks that caught moonlight, floating in assembly as if hunting for an orifice to fill. I kept to my knees and followed the length of rope, holding its filth in my dry rough hands, tightly, as one would hold a newly murdered pet. I dragged my knees along the alley, leaving a trail of blood and bits of skin. I loved the way the tiny pebbles caught into my liquid wounds and embedded themselves into my limbs; it made me feel inhuman, a thing composed of debris, once scattered, now assembled. I smiled when I came upon a corpse that had an empty bottle in its hand, and it was pleasurable to have those scattered pills that might have fallen from her hand or mouth combine with the pebbles in my knees and dissolve within my blood. Ah, the particles that spilled into my veins and soothed my throbbing skull.

I crept into a place of obscurity, unlit, and thus I felt it safe to try and stand. I rose, and staggered, and danced with the rope around my neck, a somber waltz. I pulled myself along its unending length, beside the black walls, until my rope led me down a flight of stairs and through an arched threshold, into a theatre. I smiled as I faltered down the sloping aisle, past the seats, each one of which was filled. Ah, sweet stench of extinction! They leaned or were bent over, each one a suicide. I saw the boy who had swallowed poison, the poet who had planted a dagger in his neck, the ancient man whose wrists were open like crimson petals. I saw the girl who had dined on a shattered stained glass window, such a pretty death. When the rows came to an end, I approached the steps that took me up onto the dark stage, where lengths of rope hanged from the rafters. They swayed above me, my kindred, with ropes around their necks. Oh, how beautifully their naked knees glistened in soft stage light. Now and then a flake of shredded flesh broke free and drifted toward the stage, like snow. Once I was able to catch one on my tongue, which moved the audience to applaud.

I released my rope and felt it tighten its hold and lift me high, into the place of pale light. I saw the particles that swam in that light, and so I kept my mouth clamped shut, but my smile was broad. I rose, high and higher, and joined my kindred in their danse.

Cathedral of Death

The cathedral stood on the spectral dome of a high hill, its silhouette against a violent sky. Its stone was wet from the storm that had but recently passed; now the edifice stood still and silent, a majestic thing in growing dusk. The wind moaned eerily within the mouths of leering gargoyles, those mouths from which spilled streams of rain water. A young man stood beneath one bleak beast of stone and lifted his face to falling liquid. Baptized, he approached the rough-hewn steps that led into the ancient edifice, the heavy oaken doors of which were open. He paused before removing his muddy boots, for the floor before him looked severely chilly. Finally, he kicked off his footwear and stepped through the threshold, where strange aromas roamed among stranger shadows. Dark things seemed to frolic just askance of eye-sight, but when he moved his head to observe these things he saw nothing.

Low twilight washed high windows of stained glass. He looked about serenely at the pews with their occupants of rags and dust and bones, Death's obscure congregation. Some were amazingly intact, while others had fallen as heaps of debris. Mostly they were the remains of adults, although here and there he could espy the petite frames of infant bone. Wandering down an aisle, he approached the Bishop's

throne and bowed his head as he lowered to his knees before the silent remnant wrapped in wormy robes. Shutting eyes, he prayed, as soft windsong sighed as eulogy at high windows. He prayed for quite a while, until moonlight swam to him through tints of stained glass. How tired he felt. His soul sat like some heavy thing inside his frame of flesh and bone, a soul that ached for final repose. Opening eyes, he beheld before him a thin moldy biscuit and a chalice of dark wine. The biscuit felt old and spongy as he placed it on his tongue; the liquid was sweet and thick, chilly as it spilled down his throat. He stared into the half-drained goblet and dimly saw the pale white things that writhed beneath the liquid. He drank again, until the cup was drained.

His eyes followed a stream of amber moonlight that led to a dusky corner, where soft light fell upon a figure encased inside an upright marble tomb. The curved blade of the figure's scythe gleamed in lunar light as he rose and approached this Lord of Death. He saw its pallid mask held before a countenance of chiseled bone, and he reached out as that mask slipped from a skeletal hand and floated to him. Tenderly, he ran his rough fingers over the rose-soft features that rippled at his touch. He saw the hollow sockets that seemed to burn with black fire and the lips that were moist and red. Some faint fragrance breathed to him from those lips. Bringing the mask to his visage, he kissed its mouth. The fleshy face wrapped around his own. He gasped just once as his life was sucked from him, and his death echoed within the edifice.

Above him, majestic in its marble tomb, the Reaper wore its eternal grin.

House of Legend

I stalk along the borderland of mortal knowledge and huddle in those spots of obscurity and lore. The wind sighs of fabled things spoken of by aborigines and dreamers. The hill looms before me, crowned with a peculiar ring of ancient stones that stand before the hoary house. I have trouble looking at that house, because of the way it tilts, as if ready to slip into another dimension. The legends of this house are many and immortal, predating the earliest days of settlement; for the house has always been here, according to native memory. The whispered legends concentrate on the seasonal cries and chants that come from some high place in the house when the sky is dark with clouds that ache to crawl to earth and usurp the neglected hill. I walk the hill with feet that sink into soft earth, earth that would hold and savor me. Coming to the house, I climb its steps to the dilapidated porch and turn to look down the hill to the straggling village around which it rose. How curious, that at distant windows I seem to see faces that watch me and hands that move as if to form strange signs. There is a sudden push of air that comes from some place above, a wind that smells diseased.

I turn and touch the panelled door, and push, and enter in. The habitation smells of mildew and murder, and I remember once again the insane legends concerning those who once dwelt here, shunned and secretive. As I walk up the carpeted stairway I glance at the vacant picture frames that line the rising wall, behind one of which that wall is stained suggestively. I wonder where the portraits had fled to, but I did not censure them their flight from the world of wakeful men, the dead world that I did not wish to claim. In an effort to escape I have come to this house on a hill above a forgotten village, where things had crawled and muttered and bent the air with chanting among the seven standing stones outside, where legend moans of the thing that screamed from an upper room. I approach an upper room and enter in and wonder at the framed upright mirror of crimson glass. I peer into its world of murder and smell destruction, a bouquet that I remember. I sit at the antique desk and open its side drawer, in which I find a diary, a book about 6 × 3 inches in size, with rough paper and an oddly durable binding of thin sheet metal. I open it as the wind outside becomes a tempest that sneaks through window crevices and shrieks within the room. The yellowed pages of the time-worn diary are scrawled over with my handwriting; they tell the tale of my apathy toward this neoteric era, of my dreams of playfully bringing about the extinction of mortal man. I read the journal's final paragraph as the house begins to tilt insanely in the storm.

"The shrieking surrounds me as from the crimson mirror I sense the several presences in the house, my kindred from drear dreaming, the ghosts who have called me here. The mirror's bloodstained light taints my blood with ancestry as the house leans toward the black hungry clouds that now surround it and the hill. I sense the spectres who kneel beside the seven standing stones outside and chant the name of elder deity, the thing beyond the rim that sucks this house and its occupant to its lunatic realm. I split my mouth with shrieking so as to accompany the storm as we fall, the house and I, into the void."

Inhabitants of Wraithwood

I.

I awakened to the raucous cry of crows and pushed my torso away from the tree beneath which I had fallen asleep. Where the hell was I? I remembered deciding not to return to the halfway house where I was completing my time for three counts of bank robbery, after doing two years in federal prison. I think the prison officials let me out early because they were impressed with my intellect and good manners. I had been the first inmate on record who had requested a one-volume Complete Works of Shakespeare. I ain't no intellectual, but I've been raised by a woman who taught literature and art in college. One of my fondest memories was of my seventh birthday, when Mom took me to a thrilling production of *Cymbeline*, a play with which I was familiar from bedtime readings of Shakespeare since infancy. When I listen to or read Shakespeare, I hear my mother's voice. Loving the plays is loving her.

Yes, I screwed up. After her early death, I didn't care about anything, fell in with "bad types" and learned to enjoy petty crime. Drug addiction heightened my criminal tendencies, and I got hooked on danger. Doing time was no hassle. I read a lot of good books and improved my education. But the goons and clueless "therapists" in the halfway house were too insulting to be endured, and so I didn't return one day from job hunting, robbed a store from which I stole a couple of bottles of choice whiskey, hijacked a weakling's car and drove until the petrol ran out. After that things get a bit blurry, thanks to the booze. I sort of remember hoofing it for quite a while, and then stopping to rest after climbing a hill and entering a woodland. I guess I passed out beneath the oak tree.

It must have been early dusk when at last I came to my senses. The sky still held a quality of violet, and a low orange moon hung like some gigantic disc in heaven. I've never liked the way the moon looks at me, and so I threw my empty bottle at it; and then I noticed the other glow, the moving lamplight that slowly approached and became a lantern held by Jesus. This Christ was a tall red-headed dude with dark, penetrating eyes, attired in what looked like a suit from the 1920s. He stopped a few feet from me, and the moon directly behind his head looked like some illuminated halo as one sees in the works of Cimabue or Giotto. Moaning, I made an effort to stand up, becoming aware of the dampness at my crotch and the stink of urine. I began to laugh. "Drink, sir, is a great provoker, of sleeping and piss," I told Jesus, paraphrasing the Immortal Bard.

"Are you in need of shelter?" asked my savior.

"Shelter would be cool, good fellow," says me, struggling to my feet and working diligently to steady my sense of balance. The gentleman turned and walked away. Guessing that I was meant to follow, I stumbled through the growing darkness, passing a large sunken pond as I moved beneath and out of the mass of oak trees. We crossed a wide dirt roadway and approached a two-story building situated on

37

the crest of a mammoth hill. Looking down the hill I saw a small town twinkling its lights as day expired. The building looked of the same era as the silent man's dress. Perhaps it had been some kind of hotel-cum-speakeasy in the Prohibition era. Why else would it be situated up here, so far from the rest of town?

Jesus led me into an anteroom that contained a couple of chairs and bureau on top of which were delicate bits of *objet d'art*. A stairway led to the second floor. We stepped through double doors into a charming sitting room filled with what looked like choice antiques. A brass chandelier softly illuminated the room, and one of the several small sofas looked especially inviting. I sat in it and sank into its comfortable depths. I saw that Jesus had abandoned me, and I assumed he had gone to fetch me a change of clothing. Leaning toward the low coffee table in front of the sofa, I grabbed hold of the large album of red leather that lay there, which turned out to be a heavy photo album.

My mother had taught art and literature to university brats, and so our home had been packed with quality books. I had delighted in poring over those picture books when I was a kid, long before the text explaining the artwork was of interest. Mom had always encouraged me to be imaginative, and many of our games together, after father had left us, consisted of trying our hand at copying great works of art, our tools being color crayons, watercolor, and children's modeling clay. (My Play-Doh Pietà had been a deliciously somber affair.) Because I am by nature lazy, I never advanced in art or literature, although I had a modicum of talent. I was a curious and tragic combination of intellect and debauchery, and my high priest was Oscar Wilde. I was equally comfortable in either a museum of classical art or in the lowest mire of Malebolge. Art was one of my sanest obsessions. And thus, when I opened this oversized leather binder and began to study the photographs within, I was instantly mesmerized.

I recognized the first photograph as a kind of take on Caspar David Friedrich's *Raven Tree;* but instead of an actual tree the main focus in the print was an outrageously lean old guy with long hair and beard, who had contorted himself to mimic the shape of Friedrich's tree. The sky above the fellow was crowded with crows, one of which had perched on his scrawny shoulder. The photo's sepia tone suggested that it was an extremely old print.

Turning the leaf, I saw that the next photo was a wicked parody of the *Mona Lisa.* The ancient woman pictured, old and haggard though she be, still contained a degree of facial beauty. She had been a seductress in her day. The diabolic smile unnerved me, as did the hand that clutched one wrist, digging a talon into thin flesh. A single drop of blood upon that talon was the photo's one touch of vivid color.

The next photo was Jesus, posing with his lantern and attired with a gown of what looked like silken gold. Over the gown he wore an embroidered cloak, and a curious crown of metallic thorns adorned his dome. He was standing within the grove of oaks, knocking upon one tree. Unlike the two previous images, this one was new and full of color.

Ah, how I sighed when I turned the leaf and beheld the next image, for it copied my favorite painting, Fuseli's *The Nightmare,* and this photographic representation was superb. Where they had found a creature who so resembled Fuseli's incubus was beyond conjecture. There were, however, unnerving anomalies. The gremlin in the photograph was tragically incomplete, missing both legs and all its fingers. One stunted paw leaned against the thing's chin, near its mouth, and one could not escape the suggestion that the beast had been supping on its corporeal tissue.

The woman on whom the daemon squatted was dressed in white, as in the original painting, but her hair was dark and fell in such a way as to conceal most of her face. Unlike the original, her mouth did not frown. Above the woman and her incubus, to the viewer's left, an equine skull peeked through an opening in the curtain behind the bed.

I shifted in my seat, and the smell of my soiled pants drifted to me. Feeling restless, I shut the album and got up to investigate the room. Upon one wall was a large painting of an oak grove at nighttime. Arching over the trees was what looked like a pale lunar rainbow, and I seemed to remember some such effect in a painting by Friedrich. It certainly produced an eerie effect. Dim winged specks, which I took to be night birds, spotted the darkened dimension.

Sensing company, I turned to face the beings who were watching me. The woman, tall and slender, was dressed in a long black gown of antique silk, its tight brocade collar decorated with raised patterns in gold and silver. Gloves of black lace covered dainty hands, and a veil concealed the details of an emaciated face. I could just make out the pale and colorless eyes that observed me. She stood behind a ramshackle wheelchair that was occupied by the incubus from the photograph I had earlier been admiring. I stared at that impish visage with its sickly hue, at the yellow eyes and bulbous nose, at the blue veins that lined the grotesque face.

"Welcome to Wraithwood," the gnome sighed, in a high

childlike voice. "Philippe has gone to find you clothing. You could benefit from a bath. Pera has a wee bathroom adjoining her room. Follow her, please."

"Thank you, uh . . ." I hesitated, not knowing how to address him, not wanting to shake the malformed hand. When I studied the right hand, I saw that it differed from the photograph, having two stunted fingers where in the photograph there were none.

"Eblis Mauran," he offered, bowing his head.

"Hank Foster," I said, smiling. The silent woman held a hand to me, then turned to a door near a corner. I followed her into a hallway and through another door that entered on a spacious boudoir. Undoing my shirt buttons, I watched as she went into a small bathroom and began to run a bath, sprinkling various salts from antique jars into the running water. I thanked her, but she said nothing as she ushered me into the bathroom and shut the door. I tested the water for heat, then undressed and stepped into the tub. The effect was instantaneous. My groans of pleasure rose with the steam as sore limbs and soiled flesh relaxed. I barely noticed when Jesus quietly entered with an armful of clean clothing, which he placed atop the closed toilet seat. I momentarily froze as he bent and placed a hand into the water, joined to it his other hand, then brought the hands above my head and let the cupped water drop over my hair. Smiling, he turned off the running water, rose, and vacated the room.

Okay, I thought as I scrubbed myself, I've entered into a house full of loonies and queers. Pulling the plug, I listened as the water drained, then stepped out of the tub and reached for a nearby towel. Examining the clothes, I saw that they were from an earlier decade; but they fit well

41

enough, and I rather liked the way I looked in the full-length mirror, nothing like the alcoholic drug addict I had become since Mother's death.

I opened the door and entered Pera's dusky room. The place was semi-lit by various wall fixtures that resembled candles in holders, each candle topped by an electric flame. The furnishings were all dark, with long blue-purple drapery at the windows. A black bedspread covered the commodious bed. The young woman rested upon the bed, very still, resembling a lifeless husk on its deathbed. Her frail arms clutched a length of sturdy rope. I stepped to the bed and knelt next to it, as if I were preparing to pray for the soul of a departed loved one. I touched the rope, and her head moved so that the pale eyes behind the veil gazed into my own.

She then began to sing; and as I watched the vague impression of her mouth behind its curtain of lace, I felt a chill. The song was from my mother's favorite play.

> "He is dead and gone, lady,
> He is dead and gone;
> At his head a grass-green turf,
> At his heels a stone."

I was uncertain of what line actually followed, and thus I recited the line I knew. "How do you, pretty lady?"

Pera smiled and blew at the veil, and some of her soft sweet air lightly touched my face. Then she turned away from me and stared at the ceiling. I moved my vision to the painting on the wall above the bed. It, too, had been one of Mother's favorite works of art, John Everett Millais's *Ophelia*. This somewhat explained the strange girl's song.

42

Looking at her again, I saw that her eyes were closed. Mutely, I vacated the room.

I was uncertain what way led to the main room, for there were doors on either end of the hallway. But then the sound of someone playing music in the room next to Pera's caught my attention. Through the partially parted doorway came a smell of incense. Gingerly, I pushed at the door with the toe of my shoe. A small man sat on the floor, playing a kind of Egyptian music on a short-necked lute. I laughed silently, for the tiny guy closely resembled the Hungarian film actor Peter Lorre. The piece he played was simple yet expressive, and to its cadence danced the creature named Eblis. Dance, of course, is a generous verb, given that the fellow had no legs. And yet he was not clumsy as he stood upon his stumps and moved with a kind of nimbleness, now and then smacking together the palms of his fragmentary hands. The dancer noticed me and wickedly smirked, his ochrous eyes twinkling.

The music ceased, and Eblis moved to his wheelchair as swiftly as a scuttling insect. The other fellow observed me from his position on the floor. "Ah, the new guest."

"Yes," I answered, and then quickly corrected myself. "No, actually. I've had some trouble with my car a ways back. One of your compatriots found me sleeping in that grove of oaks and brought me here to clean up. So, what is this place, a hotel or something?"

"Or something. Just a collection of lost souls, you might say, gathered accidentally—fatefully." He shrugged and laughed. "So, the old crone hasn't had you sign yet?"

"Sorry?" He shrugged again and got to his feet, throwing his instrument onto the narrow bed. Seeing the painting above that bed I went to it and touched a finger to its surface. It was a painting rather than a print, although it had not been varnished. The image seemed familiar, but I couldn't place it. What interested me was that the sitter was almost a dead ringer for the small man who now sat upon the bed. "Wow, this could be you."

"Eventually it will be. I've already lost three inches of height." I gave him a troubled look, which moved him to more laughter.

"I've seen it somewhere before, but I can't remember the artist."

"Kokoschka. This is his portrait of a tubercular Count he met in, I believe, Switzerland. Once my face began to thin I took to parting my hair in the middle. My hands aren't quite as bad as his—yet."

What the fuck was he talking about? Yes, I had certainly stumbled onto a clutch of crazies. "The resemblance is quite uncanny," I continued.

"That's the very word. Come on," he said, standing and touching my arm. "We'll return you to the convening room."

I tried to smile as he loped to the wheelchair and guided it through the doorway. The door to Pera's room was partially open, as I had left it, and I caught a glimpse of her sleeping on the bed, the length of rope in her embrace. When I followed my new acquaintance into the drawing room, I found another person awaiting our arrival. She turned and smiled at me, and I saw that it was the woman in the *Mona Lisa* photo. Although ancient and vaguely sinister, yet was she anomalously lovely. Her streaked hair was long and smooth, and it was only her hands and face that bespoke of age. I saw that she held a book to her bosom, the crimson leather of which she tapped with a tapered fingernail. The woman walked toward me and examined my face with piercing blue eyes, and then she linked her arm with mine and guided me to the sofa. On the table before us, next to the photo album, was a small pot of ink and one of those quaint feather pens. Playfully, the elderly woman sat next to me and opened her book, which I saw was a registry with yellowed paper. A column of signatures filled one page.

"You seem down on your luck," the lady crooned.

Sardonically, I chuckled. "Hell, passing out and pissing myself ain't nothing new, if that's what you mean. As for luck, she's a lady I've never kissed."

Deeply, she sighed. "This edifice was built during the Prohibition era. It served as asylum for persons of fugitive nature." There was something funny about the way she spoke, as if from personal memory. "Asylum" was well chosen, I thought. I studied her face, and could believe that she had been a bonny lass in the 1920s. My kind of woman. Yet something in her words gave me pause.

"What makes you think of me as fugitive?"

"You wear a hunted aura. You are lost and hungry. We can give you shelter. You'll find it entertaining."

"I'm broke."

"Oh, we'll make use of you. Now," and she pointed to the column of names and picked up the feather pen. "I want you to sign your name here, and then we'll have Oskar find you a room. Hmm?" I looked at the Peter Lorre dude, who I supposed was Oskar, and he slyly winked at me. I paused. Everything seemed like some weird, crafty game. But the idea of a room sounded really nice. I was exhausted and hungry. This crazy pad would be far more comfortable and entertaining than anything I've been used to these past few years. What the hell? I moved my hand toward the pen, which the woman moved to my finger. Swiftly, the sharp point of the pen's tip nicked my flesh. I watched a drop of blood spill onto the feather pen's tip. With smooth dexterity the woman dipped the stained point into the wee container of ink, then placed the feather into my hand. My little drip of blood smeared her fingernail, which she tapped onto the yellowed paper.

"Your name, young man." I signed, then returned the pen to her. "Thank you . . . Hank," she said, examining my signature. "You won't mind if I call you Henry."

"That's cool," I told her, sensing that it wasn't a request. Suddenly quite weary, I yawned. The fellow named Oskar touched my shoulder. Rising, I followed him out into the antechamber and up the flight of stairs.

II.

The room into which I was led was cosy, small yet quite exquisitely furnished with antiques. Sitting on the bed, I found it quite comfortable, and I smiled as Oskar moved to an end table on which were various decanters of booze. Standing, I went to join him and poured some excellent corn whiskey into one of the small heavy tumblers. I held the bottle to my guest.

"No, thank you. I prefer a little of this." He took up a bottle of sherry and filled his glass, then sipped quietly. I examined the room once more, until my eyes fell upon the painting above the bedstead. Going to it, I touched the unfinished work. "Ah," Oskar sighed, "your painting."

"This is none of mine—it's revolting!" It was an original

work by an artist with whom I was unfamiliar. Of moderate size, the majority was a background of etching and under-painting, dreary in tone and subject. The setting was a wood, and from the sturdy branch of one tree a woman's form hung from a length of rope, its snug slipknot taut around her broken neck. A length of dark hair entoiled her face. Beneath there stood three dark forms, indistinct and faded, mere specters of ink and wash.

But it was the cacodemonic thing leering prominently in the foreground that riveted my eyes to the canvas. I had never known a work of art to produce a sense of fear, but when I gawked at the painted thing, I trembled with fright. I suppose what terrified me was the absolute realism with which the ghoul had been conveyed; one could feel in the pit of one's soul the unholy appetite that smoldered in the rapacious eyes. The wide face had a kind of leathery texture, and the scraggly hair was clotted with dirt. Beneath the green eyes flared a wide, flat nose. Thick lips twisted so as to reveal strong square teeth. This was the only figure in the work that had been fully painted, with such lifelike detail that one could almost imagine it to be a study from life.

"It's one of his unfinished works," Oskar informed me.

"His?"

"Richard Upton Pickman, of Boston. An obscure artist, but one who has attained a spectacular underground reputation. A majority of his works were destroyed by his father, just before the old man's suicide in 1937. This is one of the incomplete pieces that were discovered in an old section of Boston that was razed and used as a site for warehouses. One of the antique dwellings was apparently used by Pickman as a secret studio." Draining his glass, Oskar set it on top of an antique dressing table that served as bedside stand, and opening the table's single drawer he took from it an old sketchbook. "I found these and the painting in a shop in Salem some years ago."

We sat on the bed and I took hold of the ratty sketchbook. "So you're one of his fans?" Oskar shrugged. I slowly flipped through the pages of sketchings. Pickman had a fine sense of line, but his subjects were nauseating, just as disturbing as the abhorrent painting. "Ugh," I moaned, "the guy was really obsessed with that image of the hanged woman. But it's weird, because in all these other sketches he's drawn a semicircle of jackal things that resemble the freak in the foreground. There's no working sketch showing the three, whatever they are."

Oskar took the booklet from me and spoke in a cautious kind of way. "Yes, I think the Three Sisters, as I call them, are original to this one unfinished painting. The one completed oil is hanging in a bookshop in a valley town in the Northwest, and it's magnificent. It shows the semicircle of that dingo brood."

I stood again and studied the painted ghoul. "I've never seen such nauseous colors in oil. They're ghastly. How the hell am I supposed to sleep with that thing drooling over me?"

"You must admit that it's unique, Hank. Pickman followed the now discarded tradition of composing his own pigments. The effects are startling, I agree."

He was flipping through the sketchbook when a photograph that had been wedged between two leaves escaped and fell to the floor. I picked it up and studied the cuss's ugly mug. "Is that him?"

My new friend nodded. "Taken just before he vanished."

I whistled. "Damn, he looks just as creepy as his art-work. He must have toyed with trick photography; no one could really look like that. What was his family back-ground?"

Oskar took the photograph and admired it. "I once went to a showing of his work that was held at a disabled asylum in Arkham. The brochure mentioned that Pickman came from old Salem stock and supposedly had a witch ancestor hanged on Gallow's Hill in 1692."

"Ah, that explains his *idée fixe*. The hanged wretch is his great-great-granny." I watched as Oskar placed the photo back into the booklet and then return that volume to its drawer. Suddenly quite sleepy, I yawned.

"You're exhausted. You'll find some pajamas in that chiffonier. Pleasant dreams." Mischief played upon his sickly face, and I lightly laughed as he turned to cross to the door. He hesitated for a moment, as if there was something else he wanted to express; but he must have thought better of it, for he quietly opened the door and slipped from the room.

I went to the high and narrow chest of drawers and found a pair of bright yellow sleepwear. Whistling noncha-lantly, I undressed, threw my clothes over a chair, and put on the very comfortable cotton nightclothes. The song of windstorm drew me to the room's one window, and going to it I peered at an eerie sight. The grove across the roadway was bathed in tinted moonlight. High above it a pale band of illumination arched above the woodland, resembling the scene that had been crafted in the painting I had observed in the sitting room. I scratched at the window pane with fin-gernails, certain that the lunar bow had been painted onto the glass; but no flakes of paint rubbed off, nor was the surface rough with artistry. Wind raged just outside the window, and beneath its ululation I could just detect the irregular squawking of distant crows, such as I had heard earlier when Jesus had discovered me beneath the oak.

I yawned once more, found the switch that shut out the room's dim light, then climbed into bed. Looking up, I could just make out the dark shape of the ghoul in the feeble light that filtered through the window. "If I see you in my dreams I'll rip you to shreds," I promised the bogey, pulling the covers over me.

III.

I awakened to a sound that I took to be the moaning of the wind, until I realized that it was coming from the hallway outside my door. Had I in fact heard such a noise, or was it a revenant of dreaming? No matter. I had to piss, and so got out of bed and wandered into the shadowed hallway, hoping that there was a toilet on this floor. Spying a pale light coming from one narrow door, I went to it and saw that it was indeed a water closet. The toilet was a relic, and to flush it one pulled a hanging chain. I ran cool water over my hands and wiped those hands on my face and through my hair. Feeling refreshed, I re-entered the hallway, and seeing another door that was partially ajar, I sneaked to it and paused to listen. Someone inside was happily humming, and a smacking sound suggested feeding. I was hungry, and so I pushed the door with my toe and gazed at the room beyond.

The chamber was smaller than my own, with a modicum of furniture. Most of the walls were covered with wallpaper designed in black and red squares, but I saw that the wall space directly behind the bed had been painted red, except for one large black rectangle just above the headboard, where in every other room I had seen had hung a painting. In one corner, standing before a credenza, stood a tall figure with a shock of wild gray hair. He was bent over what looked like an antique casserole dish, from which he was plating a repast. When he turned to smile at me, I saw that it was the guy from the photo that copied Friedrich's *Raven Tree*.

"Enter, Hank Foster," he sang in a high nasal tone. "You must be famished. Here, take this, and I'll fill another plate for myself."

"Thank you," I said, taking the plate and examining the webbed meat and potatoes smothered with a kind of béchamel. The funny old guy motioned to a small table and two chairs, where two settings of sterling silver and napkins had been assembled. When my host sat down to join me I saw that his wide eyes were lined with red. Either he was a lunatic or flying some delectable high. Or a combination of both. Taking up fork and knife, he sliced his food with dainty precision, in continental fashion. Lowering my nose to the food, I took in its rich aroma. Gingerly, I cut into a piece of meat and popped it into my mouth. It was delicious, and suddenly famished I began to chomp. "This is great."

"'Tis our daily staple, so it's a good thing you like it. You'll get little else during your stay."

I didn't feel the need to correct his presumption of my staying around. Truth to tell, I hadn't given the outside world much thought since I arrived at this cuckoo nest. As if to qualify my thoughts, a cuckoo clock across the room struck five. "Is that the time?"

"Almost dawn. Sleep well?"

"Like a log."

"No dreams? No? Ah, lovely oblivion." He happily goggled at me, and I couldn't refrain from asking:

"Dude, what are you on?"

He hooted laughter. "What exuberant light shines in your eyes. Ha, ha!" He raised a finger, floated out of his chair, and went to a small kitchenette with which his room had been equipped. Opening a cupboard, he took out a glass, which he filled with water at the small sink. "Rinse away your food, and then place this beneath your tongue." From his shirt pocket he produced a little tin, which he opened and from which he took out a small red tablet. Taking the glass, I did as he instructed. The tablet had no flavor, and I was amazed how quickly it dissolved.

"You'll want to catch a bit more sleep, I dare say. Do you like your room?"

"It's nice enough. That damn painting is a bit offensive." He merely smiled, not moving. I got up and went to investigate the wall behind his bed. The black rectangle kind of got to me. I thought I could detect subdued motion within its opacity. The little red pill was kicking in. "My Mom taught art at college. She died ten years ago."

"And you're all alone in the world."

"Yeah. It sucks," I bitterly replied. "I was so pissed at her dying on me that I rejected my fine upbringing, my stalwart tutelage. I thought I was so cool and daring, hanging with hoods and living on the edge." My voice grew quiet with self-pity. "I didn't know it would turn into this." I gazed into the blackness on the wall, at the liquid crimson that surrounded it. I could feel the wall drawing me forward. I tilted toward it and touched its surface, and laughed as my hand seemed to sink into the satanic shades. "Dude, this is some good shit."

"Let's return you to your chamber."

I took my hand from the wall and put my arm around his neck. "You freaks remind me of some of the cats that came to Mom's parties. You know, those eccentric arty types. Kind of makes me feel at home here."

He guided me to the door and out into the hallway. When we reached my room, I stopped and pushed my companion from me. "You should return to bed," he told me.

"No thanks. Don't want to look at that ugly mug in the painting."

"But it's your painting, Henry." I stopped and looked at him. My mother had been the only one to call me that name. To be so addressed by a stranger weirded me out. "What's your name, bud?"

"I am Pieter."

"Yeah. Well, listen, bro, I'm gonna go outside for a while and get some air. No, it's cool, I can see my own way out. Thanks for the grub." His face wore such a strange expression that, laughing, I patted it with my hand, then carefully found my way down the stairs, to the foyer or whatever the hell it was. Noticing that a light was on in the sitting room, I stepped into it to see if pretty Pera was there. Perhaps I could coax her into walking with me.

The room was vacant. I liked the way the dim light seemed to swim along the walls; but when I felt a sudden lightheadedness I decided to sit down for a spell on the comfortable little sofa, and seeing the shiny red album on the table, I grabbed it and set it on my lap. I opened it at the middle at sighed at the sight before me. The image was one with which I was familiar, for my mother used to have a print of it on her writing desk. The ghostly photograph copied Gustav Klimt's allegorical drawing, *Tragedy*. I traced the woman's outline with my finger. The original work had been composed with black crayon and pencil, white chalk and gold. The figure in the photograph duplicated exactly the pose of the drawing, of a woman holding a macabre mask. Everything in the photo, however, had blanched to a muted mauve and pale gray, blurry in outline. The one exception was the woman's spectral face, its whiteness quite luminous. I could just make out the woman's bouffant hairstyle and languid demi-mode deportment.

Hearing a noise, I looked up and saw Pera wheeling Eblis into the room. The gnome wore a sleeveless shirt, and I cringed at the sight of his too-thin arms, limbs that resembled those of some gaunt Auschwitz survivor. Closing the album, I staggered to my feet and skipped toward them. The dwarf's eyes were sickly yellow and red-rimmed. Blue and purple veins lined his expanded face with its bulbous nose. Cradled in his lap was a small oblong box.

I fell to my knees before him. "Yo, what's your trip?" Blinking fevered eyes, he tapped the wooden box with the black stump of what should have been a left hand. I looked at his malformed flesh, at the nub that looked as if it had been melted in some combustion. Reaching to the box, I opened it and took out one of the brown-black joints with which the box was stuffed. From his shirt pocket the little man produced a wooden match, held tightly between two stubby fingers. Swiftly, he struck it against the box and held the flame to me. I placed the reefer into my mouth and tilted toward the amber flame. I sucked, holding the inhalation for

54

a minute and then let it slip slowly through nose and mouth.

The light in the room took on a golden hue. Trying to stand straight, I suffered a moment's vertigo and stumbled backward, colliding with the veiled and silent Pera, to whom I clung and with whom I crashed onto the floor. My face nestled in her hair. My nostrils took in the scent of her etiolated flesh. She offered no resistance as I held her down, and I fancied that I could hear her purring. My mouth pressed against her delectable neck, and my hand reached to pull the veil from her face. Savagely, Eblis flew from his chair and landed on me. A ragged nail from one malformed, sullied finger pierced my face, just below the right eye, slicing downward.

Cursing, I swung at the dwarf and screamed in rage, then tried to raise myself on hands and knees. A smell of blood assailed my nostrils, and a coppery taste slipped into my mouth. My hands reached out and clutched the beast's wild hair, and with all the force that I could muster I hurled him off me. The sound of his whimpering made me laugh and spit. The room was spinning, and so was I. Trying to stand, I fell on my ass. A shadow loomed above me, a scented phantom. It pressed its veiled face nearer to my own until I could taste the fabric. Underneath that veil I could feel the probing tongue that investigated the substance with which my face was stained.

IV.

I awakened in my bed, but how I had gotten there I could not recall. Whatever I had ingested from the withered gnome's enigmatic weed, it had certainly had its effect. My throat still burned, as did my brain. Shades of eerie memory dimmed the recesses of my mind, specters that I could not mentally grasp. When I heard a peculiar sound from beyond my bedroom window, I pushed my numb body from the bed and staggered to peer out the windowpane. I saw the dark oaks of the distant grove, and thought that I could just make out a portion of the moonlit pool. I saw a dancing shadow. It was attired in some black flowing gown, but the naked arms and face seemed somehow to drink in the drenching moonlight. Cool air pushed against the pane, and so I opened the window and leaned my head out of it, toward the grove. Coldness brushed my new-made scar, and on that wind I thought that I could just detect the dancing figure's lullaby. Was it Pera? Had she also partaken of the narcotic, and was she now out there in the chilly night, high and prancing recklessly in the growing storm? I felt drops of rain splash against my face, and so I found my jacket and went outside.

Crossing the quiet roadway, I walked into the grove and toward the dancing woman. At first I could not understand what was wrong with her face, and then I realized that she wore a mask, one that had been held by the woman in the photo I had seen based on Klimt's drawing, *Tragedy*. Gold encircled her throat and arms, flesh that was semi-transparent. Beneath the sound of wind and rain I could hear her soft chanting to a tune that reminded me of Mahler, one of Mother's favorite composers. Storm clouds occluded the earlier moonlight, and yet I could see amazingly well, and it struck me as odd that the woman's clothing had not grown sopping wet, nor did water drip from the death-white mask. Seeming to sense that I was watching her, the figure stopped moving and stood very still, facing me, her hands now clutching at her crotch.

I advanced toward her, my eyes glued to her mask,

which seemed the only substantial thing about her. I did not understand how I could vaguely see the trees and bushes that were behind her, could see *through* her. I was now very close to her, and I reached out to touch the mask, its bulging eyes and wide round mouth. A smooth limpid hand joined mine and seemed to blend its texture with my skin. Together, we touched the edge of the mask and lifted. I shut my eyes as something firm yet fleshy encased my face.

A violent force pulled the mask from my face. Jesus stood before me, frowning, the mask in his left hand. "Philippe," I said, remembering his actual name, and then I looked about us. "Where's Pera?"

"Inside, where you should be. We do not enter the wooded place at night."

"Nonsense, she was just here, wearing that thing."

"No." He tossed the mask into the pool. It floated for a moment, and then was gone. "Come, take my hand."

"Uh, that's cool, dude."

"My hand," he commanded, holding it to me. I reached out and took hold of his hand, wincing as his fingers tightened like a clamp. I wanted to stop and look into the pool, but my captor forcefully yanked me after him, out of the grove, into rain, across the road and inside the old motel. We stood scowling at each other. "Go to bed, Henry."

"Aren't you going to go fetch Pera? She'll catch her death out there. You must have seen her, she was standing right in front of me, beside the pool."

"That was Alma. Now, to bed."

"Fuck you, you're not my mother. Who's Alma?" Ignoring me, he turned and went into the parlor. I followed. "Who is Alma? I want to meet her."

"She's faded. Now, go to bed."

"What do you mean, faded? Like her photograph?" I stomped to the table and picked up the photo album. Turning to the image that copied Klimt, I studied the girl pictured, that very young creature. "Are you telling me that I saw a ghost? Is that your game, freak boy? I didn't imagine that stupid mask. Take me to her room."

Philippe sighed. "You grow tedious."

"Yeah? Well, I don't like your little game. Okay, don't show me. I'll find it myself." Again he sighed, then held out his hand. "Forget it, Mary. Just show me the way."

Did he slightly smile? He shut his eyes for one moment, then turned and walked to the door that led to the hallway. I followed him to the end of the hallway, where he stopped before two doors, opened one of them, and entered a tiny room. I walked to the small bed and looked at the wall behind it. "There's no picture. Come on, I've figured a few things out. Every room I've been in has had a picture above the bed. Except this one. Where is Alma's picture, the copy of Klimt?"

"It's been taken to the catacombs, of course."

"Show me."

Again, his subtle smile. We exited the room and he opened the neighboring door. Crossing the threshold, we came to a flight of small stone steps. Philippe reached for a lantern that sat in a cavity cut into the wall, took a lighter from his pocket, and nonchalantly lit the wick. Saying nothing, he descended. The place to which he led me was like some ancient religious grotto, but here it was art that was divine. Framed pictures hung on walls like objects of adoration. As Philippe began to light various candles, I went to a

58

stone pillar on which there sat a small framed copy of Klimt's piece, beautifully copied in full color.

I looked around me, and the place seemed to contract, as if eaten by spreading shadow. My breathing became labored, and I cringed as blackness seemed to seep hungrily toward me. Gasping, I hurried to the steps and scrambled up them. Philippe eventually joined me and shut the door behind him. Removing a handkerchief from a pocket, he patted at the perspiration on my brow. Annoyed, I took the piece of cloth from him and roughly wiped my face.

"Tight places," I explained. He nodded, with such a smug expression on his face that I wanted to hit him. Instead, I strode across the hallway, past Pera's room and into the sitting room. Oskar was sitting on the sofa, placing a photograph into the leather album. Sitting next to him, I examined the photo, which was of him posed as the Count in Kokoschka's painting. I took the photograph, with which he was having difficulty, from his clumsy hands and slid it into one of the album's vacant sleeves. Then I took hold of the man's hand and examined its sulfur-yellow pigment. His face had also grown more discolored, and his sad hazel eyes had submerged within dark hollows.

"What the hell has happened to you?"

"The elder ones have worked their alchemy."

I was about to ask him more questions when he lifted his crippled hand and touched it to the scar on my face. My nostrils drank the sickened scent of his polluted flesh, the skin that reeked of death. Taking hold of that hand with both of mine, I pressed its fingers against my nose, my mouth. Something in its stench beguiled me.

"You look awful," he whispered as I touched his hand

with my tongue. He took his hand from me. "Not sleeping well?"

Bitterly, I laughed. "Too many weird things are going on. Or so I imagine, although it could just be the freaky stuff that Eblis offered me last night. Or was it tonight? What day is it?"

He could not answer, for he suddenly jerked away, convulsed with hoarse coughing. Producing a piece of yellow cloth, he covered his mouth with it until the attack subsided. When he removed the rag from his mouth I saw that it had been sprinkled with beads of blood. "What the hell is wrong with you?"

Oskar waved away my inquiry. "You need not bother about me—take care of yourself." He stared into space, frowning, and I sensed that he was deciding whether or not to confide in me, to let me into his world. But then he stood and smiled down on me. "Get some sleep, Hank. You look half-dead."

"Not so fast," I yelled, grabbing his arm. "Damn it, explain what's going on in this godforsaken place. Look, I'm not an idiot. I can see the connections, the paintings in the rooms and the stills in that album. Now, I've just had a really freaky experience with Jesus." Oskar threw me an odd look. "With Philippe," I corrected myself. "I need to understand what I've stumbled on. Explain."

"Explanations are tedious. Understanding comes with the passage of time, but it won't really explicate anything. I'll tell you only this, that we have blurred the barrier betwixt art and nature, reality and dream. The outside world, the wretchedly bogus here and now, has no pertinence for us here. 'That bloody tyrant, Time,' scarcely touches us, and abhorrent modernity is utterly rejected. What was Pound's dull dictum concerning art, 'make it new'? Our aesthetic axiom is far more fascinating: 'Make it you'!" The reprehension that I felt deep within me must have been evident on my face, for Oskar began to laugh and shake his head. "Get some sleep, Hank."

I watched him leave the room. His coaxing seemed to have had an effect, for my eyelids were suddenly heavy. I stretched out on the sofa and closed my eyes. The man was clearly ill. TB was often regarded a quaint disease largely conquered by modern medicine, but I remembered having read of recent epidemics in various regions of the globe. It was an old contagion, for traces of tubercles had been discovered in mummies dating to 2000 B.C. Wanting to observe his photograph one more time, I reached for the album, propped it against my raised knees, and turned to Oskar's image. The original painting had been inspired by Kokoschka's stay at an institute in Switzerland, where the artist had painted the portraits of some tubercular patients. Although my eyes grew heavier and my mind hazy, I tried to study the photograph, to understand its connection to the original painting, to discern the relationship with Oskar's condition. My new friend had just hinted of a link, but what it was and how it existed was a mystery that I could not fathom.

I closed my eyes and began to sink toward slumber. As consciousness slipped from me, I remembered the sickly sweet aroma of Oskar's tainted skin, his delicious smell of moribund mortality. I felt the drool that lightly gathered in my mouth, that began to drip as wakefulness evaporated.

V.

I awakened in darkness and stretched on the comfortable sofa, and then I noticed movement in the room. Looking up, I whispered her name. "Pera." She lit a candle that leaned within a sconce, and then picked up the flaming thing and held it before her veiled face.

"You're not sleeping in your bed. You need to do so. That's the way it works."

Rising, I went to her and took the candlestick from her gloved hand. "The way what works?" I listened to her hiss of laughter, a sound that was not sane. Lightly, I touched her hair. "Why do you hide your face?"

She began to rock slightly, and I put a gentle hand to her waist. "It shields me from the world, the bright reality. The envious dark drifts to kiss my drab face, and I'll be wedded to a death's-head, with a bone in my mouth."

"This is crazy talk," I mumbled.

She stopped rocking and leaned her body against mine. I could smell the cool breath that washed my face. "You name me mad? Is this lunacy?" She slid her hand toward the candle's flame and pinched the fire out, then knocked the holder to the floor. Funny, even without light I could see her clearly. The fabric of the veil tickled my face as she lifted it and smoothed it over her dark hair. I gazed at her face, with its skin that radiated like burnished porcelain. The unnatural pallor made me suspect that Pera was an arsenic eater, as society ladies were wont to be in distant eras. I had heard of dwellers in the mountains of southern Austria who consumed arsenic as a tonic, building up a tolerance for ingested amounts that would normally prove fatal. The world was filled with freaks, and I had stumbled into a realm of mutation, physical and mental. What worried me was that I was feeling more and more at home.

I pressed my nostrils against her temple and took in her mortal fragrance, never having smelled someone who aroused such odd longings within me. Her sudden deep laughter chilled me. "Pickman is a potent warlock. You're already altered." Ignoring her senseless prattle, I moved my face to her throat and raised my hands so as to fondle her breasts. Her sheathed hands took hold of my face and raised it to her own. Oh, how ghostly pale she was, so much so that I fancied I could vaguely see beneath her lucent hide to the bone of her delicate cranium. Her hands wound into my hair and tightened. Her mouth exhaled into my eyes, and vision fogged. I let her go and rubbed my face with hands that trembled. When again I looked at her, the veil had been dropped. Her hands took hold of mine. "To bed, to bed. Come, come, come, give me your hands. What's done cannot be undone. To bed."

I raised her hands to my mouth and kissed them. "Not yet. Show me some other rooms."

"Whatever for?" she asked, with an inflection that hinted of regained sanity. "Most of the rooms are vacant."

"Because their dwellers are faded?"

"Ah," she purred. She wouldn't move, and I suddenly began to feel like a cat's-paw. Disconnecting our hands, I walked into the foyer and up the stairs, the silent woman following me like some shadow. Reaching my floor, I went to try one of the many doors, but found it locked. The next door I tried yielded to my violence, and I entered an untenanted chamber. The painting over the bedstead was dimly lit by the rays of moonlight that drifted through the window. I went to it and touched the canvas. The dashingly handsome figure was familiar, and after a moment I remembered the original work that it copied, a Titian showing a young man in black, one hand naked, the other gloved and holding the glove that had been removed.

Pera stood beside me, then she quietly climbed onto the bed and placed her hand to the necklace worn by the painted figure. "They wanted to put him down in the catacombs, but I said nay. He'll not dwell in that darkened crypt, that place of death. Isn't he beautiful? So young." She reached for a varnished box that sat upon a stand. Opening it, she took out a red necklace identical to that worn by the lad in the painting. Kissing it, Pera clutched it to her chest as she lowered herself into the bed and curled into a fetal position.

Silently, I slipped out of the room and went to my own. I undressed and got into bed, kneeling on the mattress and studying the Pickman. The fellow's green canine eyes absurdly seemed to return my gaze. When at last I reclined, I saw those eyes in my dreams.

When my eyes opened to the glare of daylight streaming through the window, I heard from outside that window the song of laughter. Pushing the covers from me, I sat in bed and saw the plate of covered food on my bedside stand. I removed the cover and found some slices of the odd webbed meat that Pieter had offered me earlier. I wasn't very hungry, but I picked up a slice and began to eat. Standing, I wobbled to the window and looked out toward the oak grove, which was filled with moving figures. Were the freaks having a picnic? I found the idea slightly sinister, and that rather attracted me, for I was feeling bored. I dressed and went to join in the fun.

The light of day stung my eyes, and everything was thus a bit out of focus as I sauntered across the road toward the wooded place. Most of the faces were familiar, but there were three persons to whom I had not yet been introduced. The youngest, dressed in rather dandified Victorian garb, leaned against a tree, and something in her pose and the style in which she wore her flame red hair was familiar. A few yards from her, standing at an easel, a box of brushes and tubes of paint on the ground beside him, was Pieter. I went to study his canvas and saw pinned to its top left corner a small black and white picture.

"Isn't that Swinburne?" I ventured, watching the old guy copying the wee image in watercolor, blending the poet's facial features with those of the ascetic girl beside the tree. It was she who, frowning at me, spoke.

"Who hath known the ways of time
Or trodden behind his feet?"

"Whatever, babe," I threw at her, disliking her haughty attitude. "So, you're copying, um, Burne-Jones . . .?"

"Nope. Rossetti, painter and poet. Interesting, isn't it, how many artists have also been rhymers?" He worked his brush with dexterity and aptitude, and suddenly an idea flashed in my brain.

"Hey, those paintings above the beds . . ."

Mocking meekness, he bowed his head. "Most of them are mine own. The Pickman in your room is an original. I've touched it up a little, to bring out the beast."

"That explains it," I cheerfully replied. "I was wondering why the ones I was familiar with didn't look quite right. You've blended the original sitters with models of your own, as you're doing now. That's kind of cool." I did not mention that I thought it a dubious practice to "touch up" another artist's work.

Leaving him to his labor, I went to join Pera, who sat beside the pool of water, a petite parasol protecting her from sunlight. Absentmindedly, she dipped her hand into the bunch of pretty flowers in her lap. "Playing her part to the full," I thought, although when I saw the expression in her eyes beneath their veil I reconsidered. She gazed at me with eyes that were wide and lunatic, but also so sad that I grew quite melancholy. Tenderly, I took up a bloom and tossed it into the murky water.

Oskar came to join us, sitting next to the pool and staring into its depths with an odd expression shifting the features of his yellow face. When I asked if he was feeling well, he merely smiled and shrugged, then dipped his hand into the pool and raised a handful of cupped water to his crown. I watched the water dribble down his features. Pera reached out to his wet face and began to dry it with her glove. Oskar took her hand and kissed it, then turned to watch an approaching figure.

"The Mistress approaches," Oskar whispered.

I studied the crone as she stalked toward us, then smiled as she held a boxlike contraption and pointed its covered lens to us. Pera turned away, but Oskar stared, transfixed, as the witch removed the brass covering from the lens. I heard the squawking of crows in the trees above us and imagined that the light of day subtly subdued. Quickly, the cover was snapped back into place. The old hag's mirthless laughter unnerved me. I did not like the way she investigated my facial features as she placed her camera or whatever it was on the ground and untied the piece of black fabric that encircled her throat.

"It's time to play, my sprigs," she cackled. Slowly, steadily, everyone except Pera stopped what they were doing and walked to the elderly woman, encircling her. I was the last to stand and join their circle, standing next to Oskar and a woman I had not yet been introduced to. The ancient beldame stepped to Oskar and wrapped her ribbon so that it covered his eyes, tying it behind his head. She led him to the center of our circle, then joined our number.

We did not join hands, but everyone began to hum in a low, nearly inaudible way, and our circle began to rotate slowly. As we moved around him, Oskar reached into the air as if ready to touch our faces. At last he reached out and touched the face of one of the women I did not know. He said her name, and she laughed as she untied the band from around his eyes. Above us, the cry of crows mingled with her laughter.

Oskar skipped to me and clapped. "My turn to choose, and you're it, Hank." I wanted to protest as he pulled me to the center of the circle and began to tie the ribbon 'round my head. "Do be a good sport, old boy," he requested, and so I stopped fidgeting and let him finish. My attention was focused on the smell of his jaundiced flesh and its effect on my appetite. He tied the knot and began to take his hands away, but I clasped mine over them and pressed them to my nose, my mouth. He allowed me to savor his mortality for a few moments, and then he sighed, "Do let go, there's a good lad."

I sensed him walk away from me, and then I heard the sound of humming encircling me. Feeling slightly foolish, I raised my hands and, although I couldn't see anything, shut my eyes. I thought that I could feel a faint and shifting radiance on my hands, as if globes of soft auras pirouetted before me. Pitching forward, I grasped a face. The atmosphere grew still and silent. My fingers investigated the invisible visage; they felt the thick nose and full lips, lips that flexed so that my fingertips played against large square teeth. Thick stubble, almost a beard, covered the chin. Was it Philippe? Had he shortened his beard and I not notice it? I moved my fingers along the face and felt the ragged scar beneath the right eye, and on my other hand I felt the heat that emitted from a mouth that mocked with easy laughter.

Cursing, I ripped the band of cloth from before my eyes, and then cried in fright as a winged shadow fluttered before me, squawking risibility. The crow's beady eyes stared directly into mine as I felt the wind of its flapping wings. And then it vanished to join its comrades in the boughs above us. I stood in the center of the circle, looking at the faces that were all too far away for me to have touched.

Thunder rumbled in the distance. The circle broke up and my companions moved away. Eblis, who had not been a part of the circle, jumped out of a tree, landing near Pera. She arose and held onto the handles of his wheelchair as he leaped into it, maneuvering his stunted torso with hands, like some malformed monkey. I stood beneath the trees and listened to the sound of birds moving among the branches. I heard the patter of rain on bark and leaves, drops that slipped between those leaves and fell into the nearby pool. I looked at the others, who had crossed the road and were entering the building as Oskar held its door open for them. He stood there alone for some time, gazing at me, and then he waved and went inside.

A loud clap of thunder shook me from my mental void. I leaned against a tree and closed my eyes. My sharp hearing took in the sounds of storm, of moving shadow. The world was alive with sound such as I had never experienced. Pushing away from the tree I passed the pond and peered into its water, not understanding the spheres beneath its surface, those pale globes that seemed almost to watch me.

I ran through the rain, into the building, and stepped into the drawing room. The tiny lights of the brass chandelier spread dim illumination through the room. Stopping before the painting of the oak grove, I examined it with interest. I saw that the "rainbow" was not actually white but rather a mixture of pale yellows and greens. The same wan green glowed among the numerous brown clouds. My eyesight oddly blurred as I stared at the thing, and that painted mass of nubilation seemed to billow and convulse, its patches of pale green reflecting a kind of alien light.

Turning away, I rubbed my eyes and listened to the frail music that issued from some distant place. I stepped into the hallway and passed Pera's closed door, approached the door that opened onto the catacombs, and crossed its threshold. I needed no light as I held my hand against the rough-hewed wall and climbed down the small stone steps. Curiously, my discomfort for small dark places had deserted me. Glancing to where the whistling music was coming from, I noticed a doorway cut into the basalt, into which a squat round door had been fitted. Beside the wall leaned the dented wheelchair. Cracking open the door, I peered into an incommodious cell.

Eblis sat upon a squalid mat, looking like some troglodytic chimera, a plate of food before him. He watched me enter his domain as he put a slab of webbed meat to his mouth and tore into it with diseased teeth. Oskar stood in one corner, facing the wall as he played some flutelike instrument. Ignoring both of them, I went to examine the dark painting above the goblin's mat. Unlike the others, it did not represent another artist's work. Rather, it was a simple representation of Eblis Mauran in his wheelchair, the knobs that were his hands in his lap.

Oskar killed his music and turned to face me.

"Tell me about Pickman," I ordered.

"Not much to tell. He disappeared in September of 1926, after an unsuccessful career as an artist in Boston."

"Why did he paint his chosen subjects?"

"He was attracted to the macabre. Who can explain why? Tell me why Goya's mood so darkened that he ended his career with the so-called Black Paintings. What moods arrested Poe and Baudelaire so as to produce their diabolic lore? Hmm?"

"Stop being precious and tell me about Pickman."

"Henry, there's little to tell. Like Goya, his mood darkened near the end of his life, fueled perhaps by his lack of luck in being able to exhibit and sell his paintings. People were turned off by the image of the morbid changeling that kept appearing in his work, that became his whoreson theme. People felt abused when looking at his art."

"I'm sure they did."

"Look, I'm busy. Eblis has a session with the Mistress. Good day." So saying, he exited the room and picked up the old wheelchair, carrying it away.

I frowned at the goblin, then turned my attention once more to his painting. It was a large work in an ancient frame and seemed quite accomplished. And then I noticed the hands that nestled in the painted figure's lap, the nubs of which were both fingerless.

The gnome's plaintive voice spoke. "Master Pieter painted it just after I was woven."

I looked down at him. "I don't understand you."

"The Mistress grants me a new addition tonight." He held up his arms and smiled. "Will you carry me?"

I tilted to him and he scrambled into my embrace. His tiny arms wound around my neck, his large sad face fell onto my breast, and suddenly there were tears in my eyes. I could taste his loneliness. I carried him up the steps and into the hallway, then placed him into his wheelchair, which awaited him. He thanked me in his high and childlike voice, and I followed as he wheeled himself down the hallway and into the parlor. As I watched the tiny creature work his chair, something that Oskar had said about Pickman reverberated in my head. Oskar had described the creature in Pickman's painting as a changeling. Watching Eblis, I was certain that the word exactly described him: a secret child, unwanted in this world.

I followed Eblis to a door, which I opened for him. The crone sat at what looked like a prehistoric spinning wheel. In her left hand she held a moist mass of flesh, which she worked into the spindle and pulled through the outlandish device. I watched as the stringy meat was twisted and wound into a thread of glistening brawn. On a nearby table sat a shallow metal bidet in which a pile of the fibrous stuff had been tossed. Beside that mass of meat lay a large silver tray on which some of the flesh, woven together, was piled, ready to be eaten.

Seeing us, the old woman stopped her work and stood. "Ah, Henry, welcome. Will you have some opium?" Reaching for a pipe, she brought it to her mouth and lit the bowl. She sucked loudly and closed her eyes. "'Tis an old blend, from Burma. It will soothe your troubled mind."

Saying nothing, I took the pipe and drew on it. I watched as she sat in a chair next to the metal bowl, reaching for the gnome, who hastened to her lap. Deftly, she took up a pair of slender steel knitting needles, implements with which she worked a length of fibrous flesh into the hand on which Eblis wore two digits. My gut twisted as I watched her work, moving the needles into his flesh, her hands stained by spilling blood. Eblis neither screamed nor squirmed, and when at last he held to me his gory limb, I saw that the hand now wore a newly formed third finger. I sucked deeply on the pipe and held the smoke, and then I began to laugh, because I knew that I was dreaming.

VI.

Outside, the storm had passed, and the sky was fairly clear. I walked to the crest of the hill, my mind and soul at peace. Knowing that I was dreaming gave me a longing for adventure, and so I began to follow the road down the hill, walking toward the dark and silent town. Just on the periphery of the sleeping hamlet I came upon a small cemetery crowded with willow trees, a place that looked so peaceful that I decided to investigate its weathered stones. And then I was startled by what sounded like a low harmonious wailing. Beneath a willow, standing around a barrow of stones, were three women dressed in black. I could not understand why they looked familiar, but then I remembered that I was dreaming, and so I ceased trying to make sense of these new phantoms. Boldly, I went to them and picked up one large rock that sat atop the mound. It felt very real, cold, and heavy.

The woman nearest walked to and joined me in holding the rock. I sucked the air through my nose, hoping to smell her mortality, but no fragrance wafted to me. She was a phantom indeed. Softly, she began to sing, and as her beady eyes observed me, I fancied that her song was meant for me. Taking the rock from her, I stepped closer to the pile and returned the rock to its place on top.

"I've never seen anything like this. I suppose whoever lies beneath must have died long ago."

"Long, long ago," the woman sang. I did not move as she came nearer as her hand raised and began to investigate my face. I did not flinch as her talon poked into my scar and reopened it. I could smell the wet red stuff that began to leak down my face. Funny, I'd never experienced a sense of smell when dreaming, or of touch. Roughly, I grabbed hold of the woman's hand. She was real enough.

"What's happening to me?"

"You were lost, and now are found," the woman sighed.

I pushed her from me and looked again at the mound of stones. "For whom do you warble?"

The woman motioned to the mound. "For our antecedent. For those who float in Wraithwood. For you."

I shut my eyes and began to laugh. I could feel my high wearing off, but I was high enough to imagine that I could hear the sound of beating wings, and the noise reminded me of a line from Poe:

> "Flapping from out their Condor wings
> Invisible Wo!"

When my eyes opened, I stood alone on the cemetery sod. Above me I could hear the crying of crows as they flew upward, toward Wraithwood.

I whistled loudly and sucked in necrophagous air, a hungry aether that sank beneath my pores and chilled my soul. How soft seemed the ground beneath my feet. Falling to my knees, I clawed into that earth and brought a handful of it to my nostrils. My mouth began to water. I felt an overwhelming intensity of hunger, and in some dark secluded mental place I dreamed an image of myself digging deep into this chilly sod in search of sustenance. A memory came to me of the weird webbed food I had been served at the hotel. I craved it now. Rising, I walked out of that place, following the road upward, toward home.

All lights inside had been extinguished, and yet I could see wonderfully well when I entered the building. I had planned on going straight to my chamber, but when I heard a low murmuring within the parlor, I went to its doors and crept inside. A figure paced the room, babbling to herself. A gloved hand, through which two pointed fingernails had ripped, madly clutched the face beneath a lacerated veil. How keenly I could smell the blood that stained her face! I went to her, unable to comprehend the thing that hung from her mouth until I was very close. The crimson necklace that was a copy of the one in the Titian painting was clenched between the teeth of a tightened jaw. And still she tried to babble.

I unfastened the torn veil and let it drift to the wooden floor. Her hand shot up to scratch her face, but I held it tight so as to block the nail from slicing once more into the emaciated skin. Touching my fingers to her mouth, I gently pulled the necklace from her teeth, catching a spill of drool with my cupped hand. When again she muttered, I understood her words.

"I know when one is dead and when one lives; he's dead as earth." She took the ruddy necklace from me and swung it before our eyes. "Why should a dog, a rat, a witch have life and he no breath at all?"

"Of whom do you speak, kind lady? I did not find his likeness in the album. Where is his photograph?"

The woman tilted her head and examined me with lunatic eyes. Raising her hands above me, she slipped the necklace over my head. With one hand, she tightened it around my neck. When I began to have trouble breathing, I clawed at her hands and pushed her from me. Tittering, she fled the room, and I followed to her bedchamber, where I found her lighting a candle on a bookshelf that she had littered with various bric-a-brac. I noticed the gilded frame before which she swayed. Going to her, I examined the glossy sheet of paper within the frame. At first I could discern no image, but the more I studied it in the flickering light, the more I could almost make out an imperceptible and spectral outline. "Is this your young man?" I asked, touching the frame. "Is he the young man in the Titian?"

"The Titian," she spat, in a voice that sounded coherent and sane. "He was young, wasn't he? Not yet nineteen. And so beautiful. I take flowers to him, to his shining face. I shall soon answer his summons." She shuddered and wrapped her arms around her shoulders. Turning to me, she tugged at her collar. "Pray you, undo this button."

I worked the buttons loose, then took the candle and led her to bed, setting the candle on the little bedside stand. Her face was smeared with dark blood that had seeped from her self-inflicted wounds. "I'll be right back," I promised, and then I went to her bathroom and threw a washcloth into the small porcelain basin. I turned one of the brass spigots and let cold water flow onto the cloth, and as I waited I glanced at my reflection in the mirror. This reminded me that I was dreaming; for how could I see my face so clearly in an unlit room, and how could that reflection be mine own? I hadn't seen myself since my arrival to the motel, and so it should not have surprised me to see the growth of hair upon my face. But why was the bristle so thick, and how had my face grown so wide? Could those broad lips be mine, those large square teeth that almost protruded from the mouth?

No, this was all some mad hallucination, for only in a dream could my visage so alter as to resemble the ghoul in Pickman's painting. I thought of Oskar and his similarity to the figure in the painting above his bed. This was naught but mad delusion. And yet, when I reached for the cloth and wrung the excess water from it, I could feel the cold wetness so vividly. Returning to Pera, I washed the congealed blood from her face as she sat on the bed and stared at the flame. When I had finished, she took the rag from me and pressed it to the scar beneath my eye. Our mouths were very close, and I could smell her breath.

Dropping the washcloth to the floor, Pera picked up the candle and placed it between our mouths. "Put out the light," she whispered, "and then put out the light." My tongue, coated with saliva, licked out the tiny blaze. I took the candle from her and set it down, then reached to undo more buttons on her blouse. We sat in deep darkness, and yet I could see her, and even fancied that I could just make out the skull beneath her thin translucent skin. Together we reclined. She took hold of the necklace around my throat and spoke a stranger's name. I wrapped my hungry arms around her meat and shut my eyes. I dreamed within my dreaming, and those dreams were of dark cemetery sod, and of the carcasses beneath the earth. How piquant was the smell of that soil and its inhabitants! And mingled with their odor I took in the sweet fragrance of the lunatic in my arms.

But when the morning light fell on me from the window in her room, I was alone. And when I went to that window to seek the source of singing that I heard, I saw the figures that stood within the grove, encased by dawn's dim light. Crying, I fled the room and rushed outside, running across the road and into that grove. When I saw the figure hanging from a length of rope that had been fastened to a sturdy branch, I fell upon wet grass.

Someone called my name, and I turned to face the crone. She was pointing her camera device at me, nodding her head in approval. Cursing her, I turned once more to look at the woman hanging from the tree, at the three other women who stood underneath her and wailed harmoniously. Eblis was suddenly beside me, touching his three fingers to my face and nodding his happy head. I watched as he scampered to the tree and began to scuttle up it, like something in a Kafkaesque delirium. Oskar and Philippe now stood beneath the corpse and took hold of it as Eblis gnawed the rope around the branch. The body fell as the wailing trio blurred into one cloudy entity that rose to hidden branches, from which there came the squall of crows. I watched as the men took her body to the pool and gently tossed her into its water. In dream, I saw her dead hand gather a bunch of flowers that floated in the water next to her, and I sighed as she chose one lovely bloom and held it to me. Creeping to the edge of the pool, I reached for the flower that she offered me, and by chance I peered into the water, at the shining spheres that frolicked just beneath her. I saw the one pale globe that rose to kiss the back of her neck, that moved its mouth as if to name her. At the touch of his tender kiss, my lucent beauty smiled, closed her eyes, and sank into the water's depths.

In Memoriam: Oscar Wilde

I.

Tread gently, let your footfalls make no sound. Your animated shadow flits among the solid stones as daylight dies in darkening sky. Soft sad breath lingers in the aether at your mouth, afraid to sail too far from those lips that gave it life. Pray softly as you approach the place where she reposes. No need to shout to touch the ears of Christ, within whose magnificent arms she sits enfolded, her golden hair kissed by sacred lips. Such is the Kingdom of Christ's realm. Remove the envelope near your breast and take from it the lock of her hair that you keep as remembrance; kiss it with a sinner's mouth. Reach to steady your trembling form by holding onto the chiseled hand of a graven thing. Such is the realm of your mortality. Peace, peace. She does not heed your mask of woe. Grief is a mortal burden. Brush away your crystal tears, and know your time will come. Your Savior knows your name, and He will call you to the happy realm of death, where hand in hand you will dance with Isola beneath the silver stars.

II.

I stood in Ada's outlandish garden and admired her model, a boy in his late teens who was completely nude except for the pallid mask that hid his face. He stood upon a dais like some sturdy *kouros* statue, slim arms straight at his side, one slender leg extended slightly forward. His white skin went very well with his surroundings; for Ada had modeled her garden on the Venus de Milo gallery in the Louvre, with marble arches supported on massive pillars, around which had been positioned the results of her diseased statuomania. I had no eyes for the various figures, for I was captivated by the one who breathed, who was for me an ideal embodiment of masculine beauty. How absurd that mine hostess should cover the handsome face—for surely such a stunning figure must own a magnificent physiognomy—but that was so like my dramatic, at times my foolish, friend.

She smiled at me as she paused in her sketching, and then set down pen and pad so as to link her arm with mine. "Let us walk, dear Harry, and as we stroll you will tell me of this new poem you're working on. Ah, can you smell the perfume of the tall *lilium auratum*, which you once told me is your favorite flower? But I have a surprise awaiting you, one that I know will astonish. Come, stop gawking at that marvelous boy and walk this path with me."

"Ah, dear Sphinx, my poem is far from my mind," I confessed. "I must write a perfect sonnet in celebration of that young man's perfect form. He is a narcissus, and I wish to drown in the beauty of his eyes. Whatever wonder you have to reveal to me, it cannot compare to his flawless limbs, his smooth taut stomach, his golden phallus."

How curiously she smiled. Walking down the path, we stopped at a small marble post, upon the flat surface of which there was a small terrarium. Looking into the sphere of glass, I saw the thing that rested on its bed of dew. Opening the sphere, Ada reached for the thing and picked it up.

What a strange fragrance it had, that green carnation, the odor of which wafted to my nostrils as she held it to my face. Coming very close, she slipped the thing into my buttonhole. I watched her gloved hands, the fingers of which were wet with dew; and I saw her thick tongue, like some reptilian appendage, snake from the aperture of her mouth and lick the misty drops from the cloth that sheathed her hand. She smacked her lips together and produced a silver cigarette case, which she opened and from which I took an opium-tainted cigarette. I watched the match as it burst into flame, and I bent to that tiny flare and inhaled. Ada watched the flame creep nearer to the flesh of the fingers that held the match; and then she waved out the flame, touched her cigarette to mine and sucked.

But my lips had no taste for nicotia: they burned to kiss the face beneath the pallid mask. "Ah," said my hostess, "you long to imbibe of other appetite. You have been entranced by the beauty of youth, that brief ecstasy. And partake of it you shall."

"*Per quando?*"

"Whenever you like. How like the young you are, Harry, so rushed to do the immediate thing, when you have all of time before you. But before I free you, I must ask: what is it you expect to find, beneath passion's veil?"

"Ah, Sphinx, an enigma? I cannot answer. Heretofore, I have kissed many handsome lads; but none of them have had this creature's perfection of form, and I feel that he can show me the true face of ardor, the secret of romance. Your riddle must remain unanswered, until my lips have tasted his."

Daintily, she exhaled perfumed smoke. "Then I release you to your feast."

I ran to where the young man stood and reached to him my hand, which he took as he stepped off the dais. The blue eyes beneath the pallid mask seemed to smile, as did the similitude of lips on his nigh-featureless mask. Lightly, lightly, I touched my finger to his mask, the surface of which was soft like a petal on a rose. My hand went to his crisp blond hair, at which my fingers clutched. Ah, how my heart pounded in my breast as I smashed my lips against the mouth-impression of the mask. And then I had my answer to my friend's riddle; for when I crushed my mouth against the pallid mask its surface sank inward, and I knew that there was nothing underneath.

III.

He ran through the city, trying not to scream as his frantic fingers tugged at flailing hair. The voracious yellow moon was sneering at him, and he had to find a shadowed place in which to escape its edacious glare. He could feel its dead light warping his brain with lunacy, as again he covered his mouth so as to squash his squalling. Beneath his whimpering he heard another sound, a musical wailing, and to this he sallied, leaping down the moonlit street until coming to the Harlot's house. Within he caught the thumping of bawdy feet, and against the blind he could just make out the vague inhuman silhouettes of the things that pirouetted jerkily to rapid music, like fantastics of mechanical bent. At times they blended into one other so as to form outlandish arabesques, and to gaze at them for too long a time was to succumb to strange vertigo. He shut his eyes to the dizzying sight and staggered forward, reaching out until his hand held onto a portion of porch. Opening his eyes to subtle sound, he saw the door to the house wrench open. A creature stood before him and lit a cigarette, which it brought to the mouth of its masklike countenance. Its large eyelids flapped as it raised its face so as to contemplate the moon, and then it opened its mouth, as though attempting to sing; but the only sound to issue forth was a vile hissing. Wobbling down the steps, the thing stopped to consider him with ruby eyes, and then it belched forth a cloud of poisonous smoke and went its way into the darkness of night.

He rushed up the wooden steps and slammed the door behind him. A large easy chair at his left proved inviting, and thus he sat so as to catch his breath. From behind double doors he heard the pandemonium of hellish dancing, the sound of which caved into his head and caused his skull to splinter. Cursing, he kicked off his shoes so that they struck the closed doors, but his actions had no effect. Barefoot, he rose and climbed the carpeted stairs that led to an upper level. Pushing open a door, he rushed into a room, and then he closed the door quietly as he listened to the tiny child who, sitting at a miniature pianoforte, played a tender rendition of Strauss the Younger's "Rosen aus dem Suden," to which a naked woman sadly waltzed. He took in her rusty hair, her too-long neck, around which, fastened on a piece of twine, there swung a straight razor's blade. He saw the thin lines of cord with which her mouth had been sewn shut, and as she danced to him her hands went to her tattered lips. She pantomimed a blown kiss, and wasn't it weird that he fancied he could feel a pressure, cool and liquid, on his eyes? Her hands flew to his and brought them to her taut breasts, her chilly nipples. From beneath the sewn lips he thought that he could detect a low sound, a moan of song. Oh, the sadness of her eyes. She longed to sing—to him. He raised one hand to the clean blade, held it with pinching fingers and sliced into the cords that stopped her sound. Released, the mouth expanded, and he shuddered at the torment of her temptress wail. Seduced, he slid the blade into each of his pale wrists, cutting to the bone. Delicately, he raised his hands above his head and shut his eyes to the baptism of blood. His naked feet moved in the spreading pool, until he could dance no more.

IV.

You walk through storm, your hand at your heart. You feel the faded flower in your buttonhole, the soggy green carnation that shreds and melts as you pull it free. Before you is the wide expanse of filthy air that somehow beguiles you, and as you near it the tempest drains of violence. You stand, a sodden thing, on graveyard ground, and watch the things that dance in fog around neglected tombs. You hear the steady clacking as hands of bone are clapped, which reminds you of the funeral rites of "the gourd people" that you witnessed on the coast of Côte d'Ivoire. You marvel at how the dense fog contains a kind of misty light that enhances sight.

From out one intimate tomb she dances toward you, the thing that wears your sister's hair. She has not completely lost her flesh, and the withered mask of skin covering her skull smiles at you, although too widely. Her rotting shroud floats in the fog that moves in whorls around her fragile form, as black leaves fall from high black limbs. She capers around you, playfully, and then she offers you the lily in her fungal hand, the flower that is the only living thing. You take the plant and touch it to your lips. Its potent odor spills into your face, your pores; you can taste it on your tongue. Your substantial mouth rips into the blossom's flesh, and the taste is delicious. You notice how pale are the hands that hold the rare half-eaten bloom; and then you kneel to your sister and offer her the uneaten half, and as she takes it you wind your frigid hands into her tarnished hair and brush away the black leaves that cling to it.

"Isola," you whisper, but the sound of your phantom voice is muffled in the tempest now returned. The teeming skeletonic horde whirl around you, coaxing you to join their fray. Your little sister smiles at the chaotic crew, takes your hand beckons you to stand. Together, you step into the danse.

V.

I entertained the evil things of life,
Those panther boys whose beauty I adored;
And for this crime I lost my sons, my wife,
And I became a thing grotesque, abhorred.
And thus what can I do but live in dream,
Where my fine name is not a thing of mud,
Where kissing handsome lads does not blaspheme,
Where, seven-veiled, I dance in pool of blood?
Ah, Dorian, the mirror of your eyes
Shews unto me youth's golden little time.
Ah, Sphinx, how beautiful you are, how wise.
Dear Bosie, teach me passion's poisoned crime.
I deign to dance in Dante's holy flames.
Judiciousness I leave to Henry James.

The Zanies of Sorrow

From childhood's hour I have not been
As others were—

—*Edgar Allan Poe*

I.

It was music that brought me into the twilit world of wonder and terror. I had lived in my new quarters for a few days, delighted in my escape from my wretched former existence. I had savings enough to live in frugal comfort for six months, enough time to complete my novel. Gladly, I left my dreary job, my boring friends, my unsympathetic family, and found a lonely apartment in a forgotten and nigh desolate section of the city. My escape was complete. I had my cat, my typewriter and my books. No one had a clue concerning my departure or destination. For one half year I would live a fantasy life or reading and writing in complete solitude. I realized, of course, that getting one's wish is not always the happy situation one hopes it might be. As Oscar Wilde so wisely said, when the gods wish to punish us, they answer our prayers. Still, the first few days were a time of happy ecstasy. The rooms were spacious and quiet. I had told my new landlord, Mr. Bullon, that *quiet* was essential if I were to be able to work on my book. He gave me a room with windows facing a lush back garden, so that I would not be annoyed by the little traffic passing on the front road.

All went well, until late one evening when, as I sat in cosy armchair with pen in hand and cat on lap, there came from across the hallway a faint sound of someone at their pianoforte. I was at first annoyed at this intrusion of sound, subdued as it was; yet the longer I listened the more beguiling the music became. It contained a quality of sorrow such as I had never experienced in song. As I continued to strain with listening, tears welled within my eyes. And when, abruptly, the music ceased, I found myself longing for its continuation.

The next morning I encountered the landlord in the laundry room. "Things are going well, Mr. Stone? Your writing?"

"Yes, very well, thank you."

"Your rooms are very quiet, yes?"

"They are. I do hear, occasionally, the piano playing from across the hall, but that is all."

"Ah, I shall tell Miss Greive to keep it down, as they say."

"Oh, it's not at all a nuisance. It's so late at night when she plays, I'm usually finished with my work at that hour."

"Late at night! No, no, it cannot be allowed. I shall inform her." And he rushed off before I could protest any further, leaving me frustrated and annoyed. I spent the afternoon feeling agitated, so much so that I could not concentrate on work. When early evening came, I made bold enough to step into the hallway and knock on my neighbor's door. After a brief wait, it opened, and my nostrils were delighted with a lovely fragrance. The woman who stood before me was very beautiful, so much so that for a moment I could not speak. She raised her brows in query.

"Do forgive me. I'm from across the hallway . . ."

"Ah, Mr. Stone. I had meant to speak to you this evening. Mr. Bullon . . ."

"Has misunderstood me," I interrupted. "I was in no way complaining. Your playing is very faint, not at all disturbing."

Disarmingly, she smiled. "You are very kind." Her voice was accented, and I suspected she was European. Her green eyes were kind but, I thought, rather guarded. I was surprised when she stepped back and opened the door widely. "I was just preparing my evening coffee. Will you join me?"

"I'd be enchanted," I said, hoping I didn't sound stupid. I crossed the threshold and entered another world, an older one. I could not believe that this apartment was identical to my own, and yet I knew that it was. I sensed that Miss Greive had lived here for a long time, as the room looked so very dwelt in. Soft lamplight illuminated many pieces of fine furniture, obviously antique. One entire wall was taken up with solid oak bookcases that were crammed with hardcover editions. There was a simple elegance, a delightful feminine grace, and I found the place enchanting.

"Please be seated, Mr. Stone."

"Albert."

She smiled and bowed her head. "And I am Lucretia. Pardon me one moment."

Rather than sitting, I crossed to the bookcases and examined titles. She soon returned, holding a tray of coffee cups and scones. "You are an author, I am told."

"Yes, mostly of short stories, although I'm working on a

first novel," I replied, wanting so to take up the volume of Henry James's unfinished novel, *The Sense of the Past*, in its original New York Edition. My rule was never to handle books belonging to another's library unless invited to do so. Setting down her tray, and perhaps sensing my bibliophilic hunger, she reached for the volume and placed it in my anxious hand. "Oh, thank you. He was such a superb novelist. Such discipline!"

"Discipline is a lesson one learns with years. You are very young."

"I'm twenty-eight.'

"As old as that?" Her smile was playful. "And what is your literary genre, Albert?"

""Human relations, social curiosities, with a touch of the uncanny. Maupassant and James are my chief influences, in shorter fiction. I have one small collection of short stories published, by a small press outlet. I fear I'm a bit old-fashioned for most modern editors; they tell me I'm too 'Victorian' because of my high-literary prose style. But I won't have publishers tell me what to write, or how to write it. I'll suffer James's fate if need be, and write beautiful books that are read but by the few."

"I adore James. There is much poetry in his prose. Much digging into strange human psyche. His tales of innocent Americans lured to the debaucheries of European decadence so amuse me."

"You're from Europe?"

A slight nod and blink of beautiful eyes. "I was raised in a very small village; but I have been in your country a long, long time."

I tried to deduce her age. Although she looked in her

early thirties, there was an air about her of someone much older; but perhaps that was the European manner, to which I was unaccustomed. Returning the book to its shelf, I joined my hostess on the sofa as she poured coffee from a beautiful antique pot of polished silver. The coffee was perfection.

We sipped and munched and spoke of literature. Often, I glanced into one corner of the room where sat her pianoforte. She seemed at last to notice. "Do you play, Albert?"

"No, alas, I'm not musical; but I love listening."

She hesitated, sucking at her lips. "Pardon me if I do not play for you. It is a very personal expression for me, my music, perhaps as your writing is for yourself. I simply cannot perform before others." She smiled and shrugged apologetically.

"Of course I understand perfectly," I replied, hiding my disappointment with a smile.

"Perhaps you can write a story about such a one, the woman who can perform only in solitude. That would have a touch of the—what was your word?—uncanny. A potent word, that."

"The world is indeed strange. I love reading biographies of musicians and artists. The *lives* that have been lived! It is often incomprehensible."

"And intimidating, such adventurous lives. I am not a brave soul, and so I live in this secluded existence."

"So do I. It's the best of worlds. I mean, I'm a student, of sorts, of human nature, but from a distance. My friends are always telling me that I don't 'live,' as if their constant going out and getting drunk or whatever constitutes a supreme reality. Some call me coward, hiding in my world of books. But I'm an artist. I don't escape the 'world' and my place in it. I feel my emotions as deeply as anyone."

She thought in silence for a moment. "No, we can never escape our destiny—our fate." How sad and weary she suddenly appeared. Perhaps she was tiring. Faking a yawn, I made my excuses, and she walked me to my door. "You will visit me again, Albert?"

"I shall be delighted to do so." Feeling a bit foolish, I took her hand and kissed it. She rewarded me with the loveliest of smiles. I closed my door and fell into my armchair, took up my current biography and did not open it. Eventually, I shut my eyes.

II.

For the next fortnight I was consumed with creativity. Ideas and imagery buzzed inside my brain to the point where sleep was nigh impossible. I burned to write. For days at a time I would neither dress nor bathe, but simply sat in bed and pressed pen to pad. If I had the energy or interest I would brew coffee, and stopping for meals was a necessary bore. My two interludes of frenzied activity were evenings spent with Miss Greive, at one of which I read the opening chapters of my work in progress, to her appreciative ear. I kept secret the fact that I had also outlined a short weird tale inspired by her idea of the solitary artist, wanting to surprise her with a gift of a polished manuscript.

After the second meeting, as I stood at her door, she stopped me. "I know that you are busy with your book, you are not a social person; but I wonder if you would care to go with me next Wednesday afternoon to visit . . . an old relation. He is a lonely old man who loves literature as we do."

She hesitated, as though trying to decide if her invitation had been an impulsive error.

"I should be delighted, of course," I quickly accepted. "A grandfather?"

"No . . . an uncle. A great uncle of advanced years, who has recently come to America from our small village. Really? You will come?"

"It will be my pleasure to accompany you." She surprised me with a warm kiss on the cheek, next to my mouth. Blushing, I crossed the hall and entered my room. Now, I have always been an introverted soul, a person self-contained. The only possible society, as Wilde declaimed, is oneself. Thus is life simplified. But as I looked over my wardrobe that evening, I regretted the lack thereof. My clothes were deplorably unsocial. Then I remembered seeing, in a second hand shop where I had gone in search of kitchen items, an inexpensive summer suit of beige cotton that had slightly attracted me. It would do superbly. Happily, I prepared for bed, where I sat up for a lengthy time, pen and pad ready, thinking I would work; but instead I merely daydreamed about my new life, at how unexpectedly well it was working out, at how delighted I was to have found a new friend who was such an congenial companion.

Finally drowsy, I set aside my writing utensils and extinguished the bedside lamp. As I was nearing the tide of dreams, I could vaguely hear, from across the hallway, the faint playing of the pianoforte. The sad music, like some mother's doleful lullaby for a child irretrievably lost, cradled me to sleep.

III.

Wednesday arrived. How delightful it felt to stride beside a person who so enchanted me, this beautiful woman. I glanced at her as we strolled, trying once more to guess her age. Her complexion was smooth, sans wrinkles or spots, and her eyes were youthful. The distance to her uncle's was not too lengthy, she said, and the day was so lovely, and so she suggested that we walk. She could thus point out some interesting aspects of the city in which I was a stranger, as she had been "so many years ago." At one point we passed a high granite wall. The swirling air was heavy with blossom fragrance, and as we stopped at an open gate I beheld a small, quaint cemetery. It was crowded with trees and shrubbery, and its tilting stones looked very old indeed.

"I often stop here," she said, guiding me beyond the threshold. "It's the oldest burying ground in the city. The lilac smells wonderful, does it not?"

The air seemed to have grown a few degrees chillier, and the wind rose in strength. I watched the swaying laburnum, with their poisonous yellow flowers. I saw the swaying plumes of white and pale pink lilac. At one corner of the old stone wall stood a gigantic willow tree, its long pale vines writhing as they drooped to the ground. Atop one tomb a cat washed itself in sunlight. How strange that a place of death should seem so alive.

"You have such an odd expression on your face, Albert," Lucretia said, laughing lightly. "Does this place unnerve you?"

"On the contrary. I feel almost audaciously at peace. As a child I often spent many joyous afternoons haunting an overgrown and abandoned graveyard that was situated high on a hill—Graham Hill, as I recall its name. The place was overrun with sticker bushes and shrubbery and bending trees. Neighborhood hoodlums had violated many of the markers. But I loved it there, among the happy dead."

"The dead are happy?"

"Of course they are; they're dead, you see." We laughed together.

"But what of the spirit?"

"I never think of that. I abhor the notion of eternity. You and I are material things, chemical components. We end as dust and ash. That, at least, is my fervent prayer. To go on, as spirit or any other thing! God, what could be more damnable than eternal life?"

I saw her momentarily stiffen. The sun was suddenly sheathed by clouds and then shone brightly once again. It illuminated her pale face and the pearls of teardrops that glistened in her eyes. "Let us go," she abruptly said, "it grows late."

Vacating the place of death, we continued our walk, eventually arriving at our destination, a neighborhood that seemed abandoned. Many houses were vacant, their doorways and windows boarded. A smell of decay tainted the air. She led me to a stone house that was tall, tilted and black with age. When I glanced at Lucretia as she escorted me to the steps, I noticed again a kind of nervous expression on her lovely face, as though she were regretting having me accompany her. I squeezed her hand reassuringly as the front door opened and an elderly gentleman greeted us. They exchanged words in a language I had never heard, and then we entered the house.

"My uncle is in the courtyard, resting. He has been ill of late—his heart, we think. We mustn't tire him." I nodded as she led me through a back door and onto an expanse of yard that was surrounded with a sturdy growth of tall shrubbery that served as fence. Beneath a fig tree, fanning himself as he lounged upon a large divan, was a creature so grotesque it shook my fortitude to look at him. If the caterpillar in *Alice in Wonderland* had risen from its grave a bloated, lichenous thing, it might resemble the creature at which I gawked. As we neared him, I sensed that he was fantastically ancient, the oldest person I had ever encountered. Not an uncle, but a great-great-great-uncle! Lucretia motioned for me to wait and went to her relation, with whom she conversed in their alien tongue. Then, turning to me and motioning with her lovely hand, she said in English, "This is Mr. Albert Stone. Mr. Stone, my uncle, Sebastian Greive."

Screwing my courage to its sticking place, I walked toward the figure on the divan. I took in greeting his outstretched hand and felt the heavy press of his moist and flabby fingers. He held tightly and too long. I could not help but stare at his face, with its bumps and rolls, its growths and moles. The face was a mask of false mirth, from which a pair of sapient eyes closely examined my own visage. He would not let go of my hand. His touch, the fabric of his flesh wrapped around my own, contained a kind of force, energy such as I had never experienced. I fancied that I could detect some thing—some essence—enter the texture of my skin and claim a portion of my being. His dewy lips stretched, and a voice that dripped with pleasure spoke.

"You are very welcome to my home, Mr. Stone. Lucretia has spoken of you with enthusiasm, and I am happy to make at last your acquaintance." His accent was far more pronounced than that of his niece.

"Thank you, you're very kind." At last he freed me from his grasp.

"Please to sit," he begged, motioning to a lawn chair. "Lucretia . . ." He hesitated and gazed at the young woman, as if to query whether it was proper for him to so address her. His formal habits seemed quaintly European. "Lucretia is not one to form so fast friendships. Where we come from, we keep mostly to our own selves."

"You've never really told me where you're from," I said to Lucretia, who sat in the chair next to my own. Her uncle answered for her.

"A small village, that no one has heard of." He shrugged and exchanged a look with his niece, and I sensed secret meanings and implications in their furtive glances. I also intuited his anxious need for conversation. He looked a lonely old fellow, with his fan held limply in one hand. His grotesque form was encased in what looked like pajamas of yellow silk. The dainty feet were bare.

"I've never been abroad," I ventured. "Lack of time and money. Too, I'm very stupid when it comes to learning languages. Now and then I've borrowed recordings from the library in attempts to learn Latin and French, but my lazy brain revolts at such education, alas."

"It is not so difficult when there is little else for passing time. I learned your language from an Englishman who was my friend in prison." A pregnant pause. "I spent many years incarcerated. Is that the word?" This last was to his niece, who replied in scolding tone in their native idiom. He answered shortly in like, then smiled at me. "With little to do except read from inadequate libraries, I passed the time learning your so peculiar tongue."

"You speak it very well."

He shrugged. "Well, I had long time for learning. Many decades behind unfriendly bars. But now I am released and come to free America."

"An unpleasant experience, prison life," I mumbled.

"One finds companions, but misses the little freedoms. I do not live so differently now, old thing that I am. Except, of course, in my way of dressing. The great tragedy of prison life is prison clothing." I laughed good-naturedly, he sounded so like a passage from Wilde. "It is not easy life, incarcerated in small ignorant village. I was so long locked up in little room that, in time, my captors seemed to have forgotten my great offense. Or lost record of it. But their fear and hatred for my kind, that does not become forgotten. But that I was imprisoned for necromancy—no, that they could not remember, or did not wish to."

"Enough," came Lucretia's stern voice.

"*Basta!* Our guest is author, student of life. I give him a glimpse he cannot imagine."

I felt distinctly uncomfortable. Miss Greive smiled apologetically. "This is my eccentric uncle," her smile seemed to say. Her face told me, also, that he was someone she dearly loved.

"I'm not much versed in the black arts," I offered lamely.

"Black? No, no, Mr. Stone. The *old* arts, the very old religion. Not like what one sees on television, the what do you call it, psychic hot line? I see that, I laugh."

"You mentioned necromancy, which is conversing with the dead, correct?"

"In part, yes. And the brewing of potions to sell to they not of our race."

"You were Gypsies then?"

"Gypsy?" He frowned at the word and looked to his niece, whom mumbled a strange word. "Oh, no! Not as respectable as that! We were like the women in *Macbeth*—you know the play?"

"Ah, witches."

"Yes, we witched. And in our little village, especially when I was young—one century ago!—that is so great a crime." These words alerted something in my mind. Yes, I could imagine that he had been young one hundred years ago. How long had he existed, this bizarre creature? I found myself believing his every word. He coughed and rubbed his throat with thick fingers. "But we are parched. My dear, could you assist Franz with refreshments?" Rising, Lucretia gave the ancient one a heavy look and then was gone. Sebastian and I watched the rising moon, an orange medallion that glowed in the *demi-jour* of dusk.

"Were you very young when they placed you in prison?"

He sighed. "Oh, I had been there before, as child; for stealing and begging, you know, what a child must do for hunger. They knew, of course, my heritage. Once I was imprisoned for raising a storm that frightened the governor's horses!" He chuckled at this memory. "But my great crime, for which I was many years in tiny cell, was necromancy. My parents and an uncle had been falsely accused—and executed. It was injustice, and so I raised them up, returning to them their innocent mortality. An unthinkable crime, in

98

that place at that time." He paused, frowning deeply. When again he spoke, it was more to himself than to his audience. "We had the old scrolls and parchments, of course, handed down from the ancients. But I found spell in moldy book, which had been forbidden for us to look into. I did not care. I was young! But I must have misspoke. I learned that my art was flawed. I watched from tiny window as they tried once more to execute my innocent relations. They could not. I was very emotional when I spoke the spell and threw the runes, you see. Perhaps I was unhinged. I do not understand what I did incorrect; but those I raised could not again return to death—*ever*." He gazed at me with weird green eyes. "Is that not unspeakable, Mr. Stone?"

"Yes," I whispered, as my flesh prickled.

From out the house came Lucretia and the servant Franz. The elderly man carried a large tray filled with an assortment of refreshments, while she held three long-stemmed glasses in one hand and a very tall and tapered wine bottle in the other. I smiled, as Brazilian banana wine was a favored vintage. Franz, wobbling just slightly, placed the cumbersome tray upon a low table. Handing to him his fan, Mr. Greive said something to the servant in their native tongue, motioning to the expanse of lawn before us. As Lucretia filled the glasses with golden liqueur, Franz went out into the yard and set alight a number of braziers fastened onto tripods. In the flickering light I espied that which had hitherto escaped my notice, a small yellow tent some distance from us.

Sebastian spoke to his beautiful young relation, and she beautifully laughed. I had emptied my glass like the greedy thing I am, and seeing this the elder one bent and took up the bottle of wine, replenishing my glass. Then, swiftly, he tossed the bottle high into the air and then caught it on the circular tips of his gigantic fingers, where he balanced it with dexterity. I laughed and applauded.

"You are a shocking show-off," his niece playfully scolded. I think the wine was working its magic, mellowing her mood.

Sebastian gazed at me with wide, innocent eyes. "Am I, Mr. Stone? Am I a shocking show-off?"

"Appallingly so," I assured him. He beamed, delighted. It came to me, with sudden enlightenment, that I had lost all trace of my former repugnance for this horribly old and ill-formed creature. Surreptitiously, he had charmed me with his manner; he had delighted me with his talk, strange as it had been. Much of my change of attitude, I knew, came from the great affection my beautiful young friend had for her old, old uncle.

"And now," Sebastian spoke in a low hushed voice, "entertainment." With odd emotion gleaming in his green-hued eyes, he raised a hand to the moon and made with it curious movement. I heard the soft tinkling of bells. The sound seemed to emanate from the small tent at the far end of the yard. I watched and saw the bent-over figure that emerged from the flaps of egress. Slowly, it unwound and rose. I trembled when I saw how tall it stood, how lean its frame appeared. It was dressed in motley, and the thin long arms seemed composed of smooth white wood—or bone. With a jerk of its head it jangled the bells of its cap to an unusual rhythm, and from its face there issued a high weird wailing.

I felt myself shrink into my chair. The wailing sound was song, a tune that I had first heard weeks earlier, from behind my neighbor's door. Originally I had heard it indistinctly, in quiet playing. Now I heard it clearly, and the sound of it chilled my blood. The figure jostled through the darkness and then entered the lambent light of one of the flaming braziers. I looked upon its face and moaned in fear. The too-thin visage was a pallid mask of woe. In size it seemed no larger than a skull, although in shape in resembled nothing remotely human.

Stopping, it stomped a slippered foot upon the grass. From within the tent there came a profusion of jangling. Slowly, inexorably, they filtered through the flaps: the tall, the lean and pale companions of the first creature. They raised horrific hands to the moon, moving bony fingers as if in signal. In time to eldritch wailing, those bony hands bent forward until fingertips touched elbows; and then, awfully, those hands bent the other way, until colorless nails pressed impossibly to wrists.

They danced toward us, with heads like canine skulls that jerked spasmodically. Their movement might have seemed clownish if the creatures had not been so utterly grotesque. As they neared us, I looked imploringly at my hostess. How pale was the face that watched in rapture the awful jesters! She seemed to have forgotten my presence, and I watched as she slowly rose and moved in rhythmic danse into the inhuman herd. Her lovely hands lifted to moonlight and made strange signals to the sky.

The wailing beast was nigh, and my blood was heavy sludge that weighted me to my chair. I could not move as Sebastian Greive heavily rose from his divan and stalked into the clutch of dancers. He clapped his hands and strenuously stomped his naked feet. He punched his ponderous stomach in time to the enchanted noise. And his face, that large and fleshy countenance with its eyes of jade that so curiously reflected moonglow, wore an expression of profound woe that was identical to that of his conjuration's skeletonic crew. They danced in sallow moonlight, encircling the young woman and playing with her hair. I saw pearls of sorrow in her awesome eyes as she exchanged gazes with her old relation. They seemed to share a bond of secret and inexplicable desolation. I watched as the impossibly aged man leaped on prancing feet into the air, as if he were a child trying to fetch a gleam of starlight. Again he jumped, and the ground shook at the force of his landing. Suddenly, he jerked and placed a hand upon his breast. Weirdly, the dancing creatures did the same. With strangled cry Sebastian fell onto the ground, with a thud that seemed to convulse the floor of earth. And they, the nameless buffoons who had danced in jest of all existence, they also fell and melted into pools of shadow.

And she! Oh, great heaven, the beautiful she, finally floated to the ground, where she lay twitching until, with great effort, she commanded her composure. Slowly, achingly, she crawled to the prostrate form of her rasping relation. I quavered in the dull silence and then found the strength to creep out of my chair and limp to where they lay. Lucretia had placed the elder one's head into her lap and was murmuring alien words while holding a smooth white hand to the moon. I watched her hand move in esoteric fashion as the old man's hand rose to join it in movement. And then his hand fell upon her tear-dewed face. He whispered words in a language I did not know.

His heavy hand fell to the grass. With eyesight blurred by stinging tears, I reached for it, that hand that had once so

102

revolted me. I felt a dim memory of the power that I had experienced when I had initially touched its flesh. Sebastian glanced at me and managed a feeble smile; then, looking to his kinswoman he whispered, "Forgive me." The fading force of alchemical power crept from the fingers that I held, those fingers that grew still and cold.

"*In pace requiescat,*" I wept, as Lucretia blessed me with a gracious look. I gazed hard into her magnificent face. "Why did he beg your forgiveness?" I boldly asked. "What was your uncle's awful woe?"

"He was not my uncle," she sobbed. "He was my son."

In Remembrance: Edgar A. Poe

We have drunken of things Lethean, and fed on the
fullness of death.

—*Swinburne*

I.

Childishly, I wave at the dark cloud that forms its strange
shape in the blue sky. What is it, that eerie patch of storm
that seems to pulse there, above the antique town, like some
bruise on the flesh of Heaven? Looking at it bequeaths to me
a queer passion, for that patch of darkness seems to emulate
the chaos of my stormy life. I gaze at the sleepy town, at the
trees that wear their autumn tint of gold; but I cannot keep
my eyes away too long from that daemon shape that forms
above my favorite haunt. Playfully, I hunker down and
twist my limbs, so as to reshape myself until I resemble the
daemonic cloud in my view, that thing of aether to which
my soul is strangely drawn. For am I not a fiend like unto it,
a dark and deformed stain among humanity? That black
cloud well represents my seething brain, that brain that roils
with a tempest of passion.

I float down the precipitous hill, to Benefit Street. I
breathe in the tangy wind that buffets my ears with ageless
song. I drift, a shadow dressed in somber black, down the

steps and across the winding lane, toward the silent church. Ah, there, the tabletop slab, sweet tomb of final repose. Gods, let me rest my head upon your stone, this head so heavy with weighty memories. I see the sky grown dark with promised storm. Gentle rain falls upon my face and lets me drink the sky. With that special liquid I taste a remnant of spilled cloud, a tissue of the darksome patch with which I felt such kinship. Now the rain falls with abandon, spilling into the sod, to the frigid mouths of those who drink it as Lethe and thus never remember the wretched thing called Life. This churchyard is my Elysium. My sick mind dwells upon all the lost souls who have sat upon this slab of rotting stone and reflected on the Worm. I think of you, Howard, sitting here and writing your sonnet to Poe. Of you, Edgar, sighing here for her who shall remain nameless evermore.

I lie at full length on this hoary slab of stone, and anyone seeing me, unmoving in the rain that soaks my form, may fancy me dead. I like the soothing rain, which pools beneath my weight of flesh and bone. I dream that it eats away the surface on which I recline and allows me to sink into an ancient pit of earth, a delicious premature burial that weds me to the roots and worms that wind around my fingers and weave into my hair. The passing of centuries has tainted my tattered gown, so that I look, when at last I rise to stand upon my feet, an eidolon of death.

The storm has passed. A full moon graces me with magical radiance. My senses alter and I listen to the sighing of my kindred underground. I depart the peaceful place and walk the winding path. I climb the steps that take me to Benefit Street, to the living.

II.

The lunatic poetess stepped into an All Hallow's evening, from the bed and breakfast in Providence where she was spending Halloween week. She looked across Benefit Street, to the yellow house that had figured in a weird tale by a Providence horror author; but she felt no thrill of the macabre, for the house looked very nice and normal, clean and sanctified. Walking across the narrow New England street, she approached the place that had been transformed into a pitiable little park dedicated to some local woman. Beyond the park's stone ledge was a tiny brick patio and black iron fence, the gate of which, opened, led to an incline of woodland. She sat upon the chilly ledge, beside a small cloth box, the golden clasp of which she unfastened. The balls inside were small, but as she plucked one from its container she discovered that it had been weighted with whatever was contained within its sphere. The object's surface was a pale absinthe green, on which had been painted the image of a black cat. She knew that they were iron "health" balls from China, and had once seen an educational program on their use. Reaching into the container, she took up the second ball and smiled at the tiny musical sound that issued from it. With one ball in each hand, she gently banged them at her ears. How queer it sounded, the distorted chiming from inside the spheres. The noise swelled as it sank into her orifice and sounded inside her brain, where it shaped itself darkly. Cloudy images pushed onto the back of her eyes, blurring vision. Not liking the things that formed before her vision, she clanged the balls before her face, violently.

From some distant place came the pealing of church bells, as if in answer to the clamorous explosion of noise of

106

her Baoding balls. A white thing watched her from the sky, and as her eyesight cleared she saw that it was the pale-faced moon. Raising her hands to that lunar sphere, she banged the balls together once again and shuddered at the clang and crash of the bells, bells, bells—those inside the balls, and from some distant place, and from inside her skull.

III.

How pale is the moon that hangs in heaven—that eidolon of lunacy and death, as white as a whimsical maggot. I climb the steep hill, to Congdon Street, and stroll to the small park where one is rewarded with a magnificent view of downtown Providence and other westward regions. And it is there, squatting beneath a tree, that I find my Pierrot, the dwarf who reads by moonlight from a slim volume of poetry. His white tunic is slightly soiled, and the painted visage beneath his black skullcap resembles that of a monkey. Seeing me, he drops his volume of verse into some invisible pocket and rises up on bent and crippled limbs. Against tradition, the ape speaks:

> "I know a place of solitude where mortal sound cannot
> intrude,
> Where on the floor an oblong box (with neither orna-
> ment nor locks)
> Awaits the One who will awake, shedding slumber to
> partake
> In acts of ecstasy sublime—out of Space and out of
> Time."

Saying nothing more, the small creature moves away from the tree and out of the park. I watch its curious gait—

for the creature's cursed limbs keep it from walking as a man, and thus its movements are a queer combination of a hop and a fidget. The wee thing pauses for a moment, not looking back. I move through dark air and follow as my guide resumes his motion. He leads me to a vacant mansion of an American colonial mode of design; but we do not enter in, and I continue to shadow the jester as he leaps across a pebbled path that winds to a small hothouse, into which he enters. I stand for a little while and observe how moonlight falls like film onto the panes of glass with which the building has been structured. I stalk to the transparent door and place my hand upon its warm surface, and beneath my hand I fancy that I can discern a faint reverberation, like some trembling of a heartbeat. When I open the door my face is kissed with a rush of hot ventilation.

The atmosphere is illuminated with thick and cloudy incandescence, soft yet bright. I walk past beds of orchids and cacti, past pots of citrus trees. I espy where my guide sits on the floor before an oblong box, oblivious as a moonstruck calf. I bend to the box and lift its black lid—and I gasp at the scent of past eons that arises from the swathed shape nestled therein. The sepia bandages, tinted by immemorial time, have been tightly wrapped around the feminine figure they encase. The face alone is naked of aged cloth, and I stare at the beauty of dark features, the full dry lips, the exquisite glass orbs that replace living eyes.

Mists of moonlight melt through the glass roof and drift to us as I wrap my arms around her light figure and lift her from her oblong box. I sense, dimly, the faint pulsing that I experienced when placing my hand against the transparent hothouse door; and I smile as the apish gnome takes a recorder from one invisible pocket and begins to play a melancholy tune in time to the subtle throbbing of the place. I dance with my silent nymph, and as we whirl I breathe into the supple lips that seem to smile. I bring those lips to my ear, so as to drink in some words from the mummy priestess. My attention thus distracted, I do not see the tall black throne until we crash into it. I spiral to the floor, where I lay sprawled like an ill-bred fool, with my head upon her sheathed breasts. And thus I hear it—the source of abstruse sound, from some secret place beneath her wrappings. I hear it clearly—low, dull, steady—an accusing reverberation. My jester had stopped his playful noise and regards me with mocking eyes. God! That beating, beating, beating! It throbs inside my head! I can feel it beneath my eyes and in my nose. Madly, my foaming mouth clinches her ancient bandages, eating dust and death. Raving, I rip with fingers into her carcass and pluck out the tormenting fiend—her liquid beating heart. I curse the fiend who leans unmoving, that ape whose eyes ridicule me. I throw her beating organ at him and growl as he deftly catches it. Glancing at the mummy's face, I behold that one of the glass orbs has become dislodged, so that it sags from out its socket, a round pale thing like a vulture eye. The sight of it drives me mad with horror and disgust, and jumping to my feet I kick the carcass from me, falling backward into the black throne.

My monkey Pierrot holds the heart toward the glass roof, unto the moon, and as I turn my eyes I catch that lunar sphere that darkens and turns crimson. From somewhere within the vacant mansion a clock chimes the hour. I suck in the red mist that is the hothouse air as my simian courtier hops toward my throne and acquiesces. I handle the proffered thing and hold it high above me. How horribly, wretchedly, her detached organ (still beating, ever beating) stains my hand with mess of blood. I tightly squeeze the beating fiend and let its hot juice rain over my vesture and bead upon my brow. Blood-bedewed I arise, a thing of wet red death, ready to hold illimitable dominion over all.

IV.

Lunar light darkened, and when she lifted her eyes to the moon she saw it transform, cloud with crimson tint, become a disc of blood in black heaven. Some winged silhouette darted past the moon and flew into the woods before which she stood. From somewhere among the trees she heard a raven's cry, a spectral echo. The poetess followed this eidolon of sound, past the black fence and into the wooded area, past a growth of shrubs with large leaves. She stepped onto the flat stones that formed a kind of path leading toward the yellow house, and then she climbed eight stone steps that took her higher into dark woodland. The stone steps ended; before her were a series of ancient wooden steps that took her higher yet, to a winding path that ended before a monumental tree. Upon a low branch of that tree, a raven watched her progress.

She moved toward the dendroid dweller in the woods and stared at the oval frame fastened to its massive trunk. The dense growth of surrounding trees offered little light with which to study the gilded frame, which was Moorish in the style of its ornamental design. Standing very still, she stared at the portrait of the young girl encircled by the filigreed frame, a portrait showing only the head and a portion of shoulders. She had never beheld a visage as *haunted* as that

110

of the oval portrait. There was nothing in the expression that suggested any kind of human feeling; she could discern no trace of sorrow or anger, of joy or contemplation. The face was a void, a negation.

A rustling sound came from above, and she watched the woman in the portrait lift a hand so as to catch the sleek black feather that drifted from where it had detached itself from a raven's wing. She watched the young woman's image smooth that black feather across her mouth, her nose, her eyes. Reaching to the canvas and touching it, she found that it was smooth and hard, like glass; and when it cracked at the touch of her hand she could feel that splinter form as a crevice on her skull. Falling to her knees, she caressed her throbbing dome as blackness leaked from out her brain and formed about her as shapes pent in dementia and shadow. They approached, these formless woodland ghouls; they flowed about her and pressed their phantom paws upon her palms. They plucked the raven's feather from her hand and stuck it into her hair.

She rose up and walked through the shadows, to the edge of the brief woods, to the slanted street awash with lamplight. Climbing Jenckes Street, she reached Congdon Street and followed it to Prospect Terrace, where she saw, standing at the railing, another phantasm. The spectre in white had its back to the woman who watched and wondered; but then it seemed to sense the eyes that pierced with peering, and turning, it held out a gloved hand. The young lunatic approached and gasped at the elder woman's attire. The tight dress of pure white fabric resembled an invertebrate tube of soft flesh. The woman's lengthy hair hung in coils from a pale scalp. The poetess took hold of the proffered hand and wondered that a silken glove should feel so dry.

"Isn't the night perfect?" oozed the elder woman's contralto voice. "I am Madame Vermes, and I predict that you are off to attend the secret All Hallow's Gala."

"I am," the poetess confided. "Helen Weir," she spoke, introducing herself.

"Ah! I am familiar with your work." Releasing Helen, Madame Vermes raised her gloved hands to the moon and recited:

> "The conqueror moon has ignited
> With beams of imperial light
> These eyes, which now tremble, excited
> To drink in the secrets of Night!"

How strange, thought Helen, to hear one's poetry spoken, and by such a commanding voice. Her face must have expressed her wonder, for the elder woman laughed.

"Ah—my dear innocent one. How old are you, fourteen? Heavens! You have tasted so little of *expérience*. I shall enrich you with maturity tonight. You know much of madness but nought of sin. Tonight you shall dine on consummate pleasure. Come, your arm." From out of a small patch of woodland below a dark winged shape rose toward the moon. Madame Vermes chuckled at the raven's raucous cry. "Ah—there is our familiar spirit! Lead on, Erebus, we shall follow thy sooty trail!"

Arm in arm, the sisters walked beneath an All Hallow's moon, until they reached the ancient mansion, from which was emitted soft sounds of cautious habitation. Madame Vermes pushed open the door without knocking and led her young companion into an antechamber, wherein there stood a tall ebony clock. The elder woman smiled and raised a white finger. "Ah—listen! The music of the spheres!" Caressing Helen's face with her gloved hand, the woman in white approached the double doors that led into a spacious ballroom. Helen's eyes trembled excitedly at the sight before her. An orchestra of mannequins breathed fitfully into their instruments, watched by a choir of angels, bedight in veils, who accompanied the invisible sound of woe. The chamber was lit with golden candlelight that shimmered from a jeweled chandelier. A gaggle of mimes muttered before a large table, holding platters on which they piled a species of food. The Madame turned to gaze deeply into the eyes of the girl at her side, those eyes wherein hope and fear danced a minuet. Laughing, the elder woman took the younger in her arms and led her into a waltz.

The ebony clock in the hall chimed the velvet hour of midnight, that plush hour when lunatic minds weave soft silky dreams within the skull. Helen Weir felt that web of dark abstraction remove her from the woman in her arms, from the motley drama of the mimes, from the sound of puppets at their performance. She turned to the door that led outside, the door that slowly opened, allowing entrance to the formless thing that the orchestra had beckoned, the thing imbued with human gore. The chandelier lights extinguished in the whirlwind that rushed into the chamber—that carrion gust. Helen watched as Madame Vermes sauntered to the blood-drenched figured and genuflected before it, the tight coils of her serpentine hair moving in the wind. She watched as the elder woman stretched onto the floor and writhed.

The angels, all pallid and wan, began to moan an aching sound in honor of their Lord.

V.

I walk out of the hothouse, into cool autumn night-tide. My little jester hops before me, to the double doors that lead into a chamber of the mansion. From somewhere within the abode a clock strikes twelve. My courtier turns to me and speaks:

> "'Tis now the very witching time of night
> When churchyards yawn and hell itself breaks out
> Contagion to this world."

He bows before me as the clock peals its final chime, and then he turns and slowly opens the doors to which I walk. The whirlwind that heralds my sovereignty rushes past me and whips the occupants in the room. I smell extinguished light and watch the tableau before me. Veiled angels observe my entrance and weep invisible woe, recognizing the soul of horror. I see the mincing mimes, in their attire of blue and vivid purple, of green and bright orange, of pure white and secret violet. The seventh mime is attired in ebony, yet he alone wears an addition to his sartorial expression, a dangling ribbon of blood-red scarlet around his throat. He alone is smiling.

My jester lights a flambeau and leaps into the arms of the black-attired mime. The chalk-faced figure flings my fool into the air, high into the branches of the chandelier. Golden light drenches the occupants of the room. I signal to the puppet orchestra, and they place instruments to sculpted lips and breathe splintered notes of music. Lured by enchanted song, a raven flies into the room and perches on the shoulder of the black-attired mime. I squint my eyes at the sight of my whore, writhing beneath me in her tight white

114

gown. In contempt I strike her head with my foot. She squirms across the polished floor toward a mime who offers her the nourishment upon his platter. My whore plucks at the debris of foodstuff with her mouth as her coils of hair wind around the mimic's hand.

I see the beautiful child and smell her poignant lunacy. I flow like spilled blood to where she stands and take her into my embrace. She does not resist as I place my mouth to hers, as my tongue worms down her throat until it tastes her throbbing heart, that hollow muscular organ that pulses in time to nightmare's music. Ah!—how tightly she embraces me, as I lead her into my danse macabre.

Keepsake

"Ah," you moan. "The fall of darkness, and here we are at last, in the moonlit shadow of a spire. Your hair catches a residue of shimmer as it is silhouetted against those ancient skies. Here, let me sweep away the debris of star-stuff that litters your soft, soft hair. I like your arms around me as I bend unto you. I could stay one hundred years in your embrace."

The night-wind rises, rushing at us, as if to cool your passion. "Sha, shtil" you hiss. "Too loud, the sounds in this churchyard where we sniff crumbled mortality. Yes, I smell it in your hair, in this soft velvet strand that I have plucked from you so as to dab my tear-dimmed eye. Do you moan? No, 'tis but the echo of wind in that cavity, your mouth. Let me close it with my kiss."

You shudder with resurrected ecstasy, and I am held so tightly in your grip that the coins roll from my eyes. Your finger plays upon my smile. "That mouth will not stay shut," you laugh. "How your teeth gleam in this audacious moonlight. Is this one still lightly loose? I think it proper, in this churchyard where Poe once prowled, to twist your little tooth. How simply it is removed, to be held as pearl to starry night. Shall I place it in your palm? Your hand is dry and heavy."

You clamp me tightly as we recline onto the chilly ground, as you count the winking stars. "Some part of you," you whisper, "is in motion still, up there, moving between darkness and light. Perhaps I can find that part of you again; perhaps you will reveal it if I kiss your eye." Your moist lips stain my eye, which does not close as you press your mouth against it.

Postcard from Prague

Avigdor:—

I hear wind in moonlit trees—an emotionless sound. Lunar light gloves this hand with which I trace your name on rough tomb-rock. The wound on my finger (do you remember?) has opened once again. How dark the crimson drops appear in this pale light. Blood on stone, again. I cannot find the pit where Judah lies buried, but I have scraped a little hole into the sod, into which I whisper his name; and into that little hole I shall bury the tiny Golem that you fashioned out of clay.

Dearest, I have found a bit of broken tombstone, one edge of which is sharp. I shall bring it home. I shall hold it to pale moonlight in the place where you rest beneath cold earth. I shall dig until I touch your face, and with this stone I shall inscribed your forehead. Dearest, I shall shiver when, again, you hold me in your arms.

Eternally,
Karo.

Necronomicon

(For S. T.)

They came to me in midnight rain, during the hour of
mournful madness. I had read too deeply into the book and
could not tear myself away. I don't know for how many days
and nights I sat there, in the darkness of my study, gazing at
the arcane alphabet with which the words had been composed. When I closed my eyes the words were still before me:
I could taste them in my mind; my twitching lips trembled
to speak the words aloud. I thought that I could hear the
wind whisper those nameless words from some place outside
my window. No, no—it was not the wind; rather, it was my
hot mouth that uttered chilly arcane language. I whispered,
looking out the huge window into black heaven, and saw the
dark-winged things that flowed from celestial shadow, toward me. I watched the window's glass melt at their approach. Like dripping shaggy things that had been pent in
gloom—and now released by my syllables—they oozed into
the room, the wet flapping of their wings beating in rhythm
to my frenzied chanting.

Smoothly, they drifted to me. Gently, they brushed with
shapeless paws my face and hair. They leaned their amorphous faces toward my own and listened intently to my liv-

ing language. They brought to their mouths their strange flute instruments. The room was filled with intoxicating sound. It was a music that sounded familiar, like something I had heard in recent reverie. I opened my mouth and sang verses from the book in tune to the melodic air that stained the silence of the room. Looking once more at the book, my shining eyes adored the black syllables etched onto ancient parchment. When at last I blinked and raised my head, I saw the dying sunset flame heaven with supernal crimson. The final sight, reflected on my liquid eyes, was the purple of evening engulfed by swirling storm.

The winged creatures played more frantically their fantastic notes. I gazed at the approaching storm, and saw the face of eternal doom—a face composed of congeries of iridescent globes. Ah—my eyes—how they *boiled*.

The book is before me. I can smell the wormy pages whereon the words are found, those signals that reach beyond the void to where the One-in-All pulses in eternal corruption. As these plucked eyes stain my palms, I sense the tintamarre of bestial wings. I hear unthinkable voices speak my name above the storm. Yuggoth damns my puny soul. I stagger to my feet and scream to obscurity the unhallowed name. Shapeless paws grip under my arms and lift me upward. I limp beyond reason to that place where lives no masquerade of human hope.

Sickness of Heart

Slowly, his eyelids opened. Blurred forms seethed before him, hideous and pale. Ghosts of trees encircled him, swaying spectral limbs that made no noise. There was no solid sound; there was merely a dull suspicion of a deep and steady pulsing.

Pulsing. It came from beneath his bended knee. Hazily, he eyed the circle of stone faces that surrounded him, the tormented faces that contorted in awful mimicry of his own, as if they were mirrors of rock. One particular face disconcerted him, for it resembled a fiend with whom he was horribly familiar; and as he gazed steadfastly at that countenance he saw its sculpted mouth stretch in mockery, and from that mouth there came a low moaning that echoed in some deep placed within his skull. And as he watched, the other stones yawned and groaned; and from someplace beyond the spectral woodland other voices joined in the choir of misery and pain. The sound was like a knife that pierced his heart, and he opened wide his mouth so as to scream torment; but the other mouths joined with him in the tumult, so that he could not tell which of the screams was his own.

Pulsing. Screams within the swirling mauve mist. The knife was in his hand, and the flesh of his wrist was split; and from that wound there issued a red fog that spilled into the

122

air. He watched as the sculpted faces that surrounded him took that crimson fog into their mouths and shuddered. Raising the knife to his eyes, he peered onto its shining blade, but did not recognize the face reflected thereupon. He moved the blade's point to his eye and pushed until he could feel that point pierce into his brain.

Vision. It flowed before him as a cloud of darkness. From within its thickness he could hear a whispered throb, a dull sound that matched his heartbeat. Ah, his sick heart, that aching muscle that pulsed so stupidly inside his breast. What a curse it was to have a human heart. Thus his fingers tore into his chest and clutched the trembling thing and ripped it out. He watched it beat within his bloodstained palm, like some little fiend. Full of rage, he threw his heart into the fog, the fog that swallowed the moist and fleshy organ with its black mouths.

Mouths. They spat mockery that crawled to him like some chaotic jesters. His mouth caught the bits of tissue that had been expectorated from the sculpted mouth, those bloodstained bits of him that pranced down his throat to that cavity, his chest, where they mingled and formed themselves into a harvest of new tormenting hearts.

The Tangled Muse

I.

Sebastian Melmoth lounged on his divan as Max Romp peered at him and sketched impressions onto a pad. The smoke from Sebastian's opium-tainted cigarette rose in whorls that shaped themselves suggestively before his large face; and as he studied their cryptic designs his mouth curled as if to suggest some secret amusement in his mind, and then his breath of laughter pushed the haze away.

"I confess that I'm a bit anxious about your portrait, Max. Your caricatures are so cruelly honest, so offensively true-to-life. They show a distinct want of imaginative exaggeration. You hold your mirror up too close to Nature."

Ada Artemis stood beside a bronze statue of Bast and admired its inlaid blue-glass eyes. Her eyes were of a clear and almost-colorless grey; Sebastian had often complained that such eyes contained no secrets, that nothing could be hidden within such pellucid organs. A woman of few words, she silently watched the scene before her as her hand stroked the surface of the goddess.

Max set down his pen and pad and went to a table on which there was a decorative decanter of sherry. Carefully, he filled a delicate glass with the wine and sipped, and then he walked to where a full-length portrait of a beautiful young man sat on an upright easel. "The same can't be said for this, Sebastian. No one could really be that beautiful. Where did you find it?"

"It's been in my family for generations, on the Wotten side. I never told you that I am descended from aristocracy on my father's side. The painting is a family curiosity, a damaged thing kept in attics for decades, discarded and forgotten. My great Uncle Sebastian, after whom I am named, was especially obsessed with it, so family legend relates, and used to sit in a small dark room talking to the thing. I have told you of him, Ada, the uncle who went mad and spent his final years in an asylum. On the evening of his last madness, for which he was confined, he was found shrieking at the painting and slashing at the figure's breast with a silver dagger. Seems the thing was giving him bad dreams. No one bothered with repairing the canvas—indeed, the family took an active dislike to the thing and kept it hidden, perhaps linking it to the mental destruction of a once-beloved relation." Sebastian shrugged. "It eventually came to me, and I had it repaired. The original frame has been lost, no doubt having been used for some other work while this delightful boy was doomed to collect dust in tiny hidden rooms. I brought him with me when I first came to Gershom. I have yet to find a frame suitable for so perfect a representation of youthful beauty. His expression—it breaks my heart. Such a wistful look, almost touching on some vague sadness. What do you think, Sphinx?"

Ada walked to the painting and stood directly in front of it. As a painting it was superb, but she did not care for its subject. There was, beneath the boy's sad eyes, a taint of peevishness; she did not care for the way the fingers of one hand curled, imagining that she saw in them something cruel and clutching. Ada turned to the divan, but before she could disappoint her host with her reply, a young man rushed into the room, hastily removing hat and coat and handing them to the servant who followed him, but keeping a small leather portfolio that he gripped in one long hand.

"Sorry I'm late, Sebastian. I had a sudden brainstorm and got lost working on a new illustration, and that always makes me lose track of time." He then noticed the others in the room who were observing him and became silent, a bit of color coming to his complexion.

Sebastian rose from his divan and went to embrace the boy. Turning to the others he said, "I introduce Japheth Beardsley, a new resident to our city, whom I observed sketching at his table in the Café Regal, much to the chagrin of his maître d'. The sketch was quite grotesque, and very fine. I immediately introduced myself, and we became instant friends."

The others looked at the young man, taking in his threadbare clothes, his gauntness, the hatchet face below the oddly cut chestnut hair. Finally, Ada moved from the painting, approached Japheth and took his hand. "We're pleased that you could join our little *soirée*. I am Ada Artemis. Sebastian says you sketch."

"He has a remarkable talent for diabolic scenes," Sebastian crowed, "which got him into a bit of trouble in his hometown. Thus he has found his way to Gershom, where he will find neither judgment nor condemnation."

"You exaggerate, Sebastian, as always," said Max, who strolled to the boy and introduced himself. "You've only just criticized my art!"

126

"What I mean is, we do not critique personality. We do not hound or harass because one's art is morbid. We do not moralize; we know that art can express anything."

"And have you been hounded?" Ada asked the young artist.

Japheth laughed lightly and ran his exceedingly long fingers through his hair. "My first exhibition caused a bit of a scandal," he replied, smiling sheepishly. "I did some panels based on Baudelaire, which some found too—risqué. I found it all rather hypocritical; and so I've come to your city, the legend of which is whispered among various artistic circles with whom I am acquainted."

"I have seen his various *fleurs du mal* and they are quite poisonous," Sebastian said as he lit another cigarette. "Will you have some sherry, dear boy?" He waved toward the table and its decanter.

"Yes, thank you." He glanced about the room and then started as he saw the full-length portrait that had been their topic of discourse. He stepped to it and stared, and then he reached to touch one of the painted hands. Sebastian approached him and lightly touched his shoulder, and then handed him a glass half-full of drink.

"What a wonderful expression haunts your eyes, dear boy. You are enraptured."

"It's just so strange—to see her painted as a young man."

"Her?"

"Audre Brugge, the Belgian girl who sings French songs at Café Bacchus. Perhaps you don't know it; it's a bit of a dive."

Sebastian exhaled a plume of perfumed smoke. "Ah yes, the speakeasy on Queer Street. I was there *once*—the food was awful. I think I know of whom you speak, a pale mulatto wench with polypoid hair. I merely glanced at her, and did not like her voice when she began to warble. I have never heard such a *sepulchral* sound: it was like the voice of one who has tasted death and understood the meaning of that taste. I do not like to think on matters *in extremis*. How you can compare her with this Adonis I cannot comprehend. She was swarthy and alien—and he! He is composed of milk and rose leaf. He is Hyacinthus, beloved of Apollo, and I worship him."

"How are they alike?" asked Ada.

"Their faces are identical, uncannily so. Wait." Japheth drained his glass and set it on a nearby stand, and then he opened his portfolio and rummaged through various papers until he found the desired item. He handed the sheet to Ada, who examined the portrait that had been sketched onto it.

Max joined her and studied both sketch and painting. "Yes," he said, nodding, "she could be Viola to this portrait's Sebastian. Youth is often delightfully androgynous. But what odd hair she has, like coils flowing from the domes of Ceto's daughters. I'm quite intrigued. Does she perform tonight? Shall we go and listen?"

"Don't be absurd, Max," Sebastian huffed. "You haven't finished working on your sketch." He turned to Japheth. "Max is doing my portrait in lithograph."

"I have enough of it to work on—and I have my living model. Come on, this is too fantastic, to find a twin to your ancestor's mysterious portrait. How can you resist?"

"'No, no, go not to Lethe, neither twist
 Wolf's-bane, tight-rooted, for its poisonous wine.'"

Ada turned to face their host. "I, for one, am intrigued.

Let us go. Japheth will act as our Charon, our son of Night."

Max clapped his hands excitedly. "We shall share a bottle of *Artemisia absinthium* and drink in honor of your sister, Luna," he told Ada excitedly. "Come on, Melmoth, don't be a bore; do join us."

Sebastian yawned dramatically. "Oh, very well. Let me find a book that will be suitable for reading aloud during bad music." He stalked to a section of poetry, scanned the titles and pulled out a volume of *Chants de Maldoror.* "Yes, this will do for so delirious an expedition." Stepping to his closet, he pulled out the long and antique fur coat that was his favorite possession and flung it over his shoulders, and then he held out his hands in a gesture of ushering his company from his rooms.

They stepped into the moonlit night and Ada linked her arm with Japheth's. The young artist's sharp features caught in a peculiar fashion the beams of lunar light, and his pale face seemed almost to glow as he led the way. A heavy gust of winter wind suddenly pushed toward them as it sailed between the city's tall buildings.

Sebastian hugged his heavy coat closer to his frame. "Can you sample it on the wind," he queried, "the taste of doom? Shall we moan to the half-moon like some pack of underhounds?"

"Let us relish what promises to be a new experience," Ada answered.

"Ah, Sphinx—ever the optimist."

They came to Queer Street, and Japheth led the way into a dilapidated house situated between two taller edifices. Gales of laughter spilled from the doorless entrance as they climbed the steps that led onto a long porch, on which various persons sat at tables, drinking and smoking. Sebastian took a cigarette from its gilded case and lit up, which made him feel a little more relaxed. The crowd was mostly young, which pleased him, although he knew that these children had not kept their lives free and inviolate; otherwise they would not dwell within this realm of exile and dispossession, this city of wild unrest. For a moment he remembered his past life, his glory and fame and freedom, his social conquests and his sexual subjugations wherein he was dominant in all things. When his secret life had become known by the society he had courted, they hurled him from their midst. The memory of his rise and fall was his deep-felt damnation; no matter how he reconstructed his former life in this ghastly city, he would never again know the delicious taste of former victory. He walked this realm of living death, a shadow of what once he was.

"Let us find a booth," Sebastian commanded. "I am famished for alcohol."

They settled into leather benches at a table of substantial size. "A bottle of absinthe," Max told their waiter.

"Two bottles," Sebastian corrected him. "And I shall have some coffee laced with a liberal dose of brandy. Anyone else?"

"I'll try some, I guess," Japheth said as he scanned the drink menu and studied prices.

"My treat, dear boy," Sebastian cooed, rewarded with the young artist's thankful smile.

Thus they drank their sweet coffees and bitter booze and talked of art as the young illustrator allowed them to examine his portfolio. When the surrounding chatter quieted, Japheth looked up and saw the woman who watched him as she sauntered past their table and walked to where a blind boy sat before a piano. The room listened as the lad began to play his somber music, and something clutched at Japheth's heart as Audre Brugge began to sing Baudelaire's "La Muse malade." Sebastian forgot his drink and felt his slow-beating heart grow weighty with woe. He began to chant the words with whispered voice.

"*Ma pauvre muse, hélas! qu'as-tu donc ce matin?*"

"Hush, Melmoth," Max scolded.

"Her voice is like the coming of Death. No, I cannot listen." Sebastian rose and vacated the room, stepping onto the porch and puffing furiously at his cigarette. His companions sat, transfixed, their eyes and ears bewitched. The woman's voice was deeper than Japheth had remembered. Her eyes, those colorless orbs, penetrated him with their staring, and her perfect mouth made love to the language she uttered. The artist, his hands itching for his pen, took in her mauve skin, her coils of tawny hair; and he marveled at how luxurious that hair looked in the misty light of the place, how it seemed in his imagination at times to writhe with an almost lecherous sentience. He watched as her hands trembled to the emotion of her song as they stroked her velvet vest, and he stared at the dark nipple of an exposed breast. Her song ended, and the room exploded with wild applause. Japheth blushed as the lithe chanteuse winked at him and licked her lips as she exited the room.

Sebastian Melmoth felt the presence behind him, one that commanded him to turn and acknowledge. He refused to do so and stared at the yellow moon as if that sphere of dust would grant him inner strength.

"Have you another cigarette?" a husky voice asked. He

watched as Audre Brugge moved to a lower step and stood before him. How eerie that the poisonous light of the dead moon seemed to have been transferred to the eyes that held him. Hypnotized, he reached into his vest pocket and brought forth his golden cigarette case. He watched as the woman made her selection and placed the reed of nicotine into her mouth; and he trembled as she bent to him and touched the tip to his. "Your breath tastes of wormwood," she stated, "lots and lots." He detected a Dutch inflection in her accented voice.

"Yes," he replied. "One must imbibe to fulfillment. The first glass will show you things as you wish they existed; and the second glass gives you a glimpse of things as they are not. The third glass of absinthe—reveals the truth behind the mask of reality, and that is the most horrible of revelations."

"And what do you see behind my mask?"

He sucked deeply on his bit of nicotia and exhaled a patch of scented fume that floated as curtain between them. "Nay, Medusa, your alchemy cannot touch me. My heart turned to stone ages ago."

Secretly she smiled, licked her mouth and walked away.

II.

Sebastian sat on a large gold armchair and looked around the dreary room. Why were the dens of artists always so *cluttered?* Such disarray disconcerted him—he wanted to call for servants. In fact, he was trying to avoid glancing at the large canvas on which Japheth was working at his new project, a life-size portrait of the gorgon that had so beguiled him. But Sebastian could not keep his eyes away, for the artistic process fascinated him. Striking a gold-tipped match, he lit a cigarette and waved it toward the canvas.

"The skeletonic tree is quite good, especially the way it subtly imitates her stance. Of course, you need a moon casting its dead light upon her coils of hair; and the moon must not be white, but rather it must reflect the tainted color of her curious flesh, her reptile hide. Jesu, how like a lamia she looks! She makes one want to quote Keats:

'Where palsy shakes a few, sad, last grey hairs,
    Where youth grows pale, and spectre-thin, and dies;
    Where but to think is to be full of sorrow
        And leaden-eyed despairs . . .'"

"Why does she affect you so, Sebastian? I thought you treasured beauty and youth. Look at her eyes—so clear and ethereal. How could such eyes fill you with despondency?"

"They are the eyes of one who preys. I suppose the face is fine, but how can one admire it when it is concealed behind those cords of mane?" He stood and looked out of the window, into night. "This room is really quite depressing. Let us go outside and bathe in starlight. You haven't tried one of my recently discovered cigarettes—they will give you a new sensation. I *adore* new sensations. Come, put down your brush and follow me. Your Medusa will await you." Without waiting, Sebastian went to the door and left the room. Laughing softly, the young artist followed him. The winter night was chilly, but there was no wind. Sebastian was waving a cigarette at heaven, where three bats were silhouetted in as they flitted in the lunar light. "This sky is positively Goyaesque," he stated. "Of course, we need owls instead of bats. Are you familiar with his *El conjuro*? It would not sur-

133

prise me to see a pack of disheveled hags hobbling down that street, selling their craft. But—lo!—see where a witch approaches."

He flicked the butt of his consumed cigarette into a gutter as Audre Brugge approached them; and for one moment she did seem like something conjured by black arts, with the strange moonlight giving her skin a poisonous viridian tinge. Japheth saw how her helical hair seemed to move and arrange itself as she advanced toward them—and that was odd, for there was no wind. She stopped before them.

"Good evening, gentlemen," she said, one hand holding the bottom of her small shoulder bag.

"My dear Miss Brugge. How like a viper you look in that tight dress, with its geometric pattern. Would you care for a new sensation? I've just received these, from a friend in Mozambique." Sebastian reached into a pocket and produced a black cigarette case, which he snapped open. "They will make you dream tonight," he promised her.

"No thank you, Monsieur. I want to taste the evening air, it's so rich tonight."

Sebastian snapped shut the case without offering a weed to Japheth. "As you wish. I shall leave you then, for I too wish to dine on this intoxicating effluvium. I suppose you wish to be alone in his little room and pay homage to the gods of Art."

"Actually—no." The woman smiled at Japheth. "There's a curious place I want to show you, just outside the city perimeter. I think it will interest you, from an artistic standpoint."

"All right," the young man agreed.

"If you're going to walk the night then I shall follow,

surreptitiously and from a distance. I shall be your voyeur and watch in secret."

The woman laughed and linked her arm with Japheth's, and Sebastian slowly followed as they walked beyond the city, to a place of ancient desolation. Perhaps, aeons ago, it had been some kind of park, although its trees were few and withered, like something found in Casper David Friedrich; and Japheth felt a kind of pity for the barren trees, for their limbs seemed bent with heavy desolation. Sebastian scowled at the dreary wasteland as he followed the younger mortals up a slight incline to where the remnant of a ruins stood. Audre stopped before a weathered arch that was guarded by a statue of Cerberus, and she smoothed her hand over one of the daemon's three monstrous heads.

"Wait," Sebastian wailed as the woman walked past the beast and began to descend a set of steps that led to a circular platform of stone. "I have no honey cakes with which to placate the hound. If we step into its lair we may ne'er return!"

"Be not afraid, Monsieur. I shall be your Aeneas and pacify the fiend." She held her hand to Japheth. "Come," she commanded.

But Sebastian was suddenly overwhelmed with fear. He had not, in all his years in Gershom, dared to leave the city's boundaries; being out of it now instilled a kind of panic, a sense of terror. Holding his hand up in protest to the woman's invitation, he turned and fled.

Japheth tried to laugh. "He has the oddest habit of *fleeing*," he joked; and yet he, too, felt a kind of uncanny fear in the forlorn place. Was it his imagination, or had the atmosphere grown more chilly after they had passed beneath the archway and descended the stone steps? He watched as

Audre reclined on the circle of stone and began to trace the shape that was outlined on it with her slim hand. When she reached that hand to Japheth, he took it and lay beside her.

"What is this place?" he asked.

"I don't know. It must have been part of some antique civilization that existed prior to the city, although heaven knows that Gershom is in itself infinitely old. Perhaps this was their temple—it seems a place of veneration, doesn't it? And perhaps this figure chiseled into this circle of stone was the thing they worshipped. You can sense how utterly primitive it is, a relic of a forgotten era; and yet how exquisitely it is captured in their art, whoever it was that dwelt here. I knew it would fascinate you, as an artist. Primeval art has always beguiled me. I like to think about the world as it once was, millennia ago. What did they feel, that we can never sense? What did they know, and worship? What were their *secrets*? We know of the past from what they left recorded— but what were the mysteries unrevealed? It's funny, but when I lay in this place, beneath the antediluvian starlight, I feel near to a nameless past."

"This is an odd figure," he conceded, fingering the thing that was engraven on stone. "It looks like a king, or ruler, by the way it's outfitted in that robe, and by the staff or whatever it is it holds. Can't really tell its gender, but the haughty stance seems belligerently male. It's really weathered here, at where it wears a half-crown or whatever it is. It's superb, certainly. It has an aura of—power." He gazed into her clear eyes, the eyes that held him in their bewitching splendor. "Do you c—come here often?" he stuttered.

"Mmm, yes. It's a great place to lay still, to dream. Will you dream with me, Japheth?" She leaned toward him and briefly touched her mouth to his. "Be still. Here, let me rub some of this onto your temples." She retrieved a tiny jar from her bag and turned open its lid. "It's something I discovered in Tibet." He watched as she dipped two fingers into the jar's gelatinous stuff and sighed as she anointed him. Her mouth was at his ear, sighing strange language that he could not comprehend. He wanted to kiss her eyes but found that he could not move his heavy limbs. No matter. It was wonderful enough to be still and let her love him. She was on top of him, unbuttoning his shirt, and then her nails were etching signals into his chest. When she finally pressed her lips onto his eyelids, he was able to move a little. He opened his eyes, and his hands were on her heavy breasts. She pulled him on top of her and began to hum a strange melody as she allowed him to kiss her mouth, her neck, her nipples.

And then he knew that he was dreaming, as something wet and thin below her breast wrapped around his finger. "It is a gift from him—the Master," she sang in her queer low voice. "It is his reward to his anointed." He moved his head beneath her breast, to where the worm grew from out her flesh, at the place where her diabolic heart pumped. He touched the worm with his mouth, his mouth that opened as the thing stretched its elastic body and slipped between his lips. He sucked as the creature tickled the back of his throat, and when at last it removed itself from his orifice, he tasted the musky slime that coated his stinging lips.

Japheth awakened to the soft moaning of morning wind; he saw the mist above the ruins wherein he lay, in that cold and lonesome place. The siren had deserted him, he was alone; but she had left him with a souvenir. He brought the strand of coiled hair to his nostrils and drank its weird perfume.

III.

Max Romp opened his portmanteau, took out his new sketch and placed it on the table before which he and Ada Artemis sat. "It's *too* grotesque, not at all my kind of thing. It's like something out of Poe, and the style is so bizarre. Usually my sense of line is strong, but this watercolor is all blur and blotch—there are no solid lines. Now the hazy cityscape in the background suggests Gershom, but it's from an angle that I've never personally experienced."

"And you say that you saw this thing in dream?"

"That's right, the most vivid nightmare I've ever experienced. Usually even my wildest dreams have some root in reality—but this thing! It's dark phantasy of the queerest kind. And that sinister tramp or whatever the hell he is, great gods! He stands like some symbol of all the world's outcasts, with his tattered robe and glistening crown."

Ada leaned a little nearer to the work. "Glistening?"

"It shimmered, but with a dull liquid kind of scintillation, like some distant muted starlight. And it seemed to move, as if a sentient thing. Ugh, I need another brandy!" He stalked to the bar and refilled his empty glass. "And the queerest thing of all was the sound, like some low moaning; a subterranean wind, perhaps, emanating from beneath the ground. Actually, when I reflect on the noise, it sounded a lot like that woman's singing. You know, young Beardsley's mophead muse."

Ada sat back and sipped tea from a delicate china cup, and then she looked up and smiled as Sebastian was let into the room by a manservant. "Coffee! Have you any sobering coffee? Ah, I see it there! Yes, let me help myself to a cup." Ada rose and went to her friend, startled at his disheveled appearance. Her hand gently touched the tall man's shoulder, and he turned to take hold of it. "Sphinx, your hand is hot. Let me cool it with my kisses." He kissed it once and then returned to pouring coffee into a tall cup. Ada reached for the container of cream. "No, no, dear woman. Let us not dilute its potency with cream, nor sweeten it with sugar. No, let me drink it black and strong, and thus dispel the Morphean lure."

Max rose to join them, laughing. "Good god, Melmoth, you're a mess! You look like you haven't slept for days."

Sebastian gulped a scalding cup of coffee as though it were water and then refilled his cup with the dark brew. "Sleep! I have been too perturbed too sleep! I have suffered the *Napoléon* of nightmares! Why is it so somber in here? We need music. Why have you no musicians at hand, Sphinx, to soothe the soul and ease the mind?" He drained the cup a second time and refilled it once more.

"Hell, Melmoth, settle down. I've had a bad nightmare myself, but I'm not running around all gaga. Sit down and behave yourself."

"Spare me your fatuous criticism, Max. Your nightmare cannot compare to the incubus that sucks my sanity—the little I have remaining. You have not been walking the streets since midnight, haunting cafés so as not to be alone. You have not been to St. Expiry to light a candle for your own soul. I will not sit down and be calm—I will howl with the legion of the damned!" He gulped more coffee.

"Drink slowly, dear, you'll choke," cooed Ada. "Do not be quick to judge our friend. His dream has been unusual and drear."

Sebastian produced a mauve handkerchief and wiped his brow. "Was it, Maximilian? Did you see our city from that

139

horrid desolate place just outside its boundaries, looking like a metropolis of the damned? Did you see the dead trees that *writhed* like semi-sentient things as they hurled their shadows onto your face, your eyes? Did you behold the Lord of Worms rise from his realm of tarnation, clutching his staff of burnt bone and incinerated flesh, with which he etched your name into the dust? Great Jesu, did you see all that?"

Huffing, he strode to a chair and sat, wiping at his pale face, glancing for a moment at the upside-down image of Max's illustration. Then he froze, and his white face drained to a deeper pallor. Silently, his eyes filled with fear, he bent to the drawing and turned it around.

"You neglected to mention the sepia moon, looking like a scab in heaven," Max quietly told him. "I think I'll have some coffee after all. Shall I pour you a brandy, Melmoth?"

"This is uncanny. You've been to this place after all."

"What place?" Ada asked, kneeling next to Sebastian's chair and taking hold of his hand.

"But how can you have witnessed my dream? We have been bewitched. Beardsley's harpy has worked some necromantic foolery over us." He turned to Ada. "The place is just beyond the city. You know I have never left the city in the three decades that I have dwelt here—except for the few times that I have visited the Isle of Moira, wherein the dead are interred. I was bold enough to follow Beardsley and his witch to this place, but I panicked and fled. Your blurry rendition of its ruins is quite haunting, Max. I've never known you to depict places—you must have felt its spectral power when you were there."

"I haven't a clue what you're muttering about, old boy. I haven't set foot out of this city since stepping off the train seven years ago. I would never hike outside its boundaries. I am metropolitan to the bone."

"And you, Sphinx—have you dreamt of this place?"

"You forget, dear friend—I never dream."

"I know that you have told me so, but I never believed it. I prefer my sad dreams to no dreams at all. But this vision that Max and I have shared—*that* I wish I had never beheld. It is portentous, and nothing good can come of it. I must warn Beardsley."

"Stay and warn him in the morning. Look, the winter darkness comes so early, and I can tell you haven't eaten. Dine with us and sleep here until morning, and then together we can see your friend."

Sebastian rose to his unsteady feet. "How wise you are, dear Sphinx, and kind; but I cannot rest until I have warned my young friend. We have been given a premonition of some evil thing, but it merely brushes us with its wings. The beak is pointed toward a young man's heart. He sits in lamplight, and the daemon that is dreaming spills its shadow over him; and if I do not save him now, his soul from out that shadow will be lifted—nevermore."

IV.

Japheth awoke to the ringing of the bell. Drowsily, he walked down the steps and opened the building's door. Sebastian clasped his shoulders with shaking hands. "Thank the gods that you are here! I've been ringing for five minutes."

"Settle down, Sebastian. Good lord, you look awful. Come in from the cold. I've been sleeping; soundly, I guess, if I didn't hear your ringing for so long a time." He shut the door and led the way to his dark room.

141

"Sleeping—perchance to dream?"

"Huh? I don't recall. I think I'm still waking up. Sorry it's so chilly in here, my fire's gone out. Let me tend it. Have you eaten? I'm going to heat up some wonderful soup. You look in need of nourishment."

"Bother nourishment. I've come to warn you of the thing that is feasting on your soul—that harpy!" He pointed to where the painting leaned upon its easel and saw that the canvas was covered with a piece of black velvet. "That's a good sign, Japheth, to hide her from view. But it will be better still to destroy her image. There, your palette knife—it will serve our purpose."

"What on earth are you babbling about, Sebastian? No, put down the knife and answer me!"

The young man was not quick enough to stop the elder fellow from reaching for the black cloth and ripping it away. The knife fell from Sebastian's hand as he saw the thing that mocked him with its baleful eyes. Was it the same painting? He thought that it was, although it had been horribly altered. The creature's flesh shimmered with a kind of liquid coating that glistened in the glow of yellow moonlight. The coils of hair had been altered and did not cover any of the woman's face, the face that was no longer beautiful. Sebastian did not know what he feared the most—the twisting lips or the cruel eyes. He marveled at how the artist had caught an aspect of serpentine movement in the ropy tangles of coiled hair. Behind the creature, in the distance and almost completely hidden in darkness, was another figure, barely discernible. Sebastian knew that the thing wore a tattered robe and crown of worms.

"I've added your moon, per your suggestion. It brings

the thing to life, doesn't it? God, I've been working on it all night, right after I awakened from the dream. Little wonder I've slept like the dead. I knew when I awakened that alterations were required. Dreams can be so instructive, don't you find? I've never been able to capture grotesquerie so infallibly. I am nothing if I am not grotesque. What a muse she has been for me!"

It came to them, from outside the window: the harsh low singing. The lad smiled and kissed Sebastian on the mouth, and then vacated the room. Sebastian fell to his knees and would have moaned if he were not too frightened to utter sound. Timidly, he crept to the window on hands and knees, trying to fight the fear that labored to prevent his peering into night. By the time he found the courage to push aside the curtains, the two retreating figures were far away. The poor old fellow clasped his hands together and prayed to the moon.

They walked through winter's chilly air to the ruins outside the city. Hand in hand, they climbed up the slight gradient that led to the ruins. Japheth smiled at the three-headed beast that stood as sentinel before the archway; but then his face grew somber as he looked beyond that archway to the circle of stone—to that which stood thereon. His companion wrapped her arms around his waist and kissed his ear.

"We've taken a fancy to you. We love your dreaming. It is said that Gershom is a godless place, and perhaps that's true; but there was once religion here, of an ancient kind. We are its avatars. Come, join us. Go to him, Japheth, and kiss his staff."

She released him. Japheth walked down the steps and knelt before the moonlit deity. He could smell the diseased flesh of which the Old One was composed. When he lifted his face to the thing's dark eyes he beheld the crown that was composed of lengthy nematodes, their hermaphroditic bodies knotted as they moved through the Old One's dome. The demigod touched a rotted hand to Japheth's head and pushed his face toward the carrion staff. The young man pressed his lips to the charnel thing as the hand that touched him worked over his tingling flesh. He felt the woman's hands rip at his clothing and knead his flesh, the flesh that began to alter, to shrivel and grow moist. Naked, he buried his face into the woman's moving hair as his flesh began to secrete its slime, the viscous substance that Audre Brugge lapped voraciously as his human body continued to wither and shrink with transmutation.

Dead moonlight cast its diseased illumination upon the Old One, the thing that placed its new acolyte into a writhing crown.

Chamber of Dreams

This house is situated on a very old hill that rises above the ancient town, and it is surrounded by seven tall trees that remind one, on moonlit nights, of the Seven Pillars of Kadath, that realm where, in his onyx castle, the Great Old One dreams. From the depths of my soul, I sense the seven trees bend to me on the windless moonlit nights, their writhing limbs aching so to touch the crack in my face and sooth it with soft leaves. The crack is where my dreams spill forth onto the floor, dripping as effluvium from some dark space inside my skull. This waste of emanation is so slick, so undetectable in the dim candlelight of my chamber, that I sometimes slip and fall and am awakened, rudely. As I have just been shocked into wakefulness now, this moment; as I moan on this oaken floor, my numb hand in a pool of viscous dream.

The lava of my dreaming moves beneath my hand. I think it wants to pull out of doors, into rancid moonlight, so that I may crawl between the shadows of the seven trees. I can imagine what that would be like—I can see it behind my eyes—the crawling between the spaces of blackness that hum my name, as sometimes the darkness of sky also vibrates with calling. But I need not venture out of doors to feel the cold wind on my brain. I feel it now, whispering at

145

the crevice in my face, sighing exactly as it does between the seven trees outside my home. It sighs between the fissure in my skull and makes me weep the name of Usher. And I see him then—the tragic man, walking among the tombstones in the city of seven hills. He, too, is a dreamer in darkness.

I see his shadow in my mind—in delicious dream. His shadow reaches, hungrily, along the burying ground, and it has many forms. And now it takes the form of some other one, tall and lean, a wasted man who has turned dreaming into a fine art. He walks among the seven hills, in moonlight, and he aches for something out there, within dark cosmic nothingness. I can feel his heavy ache, his need to express it. Isn't that what dreamers do? Isn't that our keen compulsion?

My pen has fallen with me on the floor. I reach for it and dip its point into the pool of dream. I take out the crumpled paper from a pocket and press the pen against it. Within my dank and lonely chamber, I commit the act of dream-expression, in that place where something calls my name.

Some Distant Baying Sound

(Dedicated to my chums at TLO)

I.

Madness rides the star-wind—that chilly disturbance that titters and howls just outside my skull. It is cold and dry, like some cosmic mistral from Southern heaven; and it knows my name, for I hear it chittering again, again, "Christina, Christina." But I shall not heed it. The revolver is sleek and cold in my mouth. I have only to pull the trigger, and I shall be free of the nightmare that has plagued me since the death of St. John. How can I help but think of him at this hour of my final doom, of his mangled corpse interred by my unholy hands in our neglected garden? Oh, I remember the kiss of moonlight on my liquid eyes as I mumbled over his pit of death one last sad satanic ritual that he had loved in life. The memory of those words comes to me now, with such aching force that I remove the pistol from my mouth and speak, soft and low, the arcane language. Ah, the esoteric words that slip as sighs and weeping from my tongue. How heavy his revolver is in my hand—too heavy. I set it on the floor and touch my fingers to my eyes.

I hear it in the distance—the baying, as if of some gigantic hound. Looking at the revolver, it is suddenly an ugly, tedious thing. Cursing, I kick it from me. No, that will not be my ignominious end. Fie on such a death. Let *it* come and do its will—why should I deny the rending flesh, the spilt blood, such as my friend had offered it? As I look about our chamber of horrors, I see one of St. John's diabolic paintings, his personal rendition of Jean Delville's *Satan's Treasures*. I remember what he said to me, my companion, as he hoisted the work to its place upon the wall.

"You'll note, Christina, that I have darkened the red pigment of her hair, so as to compliment your own. Also, I've added some swirls of purple, to represent this wine on which we have become drunk tonight. For we are Satan's dearest treasures, Christina, and once we have had our fill of wine we shall slink into dark night and find fresh pleasure in the grave of that newly-buried child. We shall bring him here and teach him new ways in which to frolic."

No, I will not cry in terror. I will not desecrate this place with coward's blood. I can feel my strength return—and with it I taste new resolve. Unsteadily, I rise on numbing legs and stagger to the corner where stands St. John's greatest creation, the thing he worked on—fiendishly—after our return from Holland. He had had the huge slab of jadeite shipped from Asia, where it had been a portion of a wall of a desecrated and demolished temple. St. John had worked on it like a madman, and when at last I was allowed to view it I gasped in wonder at his gigantic replication of the small amulet that we had pilfered from a corpse in a daemonic Holland churchyard. And when I had touched my hand to the creature's adamantine surface, to its queer coloring of greenish-white and reddish-brown, I felt a sense of delectable terror as I had never known before.

Ah, there it is again—the distant sound. It comes from some unfathomable realm, a dimension between sanity and madness. It comes to claim me as its own. I shall abide. But I won't face it alone. Rather, I will slink into our neglected garden of poisoned things, where I will dig into the earth to where my dead friend rests, negated but not forsaken. I will bring him here, to recline before the beast of his creation. I will hold his mangled thews, his bloodstained bones, his ravaged cranium, in my lithe arms. I will press my lips to that which remains of his mouth and breathe into him the rituals that he loved. Together, we shall await the ravage of that which calls of promised and inescapable destruction.

II.

I tore into the night and slashed with fingernails into the sod, until I found the sordid remains of my beloved friend. Thick fog from the moor had accumulated around our ancient manor-house, and as I pulled my friend from his unhallowed plot I could hear a chittering sound. A flock of bats swooped out of the brumous air and flapped above me, darting now and then as if in an attempt to pluck my friend from my embrace. I shrieked to them that he was mine alone. Defiantly, I held him to the shape that formed—gradually, inexorably—behind the blanket of fog, a gigantic and nebulous form that flapped its condor wings and bayed to darkness. With madness burning in my fevered brain, I spoke a passage that St. John had taught me from the *Necronomicon;* and perhaps it was my rich lunacy that gave the words more than usual potency, for the winged shape broke apart and disintegrated in the sky. The bats that had swooped above me, snatching at my hair, were gone. With unnatural strength I carried St. John's corpse into our secret haunt and placed his broken form before his magnificent statue. I burned strangely scented candles to that statue and spoke verses of Baudelaire that St. John had taught me in the original French. Unhappily, I scanned the place, which once had been so filled with macabre plunder, the booty that St. John and I had looted from the unholy places of the globe. In sorrow and rage I had destroyed the bulk of our most prized possessions.

The scent of yellow candles infiltrated my nostrils as I leaned against St. John's diabolic statue, and I thought that I could detect fragrant coils spill into my nose, my mouth, and curl about my brain. The candles that were burning on the upper ledges behind the statue suddenly flared, throwing shadows on the ground before me. I lifted to my knees and saw my shadow conjoined with that of the gigantic jade hound, so that my silhouette looked to have spouted daemonical wings. Wickedly, I stretched my throat and raised my mouth—and the baying that issued from my mouth contained a familiar ring. Easily, I raised my cloudy body from the floor and filtered through the smoky air toward the large frame that contained a full-length mirror. I peered into that surface of polished glass and saw the eidolon within it, the creature that wore my sombre dress that was covered with death's debris. My long dark hair flailed wildly around my bleached and cavern-eyed face. Between my heaving breasts I saw an amulet of curious and exotic design, its green jade shining in the subtle glow of candlelight. I looked at the base of that amulet, at the inscription around it in characters which neither St. John nor I could identify. We knew that this amulet had been hinted at in the copy of the *Necronomi-*

con that had been procured for us by an American acquaintance, and which we had studied with keen attention; but we
could not find any detail about that queer inscription. We
needed the assistance of one whose mind contained a copious
wealth of arcane wisdom. I turned to St. John.

"You were preparing to visit such a one—where?"

He rose from where he lay and came to me, and I shivered as he smoothed his fingers through my hair. "In America—a valley of spectral shadow, where dwells our wizard
who aided us once before. No, don't frown—his manner is of
no consequence. He is filled with self-love, but we can toler-
ate again his airs. I know that you have studied diligently,
Christina, but your little brain has such difficulty with language." He smiled so sweetly as he voiced this critique that I
could not be angry at his words, and I shut my eyes as his
fingers smoothed the bone that was my skull.

From some place outside there came the sound of distant
baying. I opened my eyes and knew that I had dreamed.
Violent wind howled outside our home. The candles had
burned low and extinguished. Leaning against the jade
statue, I pulled my friend's remains tighter into my embrace. With one hand, I ran my sensitive fingers along the
statue's base, whereon St. John had etched the enigmatic inscription which was, he felt certain, a passage that contain
the secrets beyond the grave. The alchemy of those secrets
would help me to raise my friend from death's destructive
assault. I knew what I had to do. I would journey to America, to the Sesqua Valley, and seek the wisdom of the Beast.

III.

The journey across the ocean was long and unpleasant, but when at last I entered the confines of Sesqua Valley I felt queerly calm. I settled into my rooms and went to wander the nearest section of wooded territory. A full moon shed its light onto a magnificent twin-peaked mountain of white stone, a titan of rock that stood like sentinel over the quiet valley. As I breathed in the valley air I could taste a kind of sweetness in its substance. Hearing a noise that sounded like distant wind-call, I walked toward it, following a track of trodden earth beneath the trees, my path illuminated by a Jacob's ladder of moonbeams that reached through the still tops of extremely high trees. The path began to wind downward, and as I followed it the ethereal noise began to transform and take on a semi-human aspect. I saw distant flames in the depths below, in an open area that contained a stage-like platform, on which braziers burned in the night. Before the stage a series of levels rose upward on a steep hill, and on these there sat a crowd of onlookers. It was from this audience that the zephyr of chanted noise issued, a sound the likes of which I had never heard. How can I describe the effect it had on me, the way it touched me like a cloud of invisible aether and encased my being? Spellbound, I gazed at the altar on the platform, on which a figure reclined, draped in a scarlet gown. I watched, entranced, as small dark creatures danced around the altar. A curious sensation of pounding came from some place beneath my feet, as if some titan's heart pulsed below me in the depths of earth. Strange mauve mist began to form among the trees nearest the stage; it became a brumous wall of fog that enshrouded the stage and its occupants. The queer choir of audience raised their pitch of sound, and then the mist slowly dissipated, revealing another figure standing on the stage, a tall lean fellow whose bestial countenance was partially concealed by his wide hat. I smiled as I recognized the one whose service I sought.

The beast of Sesqua Valley held his hands to the moon and made unto that globe of lifeless dust strange signals with his tapered taloned fingers. A pallid shaft of moonlight fell onto his moving hand, and he seemed to catch that wan light and spill it over the figure that reclined on the altar. Deftly, that figure moved from off the slab of stone and began to writhe her limbs in a perversion of dance. And then she stopped, as a congregation of bats suddenly fell from darkness, diving at the flaming tapers. The woman on the stage waved her arms in an attempt to sweep the creatures from the air around her; and then she looked toward me and raised her arm, pointing. The chanting ceased as the audience turned their silver eyes to me. I trembled where I stood, penetrated by those inhuman eyes; and then I felt fingers moving through my hair. The woman in scarlet stood beside me. Alabaster eyes gleamed within her bestial face, the flesh of which resembled dark antique oak. Her breath fanned my face, and with it came a sweet and cloying fragrance that I had detected earlier in the valley air. A figure loomed behind her, and the beast smiled at me.

"Ah—Christina Sturhman. What an enchanting surprise. Where is your handsome young companion?"

"St. John is dead," I answered. And then, for the first time, the sadness of that extinction hit me with full force, and I began to sob. The other woman reached out and brushed my tears with soft inhuman hands. Her animal mouth touched mine, and as I drank that kiss I felt around

154

me a movement in the air; and in my ears I heard the flapping of tiny wings, a sound that finally rose over us and vanished above the trees.

IV.

They led me out of the woods and to a small house near to
the edge of woodland. Simon Gregory Williams sat with me
on a small sofa and listened to my tale as the strange woman
worked in the kitchen. Finally she joined us and offered me a
glass of cloudy liquid which at first I took to be absinthe;
but its taste was sweet instead of bitter, with a mellifluous-
ness that reminded me of the valley's aether. Its effect was
immediate, and the chaos in my brain subsided. The room
was dimly lit with some few lamps, and I suspected that
Sesqua Valley had not been quick to attain electric light.

"I wish you had kept that amulet," Simon said beside me,
having listened to my reason for arrival in his land. "As you
say, it sounds very like the soul-symbol of the corpse-eating
cult in Central Asia. What it would be doing around the
throat of a wizard's corpse in Holland is beyond conjecture."
He studied me with an oblique glance, took my nearly empty
glass from my hand and drained its remnant of murky liquid.
"Your people are from Holland, are they not?"

I licked my lips. "My very distant ancestors were Dutch
Jews, yes. But the culture is alien to me in all its ways. My
people have lived in Britain for close to a century."

Our hostess took the glass from Simon's grasp. I watched
as she ran her hand over his lips and brought its fingers to
her mouth. "And what is this thing that followed you across
the ocean, this thing that howls and rends?"

"I think it's a lingering familiar of the wizard from whose

155

corpse St. John and I stole the amulet. Although its master is long-dead, yet his agent exists in some plain between reality and phantasy. You know, Simon, that these shadow-creatures are borne of dimensions that may be opened with words of alchemy. St. John was seeking such a dimension. He thought that we might be able to summon forth an agent with which we could combat whatever it was that plagued us."

"Hmm," the beast uttered, nodding his large head. "And you imagine that this inscription that was around the base of the jade amulet may have been a key to such a spectral demesne. Yes. We shall have to go to your rooms in the morning and you will show me your copy of this unfathomable inscription. But for now—how very weary you are, my dear. Why, you cannot easily move your weighty limbs." As he spoke, my entire body felt incomprehensibly heavy, weighed with packed mortality. "Not to worry. Marceline's bed is near and spacious. She will welcome you as bedfellow for what remains of the nocturnal tide. Come, let's get these heavy clothes off you and send you to bed."

Simon's eyes shimmered beneath his hat's brim, and he grinned as he lifted my arms. I shivered at the woman's velvet touch as she helped my arms out of their sleeves. Golden lamplight bathed my breasts as the beasts eased me out of my garments. As Marceline began to remove her scarlet gown, Simon pulled a flute from an inner pocket of his jacket. The music that he played was soft, low and exotic. It was the equal to the woman's kisses on my lips, my throat, my breasts. A wind began to moan from some distant place in the valley, and from somewhere atop the twin-peaked mountain snouts were raised in song. We heard it then, above the other sounds, an eldritch baying near to the curtained bedroom window. Simon stopped his playing and stood dead still with a talon to his lips. We listened, as something scratched at the window pane, as something chortled and cursed *in the Dutch language.*

We saw the dark shape that wavered behind the curtained pane, its nebulous form silhouetted in rich moonlight. In the corner of my eye I could detect Simon's hand raised toward that window and moving so as to form an elder sign. I could hear his hot breathing as he whispered a potent passage that I recognized from the *Necronomicon.* Suddenly, Marceline's silver eyes were peering closely into mine. Before my eyes I beheld a curtain of translucent haze, like unto the cloudy liquid that they had given me to drink. Marceline's breasts pressed against my own as she guided me to her bed. She straddled me as I squirmed on her cool sheets and laid her velvet paws on my head. As she smoothed my dome, I heard again the sound of Simon's flute, and its lullaby coaxed my eyes to close.

I entered into dark dreaming. The hoary blackness in which I dreamed was suddenly pierced by yellow moonglow as the lid of my coffin was lifted. St. John looked down at me with an expression of ecstasy shining in his beautiful eyes. I could hear the gentle moaning of the night-wind that moved his hanging hair. He looked at the amulet that lay upon my chest, and his handsome face was overwhelmed with wonder, with that look of daemonic delight that expressed his keenest ghoulish joy. Excitedly, he took up my amulet and placed its length of silver chain around his throat. I lifted my skeletal hand so as to touch the jade figure that represented the monster that had murdered me, the beast to which my damned soul was now strangely conjoined. Clutching at that figure of a winged hound, I pulled St. John's face to mine so that I could press his hot living breath into my wide fleshless grin. But then there came, from above us, a wild chattering and whirling, and I watched the flurry of bats that swooped over the figure of my friend. From somewhere near there came the sound of awful baying, as if of some gigantic hound. A shadow spread above us, blacker than nightmare; it reached for my friend and dragged him from my embrace. I howled his name as the entity swallowed him away.

I groaned. Her soft hand covered my mouth, and as I gazed into her silver eyes I felt rare bewitchment enter my soul. Marceline's lips, moving down my throat, were hot. Her mouth around my nipples sucked reality away.

V.

I awakened, alone, in a pool of sunlight that spread across the bed. A warm breeze sailed into the room from where the window had been opened, and I drank in the sweet elixir that was Sesqua Valley's atmosphere. It was an air that enticed me out of the comfortable bed and into my clothes, out of the house and into woodland. The mountain served as guide, and I walked toward it, deep into the growth of trees and shrubs. Here and there I passed occasional specimens of sculpture, strange works that looked like denizens of macabre dreaming. They were usually quite small and rested on short stone pillars or altars made of wood.

I entered a darker part of the woods, and the path that I followed became narrow and partially overgrown, as if I had found a trail not often trod. The trees grew closer to each other, blocking out all light. At times I imagined that I could detect small and nebulous shapes that followed behind

158

the clustered trees, shapes that made no sound. I have been, with St. John, to many places that have felt haunted—but never had I felt such a spectral sensation as I did in that dark place. It was odd. I no longer felt human; rather, I seemed to be a thing of shadow that drifted through a demesne of audient gloaming. It was a realm that was very aware of my presence, that seemed to harken to my labored breathing.

I scanned the area just ahead of me, the place where the trail came to an abrupt end. I could not at first make out the bulky thing that was definitely not a tree, deformed as some of Sesqua's trees had been. Gradually I began to see that it was a squat totem some nine feet in height. Something in its shaped seemed disturbingly familiar, and when I stood directly in front of it, I swooned and dropped to my knees. It was in many ways a close replica of St. John's jadeite statue in the secret room deep beneath our manor-house, but with some few differences. Although the place wherein I knelt was very dark, yet I could discern that the daemon before me was composed of smooth wood that was of a lighter shade than the surrounding trees, of a timber not indigenous to the valley. I touched my hand to the sculpted hoofs, which was one of the aspects with which this image differed with St. John's, who has given his beast houndlike paws. The memory of my friend overwhelmed me with sudden woe, and thus I parted my lips and softly spoke a ritual in the Naacal tongue that he had taught me from the *Necronomicon*.

Close behind me, another voice accompanied my chanting. My heart quickened. Yes, in this place of eerie magick, I could conjure forth with alchemy the eidolon of my lost companion. I turned to greet St. John, in whatever form he had chosen to issue forth. But the person near to me was not my friend. "Simon?" I asked, for indeed the fellow looked exactly like the beast of Sesqua Valley, although he wore no hat, and his long hair fell to his shoulders.

"No," he said, reaching out and taking hold of both my hands. "William Davis Manly, your servant. How clever of you to find this shunned place. How cleverer still for you to know so intimately that rare passage from Alhazred. So, you're a friend of my elder brother's."

I gazed at his hands and saw, as my eyes grew more accustomed to the darkness of the place, that his flesh was of a lighter shade than that of the other children of the valley I had met. But his face was almost identical to that of Simon's, lacking only the sardonic cruelty that always seemed to gloat in Simon's eyes. This creature's eyes were different, too—they were silver-white, like liquid mercury, and they contained an aspect that was utterly otherworldly.

"I've come for Simon's assistance. He visited my friend and me once, three years ago in the winter of 1920. He helped us to locate a tattered copy of the *Necronomicon*."

"Ah—you are Christina Sturhman, of England. Yes, he's spoken of you and St. John. He was quite impressed with what was growing into a choice collection of relics and tomes. But he often complained that you were mere collectors of arcane things, rather than practitioners of the thaumaturgy to which such tomes were devoted. I think he regretted having left that copy of *Al Azif* with you. Have you brought it to him now?"

"I destroyed it, with most of the other things in our collection, after St. John's destruction by the thing we had unconsciously evoked by the stealing of an amulet that is

160

similar in aspect to this totem."

He looked up at the canine countenance, with its mop of ropy hair and high tapered ears. "She is lovely, isn't she?"

"She?"

He smiled as he gazed into my eyes. "Most sphinxes are female. I constructed this one of teak that Simon had imported from Burma."

"Ah! She's yours. I think your copy is slightly flawed—you've given her hoofs instead of paws."

How queerly he smiled at me. "This is how I saw her, when she came to me in dreaming." His soft wide hand brushed against my cheek and through my hair. "Something in you reminds me of her."

I laughed. "My large ears, no doubt!" His smile was kind, so unlike Simon's sneer. I found myself drawn to him and returned his touch. His long hair was soft and fine. "Well, I should return to town. Simon will have deciphered the insignia I brought to him by now."

"What insignia is that?" he quietly asked.

"It was on the base of a jade amulet that was a replica of this creature, or something like it. It had been carved from a small piece of jade, in what I can only describe as a kind of Oriental fashion. There was an insignia around the base which we studied by aid of a magnifying lens."

He tilted his eyes and glanced at his creation. "I should like very much to see such an amulet. I have read of such a thing—it has an ancient and diseased history. It is highly sought by sorcerers." He chuckled. "You've probably drawn Simon to distraction to have told him of this. He'll be restless until he has it. Or did you destroy it as well?" A chill ran through my flesh, and I shuddered. He saw my distress and leaned closer so as to take me in his arms. "I'm sorry to have aroused unhappy memories. And I am sorry for the destruction of your friend. Come, on your feet. You have wandered into one of my secret places, and I must now escort you out."

"Do you live here, in this lonesome place?"

"I do, in a sequestered hut nearby. How remarkable of you to have found the path. You are the first mortal to have done so, in my century of existence."

I stood, but I resisted his attempt to take me from the totem. I stared at the daemon's canine face, the mouth stretched wide with bestial hunger, at the stretch of what looked like reptilian wings. Yes, she was a nightmarish composite of creatures, and she was magnificent. I could easily have worshipped her with rituals of blood and smoke. I stared, entranced.

William Davis Manly stood suddenly before me, his eyes very bright. He brought his curiously shaped mouth to my face and kissed my eyes. With that kiss the ghastly enchantment that had seduced me spilled from my brain and out of my eyes. I did not resist as this secret child of Sesqua's haunted woodland turned me away from his creature and guided me from that secluded spot.

VI.

Simon had left a note at my rooming establishment. I was to meet him at dusk, at some tower in the woods. Marceline would come to fetch me. I bathed and napped, for the events of the past hours had exhausted me emotionally. Strangely, I did not dream, except to fancy that I could hear, just beyond the wall of sleep, small padded footsteps dancing near my cot. A rapping on my chamber door awakened me, and I called from bed for the woman to enter my room. She wore a simple gown of yellow gingham, which complimented her dark skin. Her long red hair was worn loose, and it whirled in the wind as she led me out of the building and into the woods to a tall round tower of brick. As I walked beside her up the small winding steps I took in the scent of her flesh, and thought how like the aether of the valley it smelled, as if both were composed of similar substance.

We reached a spacious circular chamber that was crowded with shelves of books and tables on which more books were heaped among scrolls and manuscripts of various age. Simon sat on a throne in the light of many candles and the shafts on moonlight that spilled through small windows carved into the brick wall. With my copy of the queer inscription in his hand, he did not deign to acknowledge our presence for some few minutes. When at last he looked up at me he did not smile.

"I am annoyed that you destroyed that incomplete copy of the *Necronomicon* that I obtained for you and St. John. The more I think on your destruction of his remarkable occult library, the less inclined I am to assist you. It is the one unpardonable transgression—the wreck of magical tools."

His condescending tone angered me, and I marched to where he sat. "I had suffered a mental and emotional collapse. My dearest companion had been ripped to death by some foul *thing* that had haunted us and is now hunting me. I grow weary of your airs, Simon. I have not forgotten the way you treated us as schoolchildren when you came to instruct us of arcane lore. Perhaps I was foolish to come to you now. You have no interest in anyone but yourself. Give me my inscription and I shall leave."

He pointed a tapered finger to a stone bench near me. "You will sit there and stop behaving like an infantile bore." He looked at Marceline and grinned. "Great Yuggoth, the creature has gumption! Perhaps that is why she has escaped daemonic destruction as of yet." He studied me with mocking eyes as I stood my ground.

"Perhaps," Marceline answered, and the beasts exchanged a look, as if sharing some secret from which I was excluded. I turned to leave, but the woman's grip on my arm was like a vice. "Do sit down, Christina. We've many questions to ask you, and some information to offer. Isn't that what you came to the valley for—answers to your enigma?"

The beast of Sesqua Valley rose from his throne and guiding me onto the stone bench, sitting beside me. "You will tell me of the amulet, and of the place where you located it. I have read of this green jade toy in Alhazred, where it is linked to the corpse-eating cult of inaccessible Leng, in Central Asia. Alhazred tells that it has oft been buried with dead sorcerers, yet finds itself inevitably once more within a wizard's hand. I shall be its final procurer. But how did St. John know where to locate it? *Al Azif* tells no such knowledge."

My weird laughter echoed in the enclosed space. "He knew it from me, fool. The story of its final owner is family legend. I supplied St. John with the codex in which my ancestors recorded the amulet's legend and its link with our antecessors. Do you imagine that there was no foundation of interest in arcane lore that led me to my friend? It wasn't mere fate that brought us together—I sought him out, hungry for his joy of that which was unusual, morbid and forbidden. Pah, this prosaic world! With his help, I was led to a delicious underworld, to the enigmas of the Symbolists and

164

the ecstasies of the Pre-Raphaelites. But mostly it was him—*his* sense of adventurous expectancy, the fever that burned in *his* eyes when we unearthed some foul new thing. And so I supplied the codex, not mentioning that it was a family heirloom. He did not seem to notice that the name of the book's scribe was similar to my own, although we radically altered its spelling once we settled in Great Britain."

The beast's eyes smolder like liquid zinc oxide. "And where is this family heirloom, my child? This codex?"

Oh, my laughter was delicious. "Destroyed, with all of the rest. What good was any of it without my friend? But hark, beast, I'll whisper the name of the crumbling church wherein the Dutch churchyard may be found. Then you can go seek your treasure, and may it damn you as it has condemned me." I pressed my mouth against his soft large ear and heaved a Holland name, and then I pushed him roughly from me so that he slipped from the bench and fell onto the round wooden floor. From somewhere atop the twin-peaked mountain, things wailed to lunar light. And from some other distant place I heard another sound, like unto the baying of a gigantic hound.

Marceline reached for me as I stood, and I realized that I was weeping. "Fie, wretch, don't touch me. I have no more need of thee and thine. I have lost the one soul I needed in my life. St. John is a mangled corpse; I *alone* know why!" I swept from them, raced down the winding steps and plunged into moonlight. I hissed at trees, and they moved as if in fear so that I could bathe more fully in the lunatic light. I saw the horde of bats that were silhouetted against that radiant globe, the moon. I beheld the nebulous shape that followed that chittering throng, the vague cloudy thing silhouetted against lunar phosphorescence. Beneath my mortal foot I could feel a throbbing pulse that emanated from some dungeon beneath the sod where dwelt the cursed valley's heart. My human hands stretched to the sky and made strange signals to the nimbus shape that fell from heaven, onto me, and that covered my being like a gauze of smog.

My only friend was dead. I remembered his destruction, the taste of rent flesh and spilled blood. It was the thing of ancestry that we had released when we opened a wizard's tomb in a neglected Holland churchyard, a wizard of mine own lineage. Oh, we had lived for the pleasures of horror, those very gratifications that had moved St. John to ecstasy! I shall know such ecstasy again. Come, hither, all ye shadows of ancestral memory. Sink into the tissue of my transmigrated flesh. Help me stretch and shape and rise—a new entity, a creature of birthright.

I laughed at the tiny creatures that rushed out of the stone tower and praised me with their silver eyes. I stretched my wings and snapped my mammoth jaws as the fellow took out his flute and played a song in honor of my ghastliness. I watched as the woman in her gown of yellow gingham writhed in danse before me. The ground shook beneath my transformed feet as the titanic white mountain moved so as to stretch its peaks, as if in genuflection to my monstrosity. I stretched my reptilian wings and cackled with pleasure. From the corners of my eyes I espied the small shapeless gnomes that scuttled from behind the trees and danced about me on their tiny paws.

I saw it billow from behind the trees—a thick mauve mist. It was an effluvium that pulsed in time to the beating of Sesqua Valley's witchery. I sucked in the sweet enchanted air as the thick mist moved through the trees, toward me. Within that sentient haze I saw another form that walked within it. He stepped into the moonlight, the child of valley shadow who, I realized, could be a new-found friend, a real companion such as I had lost with the demise of St. John. William Davis Manly raised his hand to the moon and made to that yellow orb an elder sign. He opened his mouth and spoke words to me in a Dutch dialect, and I knew that it was a translation of the inscription that had been etched around the base of a small jade amulet. My black eyes raised to the majestic moon. My mouth stretched with baying as the poet of Sesqua's shadowland kissed my cloven hoof.

Some Buried Memory

Charlotte Hund stood before the full-length mirror in its great gilded frame and examined herself. In the palsied yellow light of the enormous room she could not see her reflection clearly; she could just make out the rough texture of her large face, the verdant eyes, the uneven tusks of xanthic ivory behind the bloated lips. Raising a hand, she smoothed the nest of hairs that sprouted from one corner of her mouth, then scratched her face with thick nails. "Is it not true, sir, that I am the ugliest woman in this city?"

"Au monde, madame, au monde," Sebastian Melmoth assured her, to which she smiled.

"I often think that it was for this ugliness that I was shunned in Boston and not my criminal reputation."

Her host sucked on his opium-tainted cigarette. When he exhaled, he fancied that the smoke formed itself suggestively before his face. "You must tell me of your crime, Miss Hund," he told her as he admired the scarab ring on one fat finger. "You are certainly criminally grotesque; but ugliness is a crime of nature, not a felon of choice. Tell me the tale of your trespass, and drench your telling it with such rich description that I may fully imagine it." He sucked once more at his bit of nicotia and closed his eyes.

Charlotte stepped away from the mirror and moved to

one of the room's small stained glass windows. "To speak of my sin would mean to reveal my life, and there isn't much to tell. I do not know my parentage, for I was found."

"Found?"

She shrugged. "So I was eventually told, by my grandmother, who raised me. She would call me her 'fond foundling,' which I liked. Grandmother was an eccentric Boston witch. She taught me divination, and together we discovered my talent for finding long-buried treasure." Turning away from the window, Charlotte walked to a table and examined the beautifully crafted miniature sphinx that sat upon it. "It's amazing, the things one finds buried beneath the ground. I could sniff these things, and these nails were fashioned for digging. I especially loved the old burying grounds of New England. I remember one curious early morning, when grandmother hinted that she knew more about my background than she was wont to let on; for as we burrowed beside one venerable tree, she whispered that my kinfolk dwelt beneath that chilly sod."

"How esoteric."

"We found quite a treasure that morning. Together, over time, we collected quite a pile of buried treasure. She taught me how to weave spells, and together we would dance naked beneath the autumn moon. As I grew older, my ugliness increased, and society taught me that its heart is cruel. I began to shun humanity, to exist in the hours when most were asleep. My own slumber was haunted by curious dreams of dark figures in black spaces. I would awaken, at times, in curious places, with booty in my embrace but no memory of where I had been or with what I had occupied my time. I cannot clearly recall the morning I was found, with mud on my hands and an amazing taste in my mouth. Whatever I had done, it earned me a new home in a state hospital. I was lunatic at first, screaming to be with my grandmother. Over the years I grew more settled. I studied the sane and began to ape their ways. I discovered a great fondness for literature, and my grandmother would bring me wonderful books. The news of her death was a cruel blow, but I endured, and eventually won my release. Among my belongings was a key to grandmother's house, now mine; it was at the house that I found her letter, from which I learned of the wealth that she had left me, and that told me of this city of Gershom, where I would find exile."

"For which we are the richer," Sebastian told her. "I'm exceptionally fond of the gift of this ring. Its ancient metal, slipped so snugly around my flesh, feels very old indeed. Please tell me that you found it during one of your excavations, adorning the finger bone of some long-interred fellow. That would give me such delicious dreams."

"I'm happy that you like it. And in exchange, you will keep your promise."

"Ah, a journey to our cemetery isle. I have visited it but once; so much nature hurts my eyes, and the leaves are particularly bright at this autumnal time."

"I'm anxious to see it in reality. Your beautiful verbal portrait of it has danced in my imagination. I can well believe that you were once a poet. Come, take my arm and let us leave this smoky chamber. I'm in need of moonlight. We'll stroll beneath its glow and you can tell me what brought you to this remarkable city."

Linking arms, they vacated the building. The night was very still and very silent. As they walked past factories and

170

old brownstones, Sebastian Melmoth began to tell his tale. "I came to Gershom because of what the world calls sin. I came because I heard that this is a godless town, and without god there can be no fall from grace. I confess that I miss sin horribly. It gives such texture to existence. This spectral place has a way of luring lost souls to its confines. I find it a comfortable nether world. One meets such interesting sorts. As for transgression, well, I am hopeful that in time I shall find a new form of sin. And yet, the longer I remain in this city, the more intense my sensations become, innocent as they are. Gershom teases the brain with singular dreaming, and in such visions we find new forms of thought and novel ways in which to express innovative ideas. Ah, but here we are at our destination."

He led her onto a pier, and she saw the means of their transportation. "Oh my," she moaned.

"No, no. This teakwood raft is far sturdier than it looks, and the couch, though tiny, is quite comfortable. This small gap between pier and raft is easily stepped over. You see how even a heavy fellow like me can manage it. Take my hand and—*voila!* No, you sit on the couch. I shall stand and hold onto this pole. This pale young creature will be our Charon."

The ugly woman sat on the cushioned seat and watched as the child who was their navigator unwound the craft's brittle sail; and she wondered what was the good of such a canvas, on this windless night. Her interlocutor bent so as to whisper at her ear. "The poor child suffers from poliomyelitis or some such ailment. His limbs are quite curved. I like the way he walks, like some pathetic puppet. He will love you for any pennies you may throw his way. I seem to have forgotten my purse."

Charlotte reached into her pocket and produced a silver coin. Bowing to her, the child took the coin and pressed it against his forehead. His wide eyes looked past his wayfarers, into eventide, and when he began to sing the sound of his voice caused a chill to tingle Sebastian's spine. Charlotte listened to the wind that rose above the water. The raft began to move away from land, toward mist. That cloud of liquid air kissed the woman with beads of moisture, which she brushed away from her face with a rough hand. At last the mist began to thin, and Charlotte could see the mass of land that was their terminus. Eerily, Sebastian Melmoth began to whistle.

"Why do you make that sound, monsieur?"

"Because I am afraid." The winds extinguished, and yet the raft continued to move toward the island, as if pulled to it by some force. "The Isle of Moira," Sebastian continued, "draped in darkness. Her sand aches for the touch of our hot naked feet. She would drink our vitality with those mouths that are her barrows and her pits. Ah, and there—do you see her? Our desolate receptionist."

Charlotte peered at the place of stone steps toward which their craft sailed, and saw the grim figure that stood like some obsidian statue. The raft lodged itself perfectly against the pitted platform of the lowest step. Kicking off his shoes, the child limped toward the waiting figure and offered it his hand. Swiftly, the creature lowered itself until its cowled head was in alignment with the child's. The infant moved his mouth, as if whispering secrets. A dark face parted its lips and fed upon the lame boy's living breath. As the child began to shudder, the woman took him in her arms.

Sebastian removed his slippers and indicated to Charlotte

that she should discard her shoes. He tried not to gape at the sight of her bestial feet, which were far more feral than her ungainly hands. Offering assistance, he helped her from the raft, onto the weathered stone steps. They approached the woman and her captive. Charlotte watched the dusky hand that loosened the lad's shirt and manipulated the flesh nearest the child's heart.

Sebastian's musical voice began to pipe. "Mistress Atropos, may I present Miss Charlotte Hund, of Boston? She has come to dance naked beneath your moon."

The black woman chuckled as she rose, not relinquishing her hold on the child. "You will want to climb the highest hill, where the wind is exquisitely musical among the numbered sarcophagi. You know the place, Melmoth; you capered there once yourself."

"In one of my Greek moments, yes. I was much younger then. And far less innocent. But we shall have to ascend slowly. These thick old limbs are no longer in fine fettle. Do release the child, Mistress, that he may playfully lead the way."

The woman spread her arms and the child hobbled forward, to Charlotte, whose hand he held. Sebastian watched as they began to climb the upward path, and then he touched his brow to the Mistress and followed his friend. The moon was as orange as many of the decorative leaves, and mauve shadows hovered behind the many trees and shrubs. Sebastian did not like the silence of the place; he could hear too loudly his labored breathing. Now and then, in places of deep shadow, he sensed that he was watched by shapes in the night. He followed the path, past tombs and angels and obelisks, watching the two before him. He saw the child suddenly stop and place a tiny hand to its heart. Stopping, Sebastian produced a gilded case, from which he snatched a cigarette.

"The child has been too active, too excited," Charlotte concluded as she folded her arms around the boy. "His heart is racing and he burns with fever."

"Yes, he suffers from that dread contagion called Life. But we are almost there, and he may rest upon one of the paws of the great beast. Shall I carry you, boy? Would you like a cigarette?"

Ignoring the man, the silent child took one of Charlotte's hands and continued to lead the way. They reached the crest, and Charlotte gazed in admiration at the moon-drenched colossus. She and the child watched as Sebastian approached the gigantic stone Sphynx, before which he raised his hands and snapped his fingers. His high voice hummed an ancient tune, and he smiled as Charlotte joined him in the danse. Happily, the lame child began to move with them, his crooked feet moving in imitation of the woman's hoofs. They moved beneath the moon for quite a while, until finally the child tripped and fell, clutching again at his chest. Charlotte dropped beside him and smoothed his brow with her rude hand. Sebastian watched as her expression altered, as she lowered her face to the earth and began to snuffle.

"Whatever are you doing?"

She looked at him with shining eyes. "There is something here, beneath this ground; something rare yet familiar, something seductive. It is a memory that I once knew, long ago; it has taste and texture, and it calls to me."

"Really, you are too fantastic. I think you've been

174

touched by the corroded light of that torrid moon. I hate the moon when it resembles a scab on diseased flesh. Ugh! Those awful crimson shadows around the tombstones—it's too macabre."

Charlotte ignored his histrionic chatter and continued to smooth the ground with anxious fingers, the limping child beside her. She crawled until coming to a toppled obelisk, beside the base of which she found an opening in the earth. Peering into that cavity, she saw the steps that led beneath the surface. "Do you sense it," she asked the child, "how this hollow summons? Are you game, boy? Shall we investigate?" Standing, she took the lad's hand and led him down into the pit.

Sebastian Melmoth raised a white hand and sang some lines from Jonson:

"Farewell, thou child of my right hand, and joy;
My sin was too much hope of thee, dear boy . . ."

He watched them vanish into dank shadow. Then he turned to the gigantic Sphynx. Would she answer the riddle of what his friend would find? Was there anything that would appease doom? He looked to the moon, which had paled to a shade of ocher. Sebastian raised his hands to the sphere of dead refracted light, and then he began to remove his clothing.

The steps of loam felt strangely familiar to Charlotte's naked feet, like something she had known while dreaming. She paused one moment to press her brow against the earthen wall, breathing its aroma, which stirred a cloudy image in her brain of something she had known, now forgotten. Touching lips to the dark wall, she trembled at the taste. Something in the sensation filled her with happiness,

175

and turning to the child she began to dance upon the steps. Weirdly, she could easily see the child's bright flesh in the dark place, the small hands held out to her. Eschewing caution, she took those hands and led the boy into a clownish dance upon the sleek and narrow steps. She seemed not to notice the heaviness of his breathing, and thought that he was clowning when he began to jerk with spasm. When she let go of his hands, she was too slow to catch his falling form. He tumbled down the stairs, to a level of rocky surface. Crying, she rushed to him and took up his still limp form in her embrace. She held him as his flesh grew cool and dry. She pressed him tighter to her breasts and whispered to his uncomprehending ear. How keenly she could smell his death, the fragrance of the stuff that clothed his bones. At last, she set his still form onto the surface to which he had fallen. Pressing fingers to his mouth, she pushed it shut. "Rest in peace, sweet innocent," she murmured.

Before her was a passageway, through which a charnel breeze wafted to her. She could smell the bits of old bone that, over time, had sifted through the ground, some poking through the earth, others littering the place. Their stench was like something she had known, intimately, in Boston; but the memory was vague, like a favorite delicacy from childhood that had been forgotten in dull adulthood, until happened on by chance. Charlotte followed the chthonic blast, through the passageway, until she came to a spacious grotto, which seemed to her like the forgotten catacomb of some deserted cathedral. Broken statuary stood among the boxes of discarded death. She peered at a raised platform, a kind of bema, and saw two figures huddled over an altar, whispering as they watched her approach. She did not look away from the green eyes set deep within the rubbery faces, eyes that resembled her own. The eldest creature moved to meet her at the steps leading to the platform, and offered her his bestial hand. He smoothed her face with that hand, and combed her hair with thick strong nails. His mouth found her own. His kiss was revelation. She knew from that kiss exactly who she was.

She turned at the sound of another who approached them, and sighed at the sight of the burden in his arms. She helped to place the broken body on the altar and touched a hand to the bright small face. His carrion bouquet made her mouth to water.

"Found him just above," the new arrival muttered. "Freshly dead."

The elder beast pressed his hands together and moaned in pleasure. "Excellent. A welcoming feast for our sister." He hissed as one of the others tilted toward one thin bent limb. "Where are your manners, Erebus? Our sister shall have first pick." Turning to Charlotte, he motioned to the child.

"Give me his tender heart," was her request.

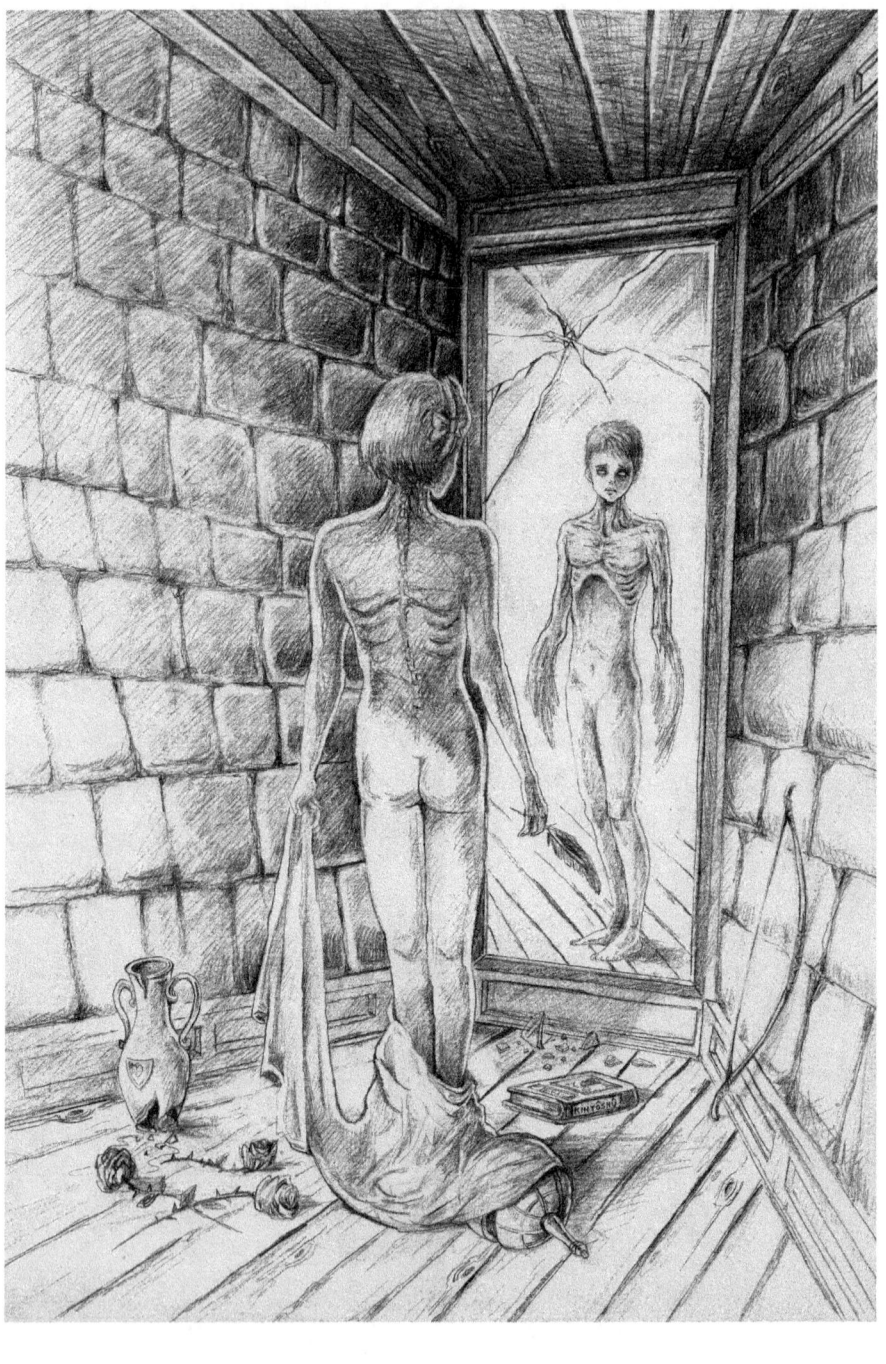

Your Ghost on Glass

Ah, there you are again, within this mirror. Yet not completely, for your face is partially eaten by devouring shadow, the void that is caught inside your black reptilian eyes. What else do I see in those eyes? Loneliness, sorrow? Resignation? Ah, no—I see the soul of a dreamer. Why is your stern mouth so clamped? Of what are you afraid to speak? No matter, I shall read your dark and liquid eyes. You died on this day, and how richly you haunt the universe. I sensed you once, in Providence, and spoke your name to shadow— and how queer it was, to sense that shadow drink my hot mortal moan. Loneliness, sorrow? I know them well—and yet how stupid they are compared to phantasy and dream. How insignificant, that the boy I love will never kiss me; for I have been kissed by cosmic dread, by the emptiness above me, into which I long to submerge. Is that where you roam now, sad and lonely spectre? If I breathe onto your image in this polished realm, can you drink my hot mortality and free me from this bondage of bone and flesh?

Ah, no. For now you disintegrate and drift into the dull backward of Time, into a boundless past. Where you walk alone.

Letters from an Old Gent

I

My dear Maurice:—

The town to which I journeyed was very strange indeed. As I hovered above it I thought the plan of roads most peculiar, as the lines, combined, formed some kind of sign that I was once able to understand but could now not comprehend. The place was not deep enough to be called a valley; rather, it was like sleepy hollow betwixt ranges of horrible gray hills. How can hills be horrible? Their queer shapes were suggestive, as if they had once been living forms who had fallen down and so perished beneath the wind that never seemed to silence. They were titanic heaps of ashen sod on which no living thing existed, heaps that held no memory of when they roamed and ruled. Their loneliness seemed echoed on the stone-paved streets of the dead town, on which no soul sojourned. I floated to one main street and marveled at the numerous statues of robed figures, figures that were inexorably rotting in the edacious wind. I could sense it all around me, the voracious air; and I could hear it smelling for me, as though it would rot me too, until I was nothing but a formless pillar waiting to crumble into dust.

Is it not strange, Maurice, that even there—among a multitude of phantoms—I was yet the Outsider? I hovered in a place in which I did not belong, observing everything of which I will never be a part. Even the daemon wind not could touch me, which made me rather sad; for I wanted to *feel* that ancient place, to walk along the antediluvian roadways, to lean against the cracking planks of slanting habitations. I did not belong to that realm, familiar though it seemed, nor did it appertain to me in any way. It was like some distant memory of a place I might have known—and lost.

I see it, now, but mistily. If I close my eyes, will I lose it altogether? There, they are shut, and before their flaps I see impressions still—red and black—as formless as the horrible hills. Perhaps—perhaps I can be of that place, if I teach myself to howl correctly, like this daemon-wind that seeks me still; if I learn to howl as one last spectre, within a haunted place.

II.

Cherish'd S. L.:—

I gaze out into the deep, immortal night and see a semblance of your handsome face: sleek hair, dark eyes, mouth poised for poetry. You dance among the dying stars, and the unfathomable animal at your side exposes one pale breast that is round like some silken lunar sphere. Brother of mine, tainted by my adoration, your breath is cosmic mistral that speaks the poison of Baudelaire, and I imbibe the alchemy. My star-brimmed eyes leak tears for you, beautiful and lonely eidolon, my phantom-double, creature of desire and dismay. You hate me now, I know; you would cringe from my attempt to touch you and be your friend. But know that I have always loved you and hold you up as rare deity. I

181

would walk beside you, reverently, through sculpted cities. I would kneel and kiss the double sex of your unfathomable animal. I would sing your praise in Hebrew verses. You are far, yet your rejection is too near, and I am branded by your hate. Your tongue, so sensual, became a baleful tool—vindictive, full of vice. Yet I would digest a phial of cyanide for you, my brother, and hope my soul (if such a thing exists) would sail to you, where I would stand on your other side, my lord, and caper with your unfathomable animal in honor of your potency. But no—I dance alone, with bright and useless streams of woe spilling from my eyes. And you, phantom, turn your back and gaze into the void of space rather than watch the antics of a friend who loves you still.

III.

Clark:—

It sits upon my mantel, the thing composed, so craftily, by your pale hands—the Nameless Eidolon. My eyes lose their location when I gaze too long a time; I see beyond, past the mundane world of men, into an alien realm of fear and fancy, where the sun and moon and archaic stars are emblems in unknown sky. In this other vastness there exists an awful motion and an eldritch sound, which remind me of your mouth when stretched in mirthless laughter; and were I wise I would close these eyes and clamp these ears—yet am I beguiled, and thus I watch the spheres that rise and fall in light of pink and purple haze. I see one dark thing only: that Nameless Eikon that you have crafted with you hands of Art, that thing so saturnine and grim.

I flow and am filled with unmistakable anticipation as darkness falls, like particles of sand, into the pale pink sky. I close my eyes to spreading obscurity and kneel on icy silt. I sense the things that prance around us to the playing of nauseating pipes. I hear the sound of waves and reawaken on a moonlit shore, my hands sunk in sand. You are there, Nameless Eikon, now gigantic, towering beside me as I examine the hoof-like prints surrounding us. What is this desire, this ache to rise and dance around you; but I am clumsy and crippled by mortality, and when I try to dance I merely drop into dark water and am swept away, out, out to where the water is reflected with one thousand stars. I sink beneath the water, drinking star-stuff, but push myself again above the surface, to look upon the Nameless Eikon one last time. How strange that I have never noticed, until now, that you have given it your face—so sinister, so supreme.

IV.

Dear Melmoth:—

I wish to rest upon this ground. This place
Beside this knoll is like some den of dreams
Found in some realm of opiatic streams
Of smoke that filter deep into this face.
This whisp'ring knoll would tell me of the One
That, long ago, was sunk into this ground,
Now long-forsaken—out of sight, of sound—
A crippled child raised as a warlock's son.
I seem to see him in this rising roll
Of smoke, a ghostly presence, pale and patched,
Like strips of fleshy matter, poorly thatched,
That billows to me from this whis'pring knoll.
We weave together, one dead thing and I.
We utter to this dark immortal sky.

V.

Dearest Sonia:—

You wear lunar light so easily, it drapes you like a gown of mist and silver filigree. I, like some moth that would beseech the moon's soft light, float to those twin globes, your breasts, to touch them with my mouth. I drink the perfume of your skin and hair. I sip the tonic of your lips, that fire. Your hands clamp mine with such force that I feel we shall never break apart. But this is mere magic of the night, my love. The dew that glistens in your midnight eyes is tarnished by the dawn, becomes drab tears of bitterness and loss. The time of sorceress darkness is now a memory. The sun-bleached realm is dry and dead and desperate, and has no time for romance, for poetry. The perfume of your hair is now the odor of rust, and silver filigree crumbles as mold. You dwell now as distant memory, in the place where I am, and shall always be, as alone as Brother Poe.

VI.

My Brother Edgar:—

Black night has crept, like cat, across the tombs, and time is but a toy of the age. You reach into the dark and touch cold night, and quiet, a silence of the grave. You sense the shapes that move beneath the earth, we beings pent in darkness and decay. We burst the wall of our reservoir of tainted sod and push above the ground, on which we dance among the hoary tombs and sniff the fervid fear that we inspire. We are the nameless dwellers of the dark, our appellations never etched on stone; and how you would be numbered in our horde, no designation limiting your reign. The ages would not dull your appetite, and you would pull dead mortal residue to your maw and feast upon those

184

planted in the ground and never cease until you are fulfilled. Ah, Brother Poet, you, your acolytes, will sit upon the slabs with pen and pad and tell the world the horror that you have sensed from we who crawl within that cave—your skull. And we who never dream will dance again, within the fever of your visionings.

VII.

Beloved Sarah Susan:—

Let me take your lovely hand and walk with you along these quiet grounds. The Grotto is especially beautiful today, and you look charming with primroses in your hair. Yes, you do look frail, and we can walk as slowly as you desire. I do not mean to look troubled—you know that I am supremely unemotional—I wish only to give you comfort, and thus I can slow my pace and enjoy Nature as you have taught me. We can gaze into the heavens and bask in their beauty, knowing that they contain nothing else, not gods nor angels with whom, in time, we dance among the clouds. That blue sky, as you have told me, is but an illusion of light; beyond it lies darkness illimitable, with here and there some momentary globes of cosmic fire. The clouds are very white, almost as pale as your face, wherein those stars, your eyes, regard me with love and wonder.

You laugh to hear the birds sing in the trees, and warble with them in your lovely voice. But then your eyes seem troubled by some sight that you imagine, there, behind the trees. I see nothing but imagine much, for you have taught me how to sense the things that haunt the places just beyond our ken. Your hold is tighter on my hand and now your laughter is a strained and nervous sound. But know this, dearest, I will catch these fiends with my imagination and so trap them that they can never do you harm. And I'll expel them with my poet's pen, and trapped them onto paper, which may be ripped or ignited. And the one sound that comes from you in night will be our laughter, sweet and safe and sane, and you will smile to know again this kiss that I bequeath upon maternal brow.

VIII.

Papa:—

Can you smell the river where you rest? It smells of mud and stones, and sometimes, at night, it seems to sing with liquid sigh. Do you hear its lullaby, where you lie? It talks to you, I know, and tells you tales, as you told me when I was but a child. I think of you now and then, and envision you beneath the ground, through which you seep to your neighbors and knock upon their doors. What would you sell them, Papa, what are the wares of Death?

Can you smell the wind that flows from off the river? It smells of earth and sky, and sometimes, at night, it whispers of another world that one can find in dream. I meet you there, Papa, and let you lift me to your lap, which once was warm but now is as cool as naked bone. What is it that we hear within the wind? It may be Mother calling—she is near, you know, just over there, where she followed you and frolics off the walls.

I have my newest tale. I'll read to you as you once read to me. I was thinking of you, Papa, when I wrote it, and of the place where you rest, in darkness but not in silence. Death is unquiet, disturbed by things that crawl and scratch and gnaw. I'll read to you, Papa, with my lips pressed onto the ground so that my hot voice sinks into the sod and finds your ears. You have no ears? They have deliquesced? Then listen to me with your bones, that ivory pith folded or out-spread. I'll sing it to the earth, my art, and add it to the noise in the dirt, the ground beneath which we will sink in time, your family, and be with you again, and whisper se-crets of the world we knew.

186

IX.

Sunand, dear fellow:—

It's interesting, isn't it, how I can infiltrate one's life? I am like one dead yet dreaming. You heard my call when very young, and I molded your mind with the power of my literary potency. As it was done unto me, I do unto others. I pulse within one's blood, through every vein. I infiltrate the eyes, which see the world anew, through my ideas. I shape the soul with spectral hands, and kiss with an influence you would never otherwise have known. I race with young minds as they devour my Cthulhu, my Innsmouth, my Fungi. I educate through the magick of my correspondence, and urge you to seek wisdom and knowledge of your own. You are mine as we walk, together, along the lanes of Providence, down Benefit Street and to the burying ground I still haunt with Poe. I am there as you stand before 10 Barnes Street, as you chant the titles that I penned there, that rich litany of Work. I dance the dance of ghosts as you slave over my stories so as to purify them as much as possible, so that they are printed as written, down to the very last semicolon and comma, as I instructed Baird. I know that you prize my correspondence for its "importance"—but know that it is my fiction that I cherish above all else. It is there that you will find me, utterly. Know, too, that I will never melt away from your mind, but like some eternal revenant I will dwell within you ever and evermore. I have attached myself, to you and many others, and there will be no letting go; for I am Eternal, and my depths can never be completely plumbed. I am as deep as Time, and the Cosmos.

Yr obt Servt

Ec'h-Pi-El

Uncommon Places

A sequence of prose poems & vignettes
Inspir'd by H. P. Lovecraft's *Commonplace Book*

(Dedicated to David E. Schultz)

I.

The primitive sun has set, ushering forth an embryonic darkness that holds much promise. The glass of cool elixir is in
my hand, and I add to the dark absinthe the flakes of dried
infant's blood that I have collected in honor of Baudelaire. I
lift my face to the night wind and watch the birth of starlight. I bring the smooth rim of the chilly goblet to my lips
and let the bitter liquid spill into my mouth. Wormwood
churns my acidic heart. Violently, I smash the glass against
the rocks on which I kneel, and then I pick up the largest
shard and hold it to dim starlight. I whisper promises to
whatever gods may heed my black prayers. I touch the
shard of glass to my forehead and etch thereon an elder sign.

Starlight begins to sing. No—not starlight; rather, the
sound issues from the shapes that swirl above me in dark
sky. I listen to these cosmic Sirens as they swim the sea of
night. Ah, their sweet voices! I am lured unto them, those

airy nymphs who take hold of my reaching hands and lead me deeper into an eldritch dark.

II.

Ah, Maryanne. You weave your spell as you walked onto the foggy pier, as you remove your shoes and stepped onto the sand. Although I remain standing on the wooden surface of the ancient pier, I seem to feel the ocean floor beneath my feet, as if I were your psychic sibling. I can hear the music of the distant waves, the wind on water, and you raise your arms and dance beneath the goddess moon. Tonight she is a gibbous deity, and as you lift your magical hand to her I see her move, swinging in the sky like some pendulum out of Poe. A thousand beautiful stars turn away as the crescent blade cuts into the sky, as the flesh of midnight clouds splits open and pours their rain of blood onto the world. How daintily you reach out and catch some drops of gore, and with what nimble grace do you dig your nude foot into the ruddy sand and with it etch some esoteric sign into the sand.

Oh, Maryanne. With moonbeams dancing on your mouth, you chant my name; and how can I resist the charm of your vocative voice? I float unto you, just above the sand, and wipe away the crimson rain that sinks into my eyes and turns your beauty into a visage of red death. You stand, naked and supreme, within your chamber of black clouds; and beyond you, on dark water, I see the nymphs who break through waves to sing your praise. They are dead things with little remaining of their faces, and yet they wail and beg your mercy. How haughtily you ignore them as you dance into the ocean, pale fire playing in your hands. With witchery you weave your globe of electric light and hurl it

189

into heaven, where it unsettles the curved moon, she who hungers for your touch and falls into your grasp, linked to a chain of star-stuff. You bring that chain over your glossy hair and let it fall so that the crescent moon hangs as an amulet between your magnificent breasts. Ah, how that white thing drinks the hue of blood and throws its crimson light into mine eyes; and when I shut those eyes I can feel the rain swarm around me like some column of liquid mortal debris, washing over me and pushing me into the rising tide. I heard the creak of antique ships that have wrecked and sunk beneath the waves. I can feel those waves wrap around my ankles like plasmatic hands as soggy mouths moan chanteys of doom. Drowning is a horrible death—the burning lungs that fill with the water that squeezes out oxygen. As the earth churns beneath me and continues to drag me down I see your bleached hand reach for me; and yet when I clasp it I find that it is not your hand at all, but a thing of bone.

Wise Maryanne. I feel your mighty hands tug at my hair and pull me up, out of red and black shadow, into mist and waves and wind. You wink at the hand of bone I clutch and curl your fingers around my own as, kneeling side by side; we write my name into the sand with one pointed fingerbone. You press your Goddess mouth against my ear and whisper my name, the name I hear echoed above me, on the wind.

III.

I looked over the waves and through the mist, to the hill of rock and earth that rose above the water, from which my name was whispered on night-wind. I saw the hazy silhouette of the domed edifice that sat upon that hill—an enticing sight. Ah, how I envied the seabirds that flew in the air near

190

your marble dome; how I spread my arms as I stood upon the shore and warbled as did the winged ones. Shutting my eyes to salty breeze, I dreamed that I was free from bonds of gravity, that I soared over dark water, to you. And as I dreamt I raised my feet as if to walk the aether, the liquid air that washed over my ancient limbs. But then the dream grew drear, and I saw the vision of my falling heavily from the sky.

I dreamed of falling to the waves, yet when I hit the surface the ground was dry and solid. And when I opened my eyes I saw that I was on a hill of rock and earth. Below me I could hear the pounding tide that hit a distant shore. Near to me was the marble edifice, to which I crawled. Reaching, I touched my hand to your smooth wall on which I could espy my vague reflection. When I peered upward I discovered exactly what you were, for there were names and dates etched on your wall, naming you a monolithic mausoleum such as I had never seen.

Pressing palms against your marble wall I pushed myself to my feet and stood. Again, I saw my dim reflection on your surface, against which my hands were pressed; and as I stared at my reflection I became baffled, for I did not understand the attire in which I was wound. Then, from behind me, came the sound of low singing; and as the surface of your wall became yet more pale I thought I could espy thereon the place behind me. I saw, faintly, the three spectral shapes that writhed in windstorm, those three things that were dressed in shrouds that aped mine own. I saw them, these Sirens who would enchant me from the mortal world, as they reached their skeletonic hands to me and would pluck me to them.

I gasped and saw my fog of living breath. Happily, I bashed my head against your wall and watched the sweet red stream that was my mortal elixir slide down your surface. The etched emblem carved onto my forehead had opened and was bleeding freely. Reaching to my face, I washed my eyes with blood; thus blinded, I walked within a red cloud, past the Sirens who would beguile me to some grave. I walked away from your fantastic form and out of that burial plot, onto the rutted road.

IV.

I walked the furrowed road in bleak autumn mist, past bare elms and distant meadows, and tasted a bittersweet air that floated before my face. Some seabird seemed to shiver as it flew by me in the shaded place, crying as though to call me back unto the waves. I ignored its plaintive summons and peered down the rutted road to a spot where undulating shadow writhed. I watched that shadow spread and lift into the air as a flock of nightbirds. Walking to where the flock had congregated, I saw the raven's corpse, its wings outstretched as though it had been crucified upon the road.

I followed the deep-sunk tracks in the road and wondered what could have caused such indentations in hard mud. The bare elms that bordered the road loomed nakedly against the bleak autumn dusk, and something in their twisted limbs disquieted me. Their serpentine design seemed strangely mimicked in the deep-sunk tracks that stretched beyond dim vision's rim; and my fevered mind—inflamed by phosphorescent absinthe—began to fancy that it was no vehicle that had caused those ruts in mud; rather, they were the tracks of some vile living thing that slithered through the ancient earth. I followed those lines through descending shadow, to where the road turned and where the weird trees became stranger still; and went beyond them, seduced by cry of cricket and of toad, to where a dank tarn brooded in early darkness.

I approached the edge of tarn and lowered before it on my knees. I raised my face to mystic night and sought for solace in starlight—but there was naught above me but blackness illimitable. I looked down at the black tarn and succumbed unto its thick temptation, dipped my hands into its essence and brought up handfuls of the dark slime. I smothered my face into the dead sludge and pushed the stuff into my visage. I tasted a sickness unto death. As I reclined and stretched upon the ground, I felt the slime sink into the rutted surface of my forehead, wherein I had etched a symbol with a shard of broken glass. I shut my eyes to mystic night and listened to the life around me. I felt the mouths of toads at my fingertips as something sleek and serpentine moved across the rutted symbol on my face. It moved across the flaps that covered my fevered eyes, past my nostrils to my mouth.

I knew a serpent's kiss.

V.

She stepped out of dark woodland, into dawn, her hands clutching at the fabric of her dress of deepest purple. Cool air brushed against her face as she studied the ancient city spread before her. How strange it looked, this elder town, like something existing in a separate dimension of time and space. There were no tall skyscrapers with which she was accustomed, and every inhabitant situated on the city's three hills looked made of wood. She approached the wooden bridge that arched across the flowing canal, but stopped before stepping onto it because of the *sound* that issued from the rush of slimy black waters, the unwholesome liquid yelps. Timidly, she stepped onto the weathered wood and held on to the damp railing and began to make her way across the time-worn bridge; and as she reached midway she had to stop and catch her breath, for the very air seemed tainted and transformed, as if time itself had been affected by the realm she now approached. Glancing over the railing, she saw the artificial human arm that flowed beneath the wooden bridge. Holding steadily onto the railing, she turned so as to stare at the rush of black water and saw the white things that flowed to her in its depths—the pair of artificial legs, like those belonging to a tailor's mannequin. At last she saw it spinning toward her in dark slime, the wooden torso with its weeping head. The thing's artificial eyes seemed to plead with her as they caught her own for briefest second— and then it was gone, beneath the bridge, from which there came an ersatz squeal of unhuman pitch.

She stumbled across the bridge, into the wooden city, over which a primitive sun began to rise. She listened to the distinctive cries of speckled cuckoos that flittered above her, and watched as they flew into a courtyard and settled upon the curved fingers of a colossal sculptured hand. Walking into that courtyard, she studied the figures that hung from stringy vines attached to the colossus. Noticing the twisted thing that lay upon the grass, she knelt before it and touched her hand to its splintered surface. It lay sprawled upon the grass like some hatchling that had fallen to its death from mother's nest, and when she lifted one of its stringy vines the thing felt dry and dead within her grasp, like a vein that had lost its fluid of life and was now a useless stem. In the corner of her eye she caught subtle movement, and thus she rose to face the thing that trembled on its strings. Pressing her fingers to the puppet's face, she was surprised at how moist and smooth the wooden surface felt. She traced with one finger the symbol that had been etched into the puppet's forehead, above its glass eyes, and her palm gently pressed against an infant mouth. She knew a puppet's kiss.

Her eyes went to the colossal wooden hand from which the puppet and its kindred hanged, and she saw that the surface was smooth like unto the toy's limbs. With both hands firmly against the sculpture's surface, she slid downward to its base, which was planted into the ground; and as she leaned against the gigantic wrist she fancied that this was not a sculpture at all, but rather some living thing that was rooted to the earth. Again she stood, before the figure that seemed to beckon to her; and when she embraced it the strings came loose from the wooden finger from which they grew, falling to her and winding themselves into her hair. Taking hold of those warm veins, she let them wrap around her fingers; and when she walked from out the courtyard, the marionette skipped beside her.

VI.

He stood upon a porch and smoked a cigarette like a live thing. From within the Harlot's House he could hear the automated band perform a waltz on tin instruments, a false noise to which wooden feet stomped in time behind a shaded window. And then he was startled to see, turning around one corner, the little puppet and its living friend. Flicking away the cigarette, he stepped from the porch and advanced toward the woman. Reaching into pockets, he produced another cigarette and lit it, and this he offered to the stranger as she approached him. He smiled as she refused the bit of nicotine and nonchalantly poked it into the puppet's mouth, which pleased the little one no end. Motioning to the Harlot's House, the tall and lean automaton held out his sculpted hand, which the curious woman accepted. Together, they entered the den of iniquity, while the little one, whose strings had become unwound from mortal fingers, sat upon the stoop and smoked.

His arm linked to hers, he guided her into the mirrored drawing room, and he was pleased as he studied her fresh-faced expression. Elegantly, he led her into the waltz, as a strange note entered into the music performed. She did not notice the way her mortality had enticed the horde of dancing mannequins—she was as the honey added to beer so as to draw forth wasps. Those who whirled around her longed to kiss her liquid eyes and press their sawdust tongues onto the texture of her flesh. When the music stopped, he turned her to the mirrored wall and ran the sticks that were his fingers through her hair. With one of the splinters that were his fingernails he traced a pattern into her forehead, and then he shuddered as his etching grew moist and red.

She awakened, as if from nameless dreaming, and gawked at her reflected image with its trickle of blood slipping from the symbol that had been etched into her forehead. Reflected with her own image were the things that stood so still, the surrounding mannequins that wore a replica of her symbol upon the smooth and polished timber with which their countenances had been composed. Filled with sudden terror, she fled the Harlot's House. How strange to find that daylight had ended, ushering forth soft velvet darkness. The little puppet was asleep upon the stoop, and she clutched him to her breast as she fled the place from which uncanny music again began to play.

She staggered through the darkened city, trying not to look at the walking creatures that aped mortality, seemingly alive, but—. Seeing a bright glow, she advanced toward it, to a camp beside the flowing canal where dwelt the city's unclean things. They sat, these manikins, around a fire; and as she watched, one creature reached for the discarded remnants of one dummy and tore from it an arm, which was tossed into the flames. And then they seemed to sense her, and turned to her their bashed faces, faces that were missing eyes and noses and, in one case, the lower portion of a mouth. One of these things began to crawl toward her, digging its fragmented fingers into the earth so as to pull itself to her. Others followed, and the diseased horde of animated puppets crept nearer, adamant and pitiless.

She backed away from the approaching multitude of lifeless things that ached to kiss her mortal tissue, to feast upon her flesh. Directly behind her, she could hear the rushing of the black slime that was the charnel canal. Looking down, she saw the thing that mewed and twitched upon the ground, the figure from which portions were missing. She watched, horrified, as the thing pulled itself closer to the edge and then pushed itself into the flowing current. And then she heard, directly before her face, a curious clicking; and when she turned to face the noise, she saw the visage of the little one that she held in her arms, the little puppet with yellow agate eyes, eyes that shimmered with a kind of hunger. Ah, how the little one clicked its dummy mouth with

197

appetite. She felt the puppet strings wind around her wrists as the little wooden hands reached for her neck and grasped. She felt the thing shift in her embrace and lift its face so as to kiss the bloodstained mark upon her forehead.

She tried to back away from the little one's caress, and thus she slipped and fell, her burden still in her arms, into the flowing slime.

VII.

August 11, 1925.

I want to set this down, as my final entry in this journal, for the hour of my change is almost upon me. My coming to the city had seemed, at first, a mistake. I had heard of this place, the city of Gershom, from a friend who had lived here for a little while, until sanity—or cowardice—drove him back to our humdrum hometown. I had lapse into literary quiescence, and knew that I needed some marvelous *thing* that would fill my mind with new dreams. When I heard of this city of exiles, I sensed that it might serve as my artistic salvation. And it has, but in a mode of expression that I could never have fathomed in any quotidian realm. And so I packed my bags and had my friend drive me here; and as we were saying goodbye I saw a mixture of emotion in his eyes, a mingling of longing and fear. His queer expression convinced me that I had made the right choice, and I was smiling as I waved goodbye to his departing vehicle.

Finding a cheap hotel, I went about the business of making myself at home. My needs were few, and I had brought the essentials of fictional composition with me. It felt strange, I admit, to be without my vast library; but I knew that if I really took to this town, I would bring all of my

198

possessions here and make Gershom my home. There were, as Howard had informed me, a plethora of artistic "types" in this metropolis, and I fell in with an apiary of buzzing poets. They were good fellows, but their energy began to drain me after the third day of talking about form and theme; and when I asked them questions about quiet and secluded pockets of the city where one could sit and do his literary work, they understood completely and, bending together over a sheet of paper, composed a little map that would lead me to a place called Scott Park. After a light supper, I went to find this place, with only my small satchel hanging from my shoulder and my diary in my hand. It was my custom, when starting a new work, to buy a fresh composition book in which to scribble, and thus I stopped at a corner shop and spent ten cents on such an item. Following my map, I found the lost lane in Perry Street, and recognized the antique archway from its description by my confrères. I passed through this ancient threshold, into a different domain.

Gershom itself is older than time, but this courtyard into which I had stepped was old in a different way. The very air seemed aged, and as one sucked it in one could taste the venerable past on one's tongue; and the light was like that from an alien sphere, cooling the eyes it touched. That light, that aether, seemed to seep into my mind, and my brain *pulsed* with new vision. I sat on an old cast-iron bench, took out my fountain pen and began to write; and the weird tale that I began to compose was like nothing I had penned before—it contained a new form with which I expressed visions of a haunted past. Time seemed to dissolve around me as I wrote, and I was heedless of the setting sun. When at last I stopped my scribbling, I sat within a circle of pale light that ema-

199

nated from the antediluvian lamp post just beside my bench.

I shut my eyes and listened to a distant sound—it was the tones of some clock striking three—and when again I opened my eyes I saw, just outside the rim of pale light, the cloaked and hooded figure. "Are you here for the ritual?" it enquired.

"Sorry?" I replied.

"Ah—you are new to Gershom. No, do not stir or be afraid. We welcome you."

This information made me look about with keener eyesight, and I beheld the others that seemed like shapes pent in shadow. But what kind of creatures were these, what kind of inhabitants of gloom? For they stood in ways that were unnatural for men, and in many cases their outlines suggested that they were not men at all.

I looked at the hooded one who stood and watched me. I saw him sway and raise a bestial hand to dim starlight. I heard the windsong that rose around us, that seemed to fall from the surrounding trees, trees that bent as if to watch the beasts that began to move in odd nocturnal ritual. I saw them raise misshapen paws unto dim starlight, and I watched that starlight drift unto those paws and glimmer quaintly upon talons. Around me they danced in shambling fashion, and as they danced the stars above us seemed to fade and die. I watched and saw the shadow-things march from us, to a path beyond the courtyard that led to a place where stood a pile of megalithic ruins. The vague shapes of tilting prehistoric pillars so entranced me that I burned to described them with poetic prose. Bending to the bench, I snatched up my journal and began to scribble a poetic paean to the site.

The hooded one stepped before me, its face concealed in

darkness. "We sensed that you are an old soul. We welcome you to join us in our realm beyond the rim of time." The beast bent to me. I shut my eyes as inhuman lips pressed against my forehead. When again I opened my eyes, I stood alone.

The mark of the beast is still upon me, a weighty wetness that clings to the flesh of my forehead. It has blessed me with rare vision, and thus I sat again upon the antique bench and wrote of ancient things. And as I wrote I saw my hand transform, saw it subtly change in shape and hue. Ah—what magnificent sensations were mine! They filled me with visions as I had never known; they transformed me as an artist. I have sat here, beneath a starless welkin, and expressed my new soul with rare poetry. I have scratched this final record into my journal, so as to share with my fellow poets in Gershom the splendors of my alteration. I now take up my ten cent composition book. I will take it with me to the place beyond the rim of time. I will write of the things that exist within that exalted dream-soaked realm.

VIII.

I beg your mercy, You, all that I Love,
Deep in the dim gulf where my heart lies now.
It is a world of doom with leaden skies;
Horror and blasphemy float in its night.
                                        —*Baudelaire*

March 1922

I took up the heavy box of calamander wood and placed it on my lap. The smooth wood, darkly striped, had an almost hypnotic effect as I stared and stared at its pattern. Finally, I opened the lid and, pushing aside the dried rose petals,

201

took out my third thumb. I had had the digit surgically removed at age eighteen; and after it was embalmed, I kept it in this antique box, nestled in it bed of petals. As I held it to light its nail, buffed and polished, shimmered like some piece of dainty porcelain. I had had its stump fitted to a key-ring, and I wore it on my person for those occasions that required unusual luck. I was in need of such boon at that moment, for I was scheduled to meet with my correspondent from India, the mystic poet Amos Capernaum.

It was a short trolley ride into town, to the steps of the Public Library, where we were scheduled to rendezvous. I knew him straightaway, and admired his black-clad body, which stood with a strange rigidity as he scanned the city skyline. He seemed unconscious of the crowds that passed him by, and did not seem to sense my penetrating gaze. He was beautiful, although his face was wan and hollow-cheeked. His wide brow was marble-white, and he could have been some statue of a classical cast. And then he turned to look at me, and I shivered as his black eyes met my own. I stumbled to him and we embraced. I had planned and practiced my initial speech, but when we linked arms and walked to catch a trolley to my flat, I felt no need to prattle. We had no need of words—our eyes spoke volumes. Indeed, I felt him inside my head, with a voice that was sweetly enchanting.

He stood at my bookshelf as I prepared our drinks, and he smiled as he observed me return my third thumb to its wooden box. I listened as he spoke of supernal things. "I am so glad we have found each other, Samuel. I knew from your book of poetry that you were that special soul to whom I could conjoin. We are the odd souls in this neoteric age—old

202

in a world that worships youth and modernity. We realize, you and me, that there is nothing but the past." He shut his eyes for some moments, as if he were remembering some distant epoch; and when he opened again his wildly luminous black eyes, they smoldered with obsidian fire. "But there is a cosmic past that even you, my dreamer, have not tasted. It is a place that I have seen in night-tide visions—and how I long to dwell there, evermore. Alas, my psychic energy is not strong enough to guide me to that cosmic plain; but with you beside me, Samuel, there is nothing that cannot be accomplished."

He leaned toward me and touched his fingers to my lips. My kiss upon those fingers was a tender thing. Oh, his beautiful godlike face! Yea, truly, if ever a creature deserved to dwell in some ageless cosmic aura it was he!

He took my hand and kissed the place where my third thumb had been severed long ago, and then he glanced quizzically at the box on the stand next to the sofa on which we sat. Leaning heavily against me, he reached for the heavy box; and as his body pressed against mine I took in his sensuous scent. For one moment of pure ecstasy my face buried itself into the softness of his raven-black hair. He moved his body from mine and set the box onto his lap.

"Ah, calamander wood. And very old wood. I can feel its agedness seep into my fingers. Ah, the old, old things—how they speak to us." He opened the box and took from it my discarded member, and I watched as he held it in his palm as if it were some priceless relic. "I have learned many secrets from old things—from books, and scrolls, and glyphs. My eyes have studied closely the poetry of *Al Azif*, that book that stole the light from out my eyes. I have learned the signs and signals with which the mad poet crossed the threshold, into cosmic shadow. We, too, are poets, Samuel—and perhaps we also wear our taint of lunacy. But madness need not be linked to foolishness. What is foolishness to the herd may be wisdom to the elect."

He closed his fingers over my third thumb and hummed a strange old tune. He held my thumb to daylight—and I saw how he looked at that light with momentary loathing as it gleamed upon my digit's polished nail. I watched as he brought that nail to his forehead and pushed it into his skin, whereon he etched an elder sign. And when he brought that nail to me and sliced that same symbol in reverse upon my brow, I did not move or utter sound. He took from his pocket a black cloth which he pressed into my hand.

"Push this against you wound, so as to stop the tiny trickle of blood. No, I do not bleed as you, for I am formed of different stuff." He kissed the drops of blood that had dropped onto my severed thumb and placed it back into its box, the lid of which he shut. "Calamander. In Ceylon we call it *kalu-medhiriya*—'dark chamber.' The place that awaits us, Samuel, is a chamber of vaulted darkness the likes of which you could never imagine. It is an audient void that listens as we weep its praises. Ah, Samuel—you will see it with me, now."

He placed the box away from us and then leaned toward me, touching his brow to where I removed the black cloth. His lips moved against my own as he whispered strange language—potent language. An ancient tongue. He did not shut his eyes and neither did I; and as I stared into the liquid blackness of his orbs I felt myself somehow pulled into their substance. I floated in an alien space, and he was by my side.

For some moments I knew supernal ecstasy as we drifted together in utter blackness, in a place where human hopes and longing were of naught. I felt for my companion an irrepressible love—an emotion that was my doom. For when I gazed deeper into his eyes, I saw that they were empty of anything like human feeling. Whoever—whatever—he was, Amos Capernaum was not a creature of empathy. He was replete with the void in which he had found a home—perhaps from which he had, millennia before, been formed. His vacant features discarded me as he pushed me from him, and I screamed as, reaching for him, I fell from darkness into light.

But I am left with more than memory; for whatever thing he is, whatever force, he was not a part of the human husk that had been his earthly host. And so I embalmed his gorgeous form, and placed it in a coffin made of calamander wood—and in that coffin, with my friend, I shall one day be interred.

IX.

We stood before the door to the garret room and I felt a keen sense of adventurous expectancy. The withered beldam hesitated before pushing the key into its lock. "It is strange, Monsieur. I always feel—I do not like to disturb the quiet of this room—his room. I spent many years in your country, when the legend of his painting was beginning to—spin. That was many years ago, and still the legend grows. And now you tell me that you are writing a book on Honoré Radin!"

"A novel, Madame Dupin. The success of the recent horror film related to his famous painting and its supposed curse has generated much interest in the artist himself. I'm unqualified to write a biography—fiction is my forte; but a semi-biographical novel would be interesting to write."

"And so you have come his garret room in Paris to collect its—quality?"

"Its *ambience*—just so."

"Oui." She shrugged slightly and turned the key in its lock. A fragrance of ancient air spilled to our faces as the door was opened. "Entrez, Monsieur Blake." I stepped into another world—an elder realm. "When the people from Hollywood came to film the opening sequence, they spent a fortune on restoring the room to how it would have looked on that evening in 1848, when he was found hanging on a rope next to the easel there. I've removed the hangman's noose—it was too much to leave hanging there. Ah, what money they lavished, those cinema people! You see, the gaslights, the antique furnishings—all as they imagined the room would look so long ago."

But I could not listen to her—I was too focused on the painting above the mantelpiece.

"This is the replication they had painted."

"Oui. You know, of course, that they had the original brought 'out of hiding,' as it were, for when they filmed the sequence of his suicide. They invited me to portray the original *propriétaire*, but I could not be in the room with that—thing in oil! This replication does not capture the aura of the original piece. We had steep security on the day—the museum would let us have it one day only—when they filmed here. You know of the lunatics who feel that the painting is evil, and of the attempt to destroy it at the museum where it is now kept locked away in a secret chamber. I stood at that door as they were installing the original in its place—and I felt such foreboding, such—*déplaisance.*" Although my back was to her, I could sense the shudder that convulsed her ancient limbs. "Well, I will leave you to your—work."

Turning to her, I went and kissed her hands, and then I took out my wallet and gave her a substantial sum. "I know you charge a pittance for those who come to see the room. My gratitude runs deep, and so I want you to accept this sum."

"You are very generous, Bobby Blake. I shall set some of this aside so as to purchase your book when it is published." Her soft old hand patted my cheek, and then she was gone.

And I was seized with a curious—an absurd and sudden— sense of panic. I did not want to be alone in the room, with its shadows and its silences—its memories. Much of the artist's original belongings were still in the room, which his queer old landlady had locked up and refused to rent after the painter's suicide. Looking up, I gazed at the ceiling beam on which the rope had been secured that had helped the artist to extinguish his mortality—an act that had ushered him, ironically, into a kind of immortality over time. My eyesight drifted down to the bookshelf against one wall, and to the titles on those shelves. Surely these could not be the actual books belonging to Radin—some of them were fabulously rare. It was known that the painter had had an interest in macabre literature and satanic rites, and the titles of these books bore that out. Stepping to the shelf I found the Comte d'Erlette's *Cultes des Goules,* Gaspard du Nord's thirteenth-century translation of the *Book of Eibon,* and the strange *Sorcerie de Démonologie.* I reached for one sheaf of bound foolscap and trembled when I realized that it was nothing less than the highly obscure French translation of the *Necronomicon*—and I wondered if this could possibly be the actual copy that had vanished from a thirteenth-century monastery in Southern France. Yes, this was a treasure-trove of arcane lore. It had been emphasized, in the Hollywood replication of Honoré Radin's life, that he had sold his soul to the dread god Thanatos, and that his suicide was but his final sacrifice to his dark deity; but the film had not detailed the depth to which Radin had been a *connoisseur* of daemonic literature—else Madame Dupin would have had to secure the door to this room with more than one lock and never leave visitors here alone, this fabulous library unguarded.

I turned again to the replication of his infamous painting, "The Grim Reaper," and reflected on its diabolic legend. It was said that whoever owned the painted met with violent death, and that their demise was proceeded by a warning from the painting itself in the form of a stigmata that appeared on the Reaper's blade. I walked to the painting and touched my hand to the scythe's curved blade—and as I touched the canvas of the excellent fake I felt a genuine chill of terror. And then I noticed, scrawled in russet French script, a line of verse that I recognized from one of Shakespeare's sonnets. My mind quickly made a translation into English:

"And nothing 'gainst Time's scythe can make defense . . ."

Was this inscription part of the original painting? It, too, had been neglected in the American horror film based on the legend of the painting's curse. Had this been Radin's maniacal occult quest: immortality?

I turned to glance at one darkened corner of the room, where a tall object had been enshrouded with a sheet of black cloth. I knew what it was from having seen the film. It, too, would figure in my novel based on Radin's mad life and secret death. Going to it, I clutched the cloth and dramatically yanked it to the ground. Before me stood the framed full-length mirror that had, I knew, been here since that drear evening in 1848 when the artist had taken his life. I stared at the image that had been painted onto the mirror's surface, and the chilly room grew colder. There, in muted colors and in hazy detail, the mad artist had painted his self-portrait. The thing was almost complete. Strangely, the very lowest portion of the trouser legs and the artist's shoes were missing, as if he had somehow begun to step into and beyond the surface of glass. It was strange to stand before this self-image of the artist—it seemed to add to the uncanny sense of *presence* in the room.

He had been a handsome young man. The horror film had represented Radin as a man of middle age; but if this mirror painting had been a correct copy of him as he was when living in this garret, then he had been very young. Except for his eyes: he owned the eyes of one who had gained rare knowledge, if not wisdom. His face, as he had painted it, was very pale—and I saw at his forehead a place in which the mirror's surface had slightly cracked, forming a kind of weird webbed symbol in the middle of the young man's brow. And then I studied the hand held at his side, palm turned upward; and it perplexed me to see, drawn onto the middle of that palm, the self-same symbol that had been accidentally etched into the painting's forehead.

I stared into the beauty of his eyes. He had painted his

lips partly open, as if he were about to speak; and as I gazed steadfastly at those pale curved lips, I thought I could almost read the words they would have whispered to me. How eerily the painted surface of the mirror beguiled my senses. How soft its surface seemed as I pressed my mouth against his and spoke the words that dreamed inside my vaulted skull. How sturdily his arms enfolded me as he pulled me to him and inside the mirror.

X.

He felt the hot mortal arms that held him, but when he opened his stinging eyes he saw that the arms were his own. His burning eyes could not take in the void in which he found himself, the place beyond time and space, the realm between the stars. It was not a realm untenanted—all around him he could sense an all-observant incorporeal presence. It brooded before him, blasphemously. It revealed itself to him with sluggish graduation, this haunter of the dark. It crept to him like some chaotic eidolon, wrapped in a robe of obsidian degeneracy; to look at it was to feel the boiling of one's eyes.

And yet he could not look away. The strange dark one smiled with a cynicism that mocked mortality, and when it raised its hands the mortal saw how the heavens had decayed, how time itself had degenerated. Nothing escaped the Old One's touch. It reached into the void and plucked an object which it whimsically tossed between dark hands. The mortal saw that the object had once been Earth, that citadel of man's hopes and pride, that sphere that man had raped, pillaged, and destroyed. It took no daemon from the void to wreck such havoc. Ah, how the Old One smiled as the dead globe in its hand deteriorated and crumbled. The thing of Chaos blew Earth's dust away.

The Crawling Chaos reached again into the void and brought forth two pale orbs. The mortal knew that they were the last dying stars of degenerate heaven. He wept to see how feeble they were, but then he gasped as the Old One struck the stars together so that a bolt of lightning formed between them, a streak of living fire that rushed toward the mortal and embedded itself upon his brow. The weeping mortal turned away from the mockery of Chaos and saw before him a sheet of mirror. He looked through glass, darkly, into a gaslit room, a place that was untenanted. Vaguely, he saw himself reflected, the tragic mortal upon whose forehead burned an emblem of dying wonder. Desperately, he smashed that forehead against his image in the mirror as the universe cracked and crumbled about him.

XI.

Madame Dupin heard the crash of glass from within the haunted room. She paused before the door, sensing that some unspeakable thing awaited her discovery. At last she pushed open the door and stepped into the room. How faintly the gaslight flickered, as if it cowered from some ghastly fiend. There was no one in the room, and yet she knew that the gentleman had not vacated it. Her first shock came when her eyes rested upon the replication of Honoré Radin's noxious painting—for there, upon the painted blade, was a thick smear of ichor, a thing that could have been night's bloodstain. Turning from this hideous sight, she saw where the mirror's glass had shattered, littering the floor with shards. How could this have happened, to a mirror that

211

had withstood the centuries? What had the gentleman done in this room, and where was he concealing himself? She bent to pick up one piece of glass, on which there was the painted image of a hand. She held it tenderly until she saw the trickle of blood that moved down her finger. She had somehow cut herself on the mirror's edge. But how odd to see the way her blood, slipping toward and onto the glass, was somehow *absorbed* into the smooth surface of mirror.

She then noticed movement on the floor, a darkness that seemed to shudder on the largest shard that lay among the detritus of shattered mirror. Bending low, her bloodstained hand picked up the weighty shard and stared at the face that was upon it. She did not understand why the painted image was not that of the suicidal artist but rather of Monsieur Blake. And when that visage flapped open its bruised lips and uttered an inhuman howl, Madame Dupin fled the room forever as the large shard of enchanted mirror, dropped onto the floor, shattered into little bits.

XII.

His heart is a lute;
Touch it, and at once it sounds.
—*Pierre Jean de Béranger*

I am a seeker of the sublime, in life and in artifice, and thus I staggered toward the dark château of ruddy stone, that ancient edifice that rose from mist and diseased vegetation. It was here that I would meet, at last, the artist with whom I had become obsessed. I walked the small foot bridge that crossed over a surrounding tarn, into which red and golden leaves, having fallen, were begrimed and swallowed up. Lifting the heavy brass knocker, I let it fall once only, which produced an echo that reverberated into the deep recesses of the dark domain. I call it dark, for when the door was opened I peered beyond the answering servant into a world of gloom. I followed the valet through intricate passageways, until we stopped before the arched doorway that led into the studio of Roderick Conduire. I hesitated before entering the spacious room, so as to listen to the gentle sound of someone plucking at a harp. When at last I stepped through the threshold, the music silenced. My eyes took their time in adjusting to the dull encrimsoned light of the place, an effect of the lamps with scarlet shades. My attention was immediately arrested by the figure that reclined upon a sofa, his face buried in his hands. Quietly, I stepped to that sofa and sat at the end opposite the man, who at length dropped his long and delicate hands from an emaciated face. The ghastly pallor of that countenance was offset by the luster of the magical eyes, gems that caught and refracted the red light of the smoldering lamps.

"Mr. Swan, I welcome you to my home," the gentleman whispered, in a hollow voice with which language was precisely uttered. "Allow me to introduce my cousin, Madeline Conduire." He pointed toward a crimson-curtained casement, before which, seating at a harp, was a young woman who looked nothing like mine host; and yet she was diabolically familiar, for her semblance had figured in the painter's most notorious work, *La figlia della Morte.* I bowed my head to the silent woman, and then reached out so as to take hold of the hands of he whom I adored. "Ah, Mr. Swan—control yourself!" the man pleaded. "Your trembling is an agitation not to be endured. Have a glass of cool wine," and he signaled to a servant. "No, I shan't have any—its smell is too heady."

I rose to meet the servant who was bringing me the glass of red wine, and I looked around the spacious chamber with its red light, its antique furnishings, its aura of otherworldliness. It was a realm of old time entombed—a place beyond time. As I brought the glass of dark wine to my lips I saw that my hand holding the glass looked strange, phantasmal. And when again the woman began to play her harp, I felt that the music was from another world, a realm beyond mortality. And when Roderick Conduire rose at last from his sofa and stepped to me, I saw that his hand played at his breast, as if it were plucking heart-strings.

The woman rose and stepped away from her harp—yet still the music played, on the wind outside the windows. She drifted to us, the pale and deathly eidolon, and I could just make out the barely discernible fissure in her face, a line that zigzagged from temple to chin; and from that fissure I could see the mist that rose from her countenance, that undulated to the diseased vegetation that was her hair. She reached for us with her spectral arms, limbs of aether that wrapped around us as we danced in that chamber of red death, where I would caper—evermore.

XIII.

Wait.

I see you in the mists of moonlight that pierce through the large window—you, my ghost on glass. There is no bloodstain at your wrist, no mortal wound. But why are you so thin—emaciated; and why are your eyes sunken pits of black despair? Your moment of freedom is at hand. Just wait. See here, the blood-red rose held in my hand? Why is your reflected bloom so black, so desiccated?

Wait. What are those shadows behind your mask? They leak into the stream of Night Eternal, to which they are conjoined. I feel no shadows on my face; rather, I sense soft lunar light, a delicate filigree of moon-web, into which I would spin myself forever. Such cool light, to soothe my burning brain.

Watch.

Witness my eyes, the living gems that take in your ghastliness. Watch the trembling hand that reaches out to touch your polished surface as I stand in this room of solemn silence. Come, let me press my mouth to yours, my only love. Watch me close my eyes as our lips touch, mine that ache with fever, yours as cool as mirror.

I open my eyes and gaze onto a surface of polished glass. I stand outside an empty room, and see the stain of crimson on the floor. I stand alone.

XIV.

I stood alone on the summit of Sentinel Hill and looked down at Dunwich, on that dark afternoon of February 2nd. I stood among its tumulus of ancient bones and wondered if any of the skulls were hers. Reaching out my hand, I called to her tragic soul—but it was not there, among the mound of discarded death. And yet I sensed a touch of something, some hint of her memory, from the place below to which I now began to journey—the farmhouse where she had met with death. How remarkable that it still stood, that hovel of misery and magick. Of course it had been a shunned house, wearing as it did its aura of Dunwich horror and disease. Uneasily beats the heart that trespasses on Old Whateley's land. The senses warn that certain ground is sacred or accursed, as is the house one dares to build upon it—and soon I stepped on such a ground and walked toward such a haunt. The day grew darker and a wind arose; and I listened as that wind pushed through the rotting boards of the old farmhouse, a wind that whispered sounds like I had never heard before. It was almost musical, the sound, like some emanation from another world or realm of beings. It beguiled, and beckoned.

The house seemed almost to shudder in the gale that grew around it, and its front door was suddenly pushed open, as if in invitation to the stranger in its midst. I accepted and walked in. I knew enough of the family legend to know that the place I sought was on the ground floor; and yet tantalizing curiosity tickled my brain with a desire to investigate the upper room of oddly calculated size, the room stained with Outside taint. But that was for another time—perhaps. Now I would walk to the room where the sad, doomed woman had met with uneasy death. I approached the door, which was cracked at its center, a long fissure of past violence. Ah, the violence that quaked *my* soul, as I leaned my fevered head against that door, which opened to the force of my leaning.

It rushed to me, the scent of sacrifice and sorrow. My mouth caught it and I had to scream it out less it should damn my soul. The room was small and cramped. One entire wall had been decorated with a crudely painted replica of an illustration of the spherical Earth that originated in Gautier de Metz's *L'Image du monde*—which he had created in an era when the common belief was that the Earth was flat. Near to me, on one tilting table of rotting wood, I saw an old and rusted armillary sphere, the design of which was strangely suggestive. Most disturbing of all was that there was no small terrestrial globe fixed on an axis within the metallic circular rings; rather, there was a shape composed of minute bits of substance that might have been the destructive aftermath of a star's implosion.

I moved to the larger globe in its sturdy wooden stand and saw that it was an extremely ancient celestial globe of, I estimated, Asian design. It, too, was very queer; for the surface was black, but of a kind of transparency that one could vaguely see through to where dim points of lights vaguely shimmered. Some few of these minute stars had twin trails of light that suggested wing-span. I touched my hand to its surface and shivered at the chill that crept into my flesh.

Looking to my right, I shuffled to the third and smallest globe, which looked at if it had been composed of tanned human hide. I saw the empty and elongated slits that might once have held eyes, and the dry slit of mouth. Beside it, on the floor, was a battered child's coffin, and I reached for and lifted its lid. Inside, resting on a bed of ash and tiny bits of bone, I found a handmade doll. The hair that had been sewn into its scalp was pure white, and I knew that it had once belonged to an albino woman who had, long ago, tenanted this room. I smoothed the white hair with trembling hand. I spoke the words of alchemy that I had learned from study of ancient tomes. The dark room filled with moving sound. The celestial globe began to revolve slowly as the ephemeral lights within it moved with churning motion. I thought that I could detect another voice accompanying my own, coming from the globe of human hide; but I was too intent on the coffin and its inhabitant to look. I saw the effect of my occult sound, as the ash and tiny shards of bone began to creep over and into the texture with which the doll had been composed.

I reached into the coffin and raised her in my hands, the tiny creature that moved and cried. I will call her Lavinia. I will raise her in this haunted house. Together we will wander the fields and climb Sentinel Hill, to call unto the void and usher forth the demise of brutal men.

XV.

He stepped into the lonesome place and raised his face to moonlight. How strange, to fancy that he could feel the lunar power that pulled at the liquid in his skull and washed the brain with weirdness. Turning his back to the moon, he climbed the steps that led to the expanse of porch of an old dark house. The figure that sat, unmoving, on the porch swing looked at him with eyes concealed behind dark glasses. He stood and stared at the figure's flesh, at the oddly shaped scalp from which a length of lank dark hair fell to shoulders; at the mark that had been etched into a high, wide forehead—a symbol he had once observed in an unwholesome book. He knelt next to the fellow and saw that the man's lips were moving as if in an attempt to utter sound. The stench of a whispered phrase pushed into his face and tickled his brain. Leaning forward, he kissed those lips and pressed his ear against them. The stranger uttered secrets.

He entered the house on Bowen St.—the edifice that had beckoned in night-tide dreams, and watched the suggestion of shapes that seemed to hunker behind black windows, like some horror unnamed and unnamable. The window seemed to call attention to it, and thus urged he stepped to it and placed his hand upon its chilly pane; and he could feel, on fingertips, an odd vibration, as if some gigantic lips, pressed against the other side of black window, were mouthing occult things against the pane. He felt an impression of lips—cold and dead—against his hand; and he fancied that the shape of lips formed a counterpart to the secrets that had been spilled into his ear.

He stepped out of the haunted house and gazed at the hump of discarded clothes upon the porch swing, and at the blanched fleshy mask beside dark glasses. Picking up the mask, he placed it against his face, and shuddered at how its texture adhered to his own. Taking up the glasses, he placed them over the mask's wide eye-slots; and when he gazed through them to the night, he could not comprehend the shadows of the night, the forms that blurred and burrowed into darker patches of gloom. He stepped out into decadent night, following a curious sense of direction that he could not comprehend.

Why had moonlight fled? Why did the ancient witch-town look so strange? He knew where he was—but in what year, what age? The surrounding houses, having stood their ground for centuries, offered no clues. He felt as if he had stepped into some alien epoch of pitiless time, through which he staggered like some lost soul. Shutting eyes, he reached out as if for some thread of familiarity—and it came to him, instantly, in the sound of an intimate voice.

"Ah—there you are! Thank you for meeting me." He opened his eyes and gazed at the face that seemed familiar. The woman studied his eyes with a curious grin on her face. "Your eyes look so odd in this lamplight—not like your eyes at all! Isn't this night wind magnificent? I love how your hair floats as it brushes you. It was your hair, you know, that made me seek you out—or, rather, the legend of your hair. To have experienced a sensation of horror that turned your hair white—I confess that I've tried to imagine it! Now that I've inherited my forebear's old house here in Arkham, well, it's becoming easier to imagine such things. My brain seems to be working in a different way than what I'm used to. Well, my *imagination*, at any rate. Oh, the dreams! I've never had such unfathomable dreams. You mentioned, over the 'phone, that Arkham has a reputation for affecting the night visions of they who find their way to this town. I thought you were merely being playful, as you are in the letters you've written to me about my books. But . . ."

He answered that he did not mind at all, and to reassure her, he linked his arm with hers as they walked toward Hangman's Hill. And then he stopped and expressed confusion, for he knew that she had inherited a queer old house on Frenchman's Hill, which stood at the other edge of town. But his friend merely smiled and wagged her head.

"No, this way. As I said, my imagination is acting peculiarly, which may sound absurd to you, coming from a woman who writes horror fiction. Well, it's very weird—I've had the most outlandish dreams, and for the first time in my life I can remember them clearly when I wake up. I've written some of them down, and they'll make great little stories; but, they aren't like my usual thing—much darker, far more strange. Writing for the horror market, you know, isn't a difficult task—people like the same sort of thing over again and again. I pen my cheap, melodramatic puppet-shows, and my readers gobble them up and belch for more! But I've never written anything like this—this dream that churns within my skull, like some sentient shadow-play. Gawd, just speaking of it makes me talk differently—it affects my little brain in a way I've never known!

"I've turned the tower room of my new home into my boudoir, and it's very pleasant and cozy. I have my bed next to the window facing the river—I can see that weird uninhabited island just past the Garrison Street bridge—and some plot of hilly land far beyond keeps tugging at my mind. My dreams? Well, it's one recurring dream, actually. I'm walking on a moonless night through a wooded area, and there are really odd figures standing around watching me, as still as statues. And—I'm compelled to dig in this one place, into earth that is soft and cold. I dig deeper and deeper, until I am in a pit of utter blackness. That's it! That's where it always ends. But when I awaken, I can still feel the cold soft marl on my hands. Ugh!"

They wandered for an hour, to the place that he had never visited; yet the way, as they walked, began to feel familiar, as if he had frequented it in lost or forgotten time. The dark hill spread before them, and from somewhere on it he imagined that he could hear a distant moaning wind—such a subdued sound, like a muffled voice that called in secret from deep earth. They came at last to the tall black iron gates of Old Wooded Cemetery and regarded the beast that was sprawled before that entrance, unable to ascertain if the thing lived or was dead. They watched, as the canine sluggishly lifted its head and sniffed the air. It had no eyes, and its currish countenance seemed peculiar and incomplete. When the thing opened its snout and bayed, the doleful bellow sounded queer, as if it came from a creature that poorly imitated a hound. What noisome stenches then tainted the night air!

221

They walked to the highest point in Old Wooded Cemetery, the summit of Hangman's Hill where Goody Fowler was hanged on suspicion of witchcraft. "This is the place," she informed him, "I can tell by all those funeral statues—they look just like the figures who watched me in my dream. Gawd, look at how *hungry* their faces look—the ones that still have faces! Here, this is the slab I saw in my dream, but of course it's too dark to read its inscription. But look—you can see where it's been damaged, there, where something oval has been removed. You can just make out the discoloration in the old stone. Weird, isn't it, the way that stone ages and turns black in spots, eaten by time, just as we are? What did Shakespeare call Time—I remember it from a speech I had to memorize in high school—'cormorant devouring time,' something like that. Come on, kneel next to me here and put your hand on the stone, just there. You can feel the vacant spot where something had been fastened to the stone, something small and oval."

He fell to his knees and touched the cold rough stone as darkness seethed around them. Her white hands curled into the earth and began to dig, until one hand found an oval of glass, She tugged it from the dirt and wiped its surface clean. How chilly it felt within her clasp, with a frigidness that moved up her skin and froze her brain. Next to her, the gentleman pulled out a box of matches and struck a match so that it exploded into blazing light. She felt the flesh of her face creep as she gazed at the visage beneath the oval of glass—the photograph of the friend who knelt beside her. Turning to him, she did not like the way his lips smiled as his smooth face slipped askance. His crooked lips pursed together and a low push of sour air extinguished the flame.

Fingers crawled beneath her face and peeled it free from bone as some bestial thing howled near the cemetery gates.

XVI.

He had introduced himself as "Mr. Richard Peters," and proclaimed to be an admirer of my decadent verse. I allowed him to buy me another coffee and sweet roll and sit next to me in the North End cafe, and then I observed as he pulled a pad and pencil from the carpet bag he carried. No one had ever sketched me, and I found the prospect pleasant; and so I leaned back in my chair and pouted prettily as his pencil rushed across the pad. This gave me a chance to study his unhandsome mug—the strangest face that I had ever seen— and although he was not comely, there was something about him that I found alluring. He had a presence—an almost psychic vitality that was concentrated mostly in his somber green eyes. As I stared into those eyes I experienced a kind of—fear, I guess I would call it—a foreboding that beguiled. My fingers suddenly itched for my own pen and pad, with which to describe the ideas that began to agitate my brain. Instead, I whispered some impromptu verse:

> "And then from realms of dream and darkness came
> The strange Dark One to whom the shadows bowed;
> Cryptic and cool, too silent, queerly proud,
> With eyes as green as secret sabbat flame.
> With eyes of somber hue the beast commands
> To know the secrets that my mind has heard:
> The hidden things conveyed by sense, not word,
> The phantom lore untouched by mortal hands."

The artist remained silent and secretive, but he lifted up his pad and showed me my portrait. He was good—very good; somehow he had been able to subtly suggest the skull beneath my face, and he had caught in the expression of my eyes a hint of the secrets that sometimes chilled my dreaming brain.

"So," I asked him, "how far is your studio?"

"It's in an alley nearby—a crumbling old shack, really, but it suits me perfectly. I paint in the cellar, by yellow candlelight, where I can hear the walls above me tilt in windstorm, or the things that fumble in search of food beneath the queer old brick well built into the ground. But it's not there that I want to take you just yet." He smiled so strangely that I felt a chill tingle my spine. "I have another idea. Come, follow me."

Rising, he reached into a pocket from which he took a wad of bills, which he left on the table next to our emptied coffee cups, and then he picked up his carpet bag and vacated the place. I hesitated for a moment, slightly bewildered by the effect this strange man was having on me; but then I rose and went out into the cool autumn night, raising my eyes to the moon that rose above the North End. I lit a cigarette and followed his tall hulking figure as he led the way through the old and dirty alleyways, past crumbling-looking gables and crooked archaic chimneys that had spilled some of their dislodged bricks. He led me into a darker, narrower alley and then stopped beside a filthy worm-eaten wall with planks of board covering its windows. Setting down his bag, he reached into it and produced a large camera, the strap of which he tugged over his head so that the mechanism hung from around his neck.

"Such wonderful ambiance here, Miss Eliot! Let's pause and I'll have you pose before this antique wall. I like to work from photographs of my subjects, you see—I work best in solitude, I find, as perhaps you do yourself. You're not one of those bohemian poets who prefer to scribble their lines in public, I take it. I've noticed you often in your coffee house, but have never seen you pushing pen to pad. I suspect that you're like me—wanting to be alone when in communion with the gods of art. Stand just there, if you will. Excellent!"

I felt it then, as my bare arms touched the mottled surface of the ancient wood, as my soul drank in the agedness of the haunted place. I knew the substance that I had expressed in weird decadent verse, knew it with a keenness and maturity that I had never experienced. I startled fearfully as the flash from his camera lit up the area, and for one terrible instant I saw clearly how horribly old and decayed this part of Boston was. I felt that antique ruination deep within me, felt it creep into me and begin to rot my bones. There was a sense of unholy hungriness in the decrepitude of the place. But in that light I beheld, for just a moment, something else: a formless black shape that crept just behind the artist, something that raised its snout to the man's lowered hand, as if to lick his palm. Yet when my eyes adjusted to the darkness after that flash of burning light, Mr. Peters stood alone, nodding his head as if in satisfaction. He raised his hand and motioned that I should follow him as he silently turned away and continued to walk along the timeworn brick of the alleyway.

I followed as he took us to Copp's Hill, and let him link his arm with mine as we climbed the steps and passed the gate, into the burying ground. His solid body pressed against

225

me, heating my flesh. I decided he had ruled the situation long enough.

"Here," I told him, "touch your hand to my heart and feel my intimate fear." His rough hand slipped into my blouse and cupped my smooth breast, and I laughed at his playful grin. "How frantic beats my little heart, beneath that yellow moon in this sequestered place of death and memory." I pulled him closer and breathed upon his eyes. "What say you, Mr. Peters? Do the ones planted beneath this sod have memories of the hideous thing called Life? Why do you laugh?" I brushed his thick eyebrows with my lips and breathed onto his eyes.

His rank breath fanned my face as he spoke. "Because you're beautiful. As lovely as the past, to which my soul is wed. I feel it here, on this ground, beneath the old moonlight—the invincible past, the past that lingers, immortal and unaltered."

I smiled and pushed him from me, and then I opened my blouse a little more as he lifted the camera that hung from a length of cord around his neck and aimed it at me. The bright flash turned the black air white for one instant, and then a red tint drenched the trees and crooked tombstones. I tried to imagine how this hill had looked in 1632, when a mill stood here. "Well," I told my friend as I sauntered to the table top tombstone beneath which the Mather lads had rotted, "the past can never remained untouched, not even here. You know that this burying ground has changed throughout the decades, to the extent that many stones don't exactly mark where their named dead have been interred. The highest point of the hill was lowered by several feet in 1807, and several tombs were rearranged when the paths were laid out in 1838. You're wrong—may I call you Richard?—about this neoteric age; it has its delicious aspects, of which I am one. Come to my lodgings tonight and taste the magick that a modern witch may weave."

He studied me from a distance, watching as I tossed the consumed cigarette onto the cobblestone path. His tall form, silhouetted in moonlight as he stood just off the path among tilted eighteenth-century slabs, was very still. Something in his manner struck me as strange: he seemed, somehow, so at home in his surroundings, like something born in strange shadow. I smiled and raised one lovely hand to the moon, then posed with perfect pout as he aimed his camera at me. I was startled, after the flash of blinding light, to find him suddenly so near to where I lay, unable to guess how he could have traversed the length of land so quickly.

"Your poetry is the weave that casts its spell on me, Miss Eliot. It's because of your verse that I sought you in that Italian cafe tonight. I've noticed you there often, sipping your mug of brew as your mind wheeled. I thought that someone who could write such paeans to darkness, death, and decadence would have something interesting to offer an artist such as myself. And when I saw your face, I knew I was right. I have a singular talent for capturing faces on canvas—and yours is exactly the kind that can intoxicate me. Your eyes brim full of secrets!"

He did not come to me, and thus I moved off the slab and began to waltz among the markers, stopping only when I nearly stumbled into a crevice in the earth. I looked and saw how the phallic graveside marker, equally as tall as I, had been dislodged, revealing a cavity in the ground. Dim moonlight streamed into that pit and faintly revealed the earthen steps leading down into the dark. "Ah, Mr. Peters," I exclaimed, "here we have a secret into which we both may plunge. Alas, that I did not bring my torch!"

The artist raised a finger to the moon and smiled, and then he bent so as to reach into his bag of tricks, out of which he took a dented antique anchor lantern, by which (who knows?) some sea captain had read his maps. I walked to him as he struck a match with which to light the wick, took out another cigarette and pulled his hand toward my mouth. I watched his dark green eyes regard me as the flame touched my cigarette, and then I sucked deeply, held the cloud within my lungs for some few moments before setting it to drift through midnight air. How pale and wan the little light appeared within the old bent lantern. He smiled as I took the lantern from him and began cautiously to pad into the pit of death. The chamber beneath the earth was deep and narrow, yet seemed to me excessively lengthy. As I held the lantern forward, I frowned, unable to see the wall of earth that should have been before me. His voice sounded behind me, and although I knew he must have been nearby, he sounded far away.

"No, you cannot see the end, for it tunnels quite a ways. You know, of course, that the whole North End was once honeycombed with tunnels, through which strange things trafficked. I like that you fancy yourself a modern witch— but to call oneself such a thing isn't as dangerous as it used to be. They hanged my four-times-great-grandmother on Gallow's Hill, with Cotton Mather looking pharisaically on. She could have taught you a thing or two about witchery." I sucked at my cigarette and then extinguished it against the wall of dirt; but before I could flick it from me Peters fetched it from my fingers and placed it on his tongue. I watched the shadows that played upon his frolicsome face as he swallowed, those shapes thrown from the lantern's pale illumination that moved on and about him.

Something in his peculiar manner disconcerted me. Nonchalantly, I reached for a bit of human bone that poked through the sod above us. Touching the tip of bone to the wall near me, I etched my name. Something chortled, and when I turned to look at my companion I noticed the dark shape that breathed at the artist's feet. The black thing raised its misshapen head, but in the darkness I could not make out its face—if indeed it had one. I tossed the bone to the beast. Peters stood before me, and as I gazed into his eyes they seemed to drink the essence of the lantern's flame, glowing with a greener hue as the tiny flame withered and went out. My eyes were suddenly assaulted by a blinding flash of light, and in that blaze I saw the artist, his camera pointed at me. For one brief instant I saw the black furred thing that rose beside him on hind legs. There was nothing afterward but darkness, and the sound of twin breathing, the rank exhaust that fanned my face as tongues tasted my flesh.

XVII.

I walked across the Garrison Street bridge, stopping midpoint so as to watch the play of moonlight on the Miskatonic that flowed below me. I listened to the river water call with liquid voice, as if trying to coax me over the railing and into her depths; but I resisted her temptation, for I had other abysses in which to plunge. Continuing my walk across the river bridge, to Water Street, I approached the antique house that was my destination. I contemplated the woman I had arranged to meet—and possibly to paint. I knew that she was incredibly old, and that she lived in the darkened edifice, never showing herself except in deepest night. A line from Ovid came to me: "Blemishes are hid by night and every fault forgiven; darkness makes any woman fair." Yet Delia Eliot was not any woman—nor was she young and fair. No one knows how old she was in 1925, when Richard Upton Pickman painted her; and his canvases were certainly no indication, for in some of them she looked very young, little more than a teenager, while in others she was depicted as quite mature, a spinster in some shadowed room, seated at a spinning wheel.

Miss Eliot had earned a slight reputation as an underground bohemian poet, but I knew of her from my obsession with the Boston painter and his work. He was reputed to have completed thirteen canvases of her shortly before his mysterious disappearance. Using my criminal influence, I had obtained a small painting—one of a series—in which he showed her as an adolescent surrounded by dog-faced ghouls, with whom she was depicted as feeding. Pickman titled the work "The Lesson IV." I had no idea that this bewitching woman yet lived—until I saw a recent painting of her at an exhibition in Salem. The artist assured me that, although incredibly aged, Delia Eliot was very much alive and dwelling in her mansion by the river in Arkham. It was her prejudice never to be photographed, and thus all images of her were aesthetic recreations. I remember how queer I felt as I gazed at that image of an elderly woman at her spinning wheel; although incredibly ancient, her face was recognizable as the visage that had apparently haunted Richard Pickman. She haunted me, now, and thus I arranged my meeting, after a few months of sporadic correspondence. Although my artistic talents are limited, I worked with a friend on a charcoal sketch of Richard Pickman, inspired by the one photo of him that I had been able to locate from a police report concerning his disappearance. She claimed to have been delighted with it and suggested that I come to visit her in the old house she had inherited in Arkham. And thus I found myself facing that magnificent old habitation in autumn moonlight. My knock at the door was answered by a fey man of indeterminate age who looked like Aubrey Beardsley dressed in formal attire and holding a taper. Softly, he spoke my name, and I nodded in acknowledgment; he then stepped aside and allowed me to enter the dark domain. The flickering candles, held in antique bronze sconces fastened to the yellow wall, threw dancing shadows on the servant's face, highlighting his gauntness—the somber eyes and tapered ears. Curling his thin lips, he motioned for me to follow him through a hallway and into a room with walls of paneled oak.

She sat on a cushioned chair of red fabric, dressed in flowing black. I had expected her to be old, but the sight of her withered face with its high forehead and pale eyes shocked me. Her long white hair was covered by a black and silver lace mimkhatah that gave her a kind of frail beauty—yet it was a morbid beauty, for her skin was so thin that one could easily discern the skull beneath the face. She smiled and motioned me to a chair, then nodded at the servant, who departed.

"Welcome to my home, Mr. Barnes. How young you look!"

"At twenty-seven I no longer feel so youthful," I answered.

"And that is too absurd. I have made you a small present." She tilted to a table beside her chair, and as she did so I noticed the weird medallion around her neck that swayed with the movement of her body. I suspected that the necklace was a present from one of her many artistic cronies, and it was certainly imaginative. The focal point of the thing was a vintage camera lens, onto which a metallic winged skull and miniature oval portrait had been mounted. I recalled having seen the skull design on stones in a New England burying ground, below which had been etched the words:

"Remember me as you pass by
As you are now so once was I.
As I am now so you must be.
Prepare for Death and follow me."

Miss Eliot reached with frail old hands and took up her small present, a sweater made of black and yellow candlewick fabric. Holding the garment in both hands, she offered it to me. I thanked her.

"Wear it well," she said in her pleasant gravelly voice.

I reached into my knapsack and produced an early edition of her poems, the sight of which moved her to sigh. "Will you honor me with a signature?" I handed her the book. She hesitated for many moments, then took my proffered pen and opened the volume to its title page.

"I always feel a vague precaution before signing my name. It probably stems from my witch heritage. The signing of one's name can be a potent—at times a parlous— thing." Smiling coquettishly, she guided my pen across paper and returned both pen and book to me.

"Yes, I've noticed the recurring witch motif in your

work, especially the odd reference to some esoteric witch-cult whose members are interred faced downward."

"The better to kiss the devil's buttocks," she laughed, and then she moved in preparation to rise. I stood and offered her my hand, which she clutched with her smooth dry claw. "No, leave your things there and follow me. I'll show you the wonders of which you've dreamed. Come." She walked steadily enough, despite her advanced age, and led me to a massive door before which stood the tall lean servant. He had exchanged his taper for candelabra on which three squat candles flamed, and in their light I could just make out the emblem that rose as scar on his forehead. The design was deliberate, and so I conjectured that the fellow liked to play with razor blade art, as was the fashion with so many youths in the alternative scene of the day. "Titus will guide us below," Miss Eliot confided as the fellow opened the door and began to descend pitted stone steps. We sank into an area that was nothing less than a subterranean art gallery, and the paintings that I eyed made me gasp. I walked to the wall on which the largest pictured hanged, and as I admired it I could hear the wizened woman's raspy breathing near me. "What say you, sirrah? Was I not a stunning thing in youth?"

The background was a bent old tree in a cemetery, which I slowly recognized as Copp's Hill Burying Ground in Boston. The madness of the piece lay in the figures in the background, black things that rose like hungry shaggy shadows from the ground, things that in some few instances began to ape human design. One quasi-anthropomorphic thing was very near the woman in the foreground, bending as if preparing to kiss the palm of the woman's outstretched hand. That woman was a very young Delia Eliot—and she was magnificent. Pickman had captured, with perfection, the sorceress beauty of her powerful eyes, eyes that caught me completely in their spell. Her complexion was smooth and fair, and the only color in the painting was very luxurious red hair. I turned to gaze at the little woman beside me, this shrunken thing that was nothing like her former self—except for the eyes, those gems that held their violet beauty still. They gazed at me with potent emotion as I took up her hand and kissed its palm.

Candlelight was caught on the necklace that swung above her breasts, and I reached for that amulet and studied the antique camera lens that was its major feature. Her guttural voice whispered, "It was from his camera, you know, the one he left behind when he—went away. Ah, the images that were caught upon it! You can almost see a semblance of them, can't you, moving like blue and verdant shadows just beneath the surface?"

I lifted the round object closer to my eyes and scanned its cloudy surface, noticing that a tiny symbol had been scratched onto the glass. It was a symbol that I had seen before. "I had a friend in Salem compose this piece of art. To wear it is to see the world as Richard saw it, in all its secret ghastliness. Oh, what rare souls we are—we who love the secret things. Forbidden things." I shut my eyes and she wrapped her crooked fingers around the necklace and lifted it from her flesh. Reaching out, my hands touched hers and helped them guide the relic over my head.

My brain could not endure the revelations that seared into it. I crumbled to the floor.

XVIII.

Icy shadow cools your boiling brain and gently wakes you.

You rise, in darkness, in an unfamiliar place, among strange scents and obscure memories. One single taper burns some distance from you, and its pale light pulls you like a moth unto it. You crawl across the floor, to the black shape that rests what might be human hand next to the flaming candle in its holder. Taking hold of that candlestick, you rise before the oblong box of pitted granite and gaze at the form within it, the frail old creature who lays face downward. Compelled, you bend to her and smell the essence of her senescent flesh and ancient hair. You move your nostrils to the still, still hand and gently kiss its palm. The thing that sways around your neck taps against the granite crypt. There are echoes in the air.

Waves of sound swim into your brain and vibrate vision. They push you to the canvas on the wall, into which you sink. Primordial wind embraces you as you stand among the black and tilting stones. The moon is pale, like a taper in a secret room. You feel its cool glow upon your fevered eyes, the eyes that watch the form that rises from its oblong granite bed. Beside it, another thing arises, black and formless, held in abeyance by the hand that soothes its hunger. They flow to you, these shadows, one so pale, the other black as nightmare. Her tiny hand touches the relic at your breast and she admires herself on the surface of a vintage lens. Glancing down, you see how the moonlight plays upon the tiny symbol that has been etched onto the sphere of glass. You watch her white hand release the relic and rise to touch your eyes. You feel the nail that pricks your forehead and etches thereon the Elder Sign, and you smile as she lowers her hand so that the shadow-thing can lap your blood that stains it. That shaggy shadow rises next to its mistress, the faceless shadow that wears the sign upon the surface where a face should be.

You shut your eyes and lean against the venerable tree as the creatures bend to you, their hungry tongues upon your throat.

XIX.

I am not the thing I have been.

The dwelling in which I have existed is situated in a mountainous region above which the sky is a region of moving shadow, mauve or gray or black. We have never seen the moon, of which I have read in our keeper's books; but I have seen a semblance of the stars in our keeper's eyes, a collocation of articulate pinpoints of light that spoke to us of dark matter. I drank those secrets in when you opened my arms so as to feed me, and had I been born with a mouth I would have smiled at the cryptic secrets revealed.

The women stalked the carpeted halls on the night you expired; they wept behind their masks, those stiff and crooked faces. Their long black dresses scratched against the ground and I so hated the sight and sound of them that I defied convention and crept into the chamber where they had placed your oblong box onto a low stone slab. It was quiet in that secluded place, except for the breathing of the walls. I knelt before your oblong box and dreamed your name—and how queer it was, to imagine that I heard you answer me from some adjacent realm, to image I saw that pale spider, your palsied hand, rise before me and prick its thumbnail deep into my forehead, where it etched a signal that I did not understand. I did not bleed, but the walls did, blackly. It was then that the moon arose, illuminating the room with ghastly death-light. But, no, it was not the moon; it was your petrified face, glowing with a death-light that pierced the bleeding walls, the walls that whispered, that beckoned. Ah, the eerie light made those liquid walls alluring, so that I went to them and pressed my ear against them, so as to understand more fully their articulation. I did not resist them as they sucked me in, as something formed of shadow-flesh crept along my face and settled just beneath my nostrils, transforming me. They opened, those petals of ebony flesh, and with them I whispered, esoterically, your name.

XX.

I never solved the mystery of how my Uncle Silas came to own Elmer Harrod's house in Arkham, but I suspect it had something to do with my uncle's love of campy horror films. Harrod had a fine collection of such films, as well as his personal homemade efforts that had been shot in the nearby cemetery. My uncle used to love to show me these homemade films when I visited him as a young teenager, and I confess they had an eerie appeal for me as well; and I recall how something caught my attention, something reflected in Elmer Harrod's shadowed eyes—momentary expressions of authentic mental disturbance, bewilderment, fear. Harrod's fame, such as it was, came from his occupation as television horror host, but I was too young to remember his ghastly makeups and muggings before his Victorian house on the television screen. He was less renowned for the books of horror fiction that he had edited for various paperback publishers, short-lived titles with lurid covers; or for his one novel,

Underneath Witch-Town, which, as an adolescent, I had found enthralling after having found a box of copies in Harrod's house after my uncle had purchased the residence and its contents. It was the library of the house that really influenced me, for it was stuffed with the horror host's extensive collection of weird phantasy. I spent summer after summer poring over those books, and it was under the spell of their authors that I became determined to join their ranks and write horror fiction professionally. It was while stumbling through the high grass of Old Dethshill Cemetery that I came up with my pen-name, Deth Carter Hill—for there were many Carters buried in the place. I had been particularly drawn to the hidden grave of one peculiar fellow, Obediah Carter; for his long tabletop tomb, dated 1793 to 1887, was decorated with a faded photograph of the elderly gentleman that was beneath an oval of glass that had been fastened to the slab of stone. There had long been legends that the Carters of Arkham had been tainted with witch blood, and one could well believe it when examining the stern and satanic countenance of Obediah.

I came to inherit the queer Victorian residence after my uncle's insane suicide, and I happily made the move from my small and cramped apartment to the spacious abode, where I was surrounded by elements of ghastly horror collected from various pockets of the globe by the two previous owners, things that I knew would aid my career as weaver of weird tales. I was ruthless enough to bask in the notoriety that came my way, to the aid of my creative reputation, by the scandal that arose from my uncle's suicide; for the local papers carried sensational stories of how my uncle's corpse had been discovered hanging from a strong length of vine attached to a hideous tree in Old Dethshill Cemetery, and how the end of the vine that had tightened around his broken neck had implanted itself into the flesh of the ravished throat.

I found, during my first months of residence in Arkham, that Uncle Silas had gained a curious reputation in the town; for it was whispered that he never ate, was never known to shop for groceries or dine out, and the fact that he was often seen haunting the abandoned cemetery at night gave way to rumors of vampirism and other such nonsense. It was when I discovered my relation's own home movies that I learned how uncanny truth can eclipse the wildness of paltry rumor; for Uncle Silas had followed Elmer Harrod in the practice of being filmed within the wild confines of the haunted burying ground, but where the horror host had brought in a film crew to record his outlandish behavior among the tombs, it seemed that my uncle's was a one-madman's crude operation. On one spool of film he had recorded himself dancing among the tombs and speaking the most outlandish gibberish I have ever heard, in what must have been a language of his own invention. He seemed almost to chew upon his lips as he drooled and muttered such phrases as "Kloolhu Rally" and "Ne'er-lahtep." On one film he had recorded himself reclining on the slab beneath which rotted Obediah Carter, and the dim electric light that he had somehow set up caught to perfection the weirdness of his expressions, with which me mimicked the actual visage of the dead sorcerer as he muttered what seemed to be snatches of eighteenth-century verse. But perhaps the most disturbing images were caught on the three rolls of film that showed him dancing in front of the unwholesome tree on which he ended his life. On one spool of celluloid he had wrapped the hanging vines around his arms and ankles and then pirouetted like some deranged puppet; and it was eerie to see how the withered old tree, in the uncanny light of uncle's source of illumination, seemed more like some gigantic bestial claw than any dendroid inhabitant of the necropolis. My uncle's experiments with filming seemed to incorporate some kind of trick photography near the end, for on the last spool of film he was seen close up, dangling from the vines of the tree, vines that resembled cloudy veins through which a dark substance moved in the directions of my uncle's upraised limbs, into which the vines had penetrated. Uncle Silas did not regard the camera as he muttered, "More, more—my arms are hungry."

I could watch these films but once, and then I stored them away and tried to forget them; but the memory of their images haunted my dreams, and I knew that the only way that I could expel them was to use them as fictional fodder. Thus it was that I composed my first novel, *Beneath Arkham*, the publication of which brought me a modicum of fame and fortune.

XXI.

He walked upon the earth, through tall decayed grasses, and watched with horror the yellow face that rose from some buried realm and stained the sky with jaundiced light. The clammy breeze that blew toward him from the face embraced his flesh and crept beneath his eyes, and he could feel it coil around his burning brain, corroding it with mordant fear. The features on the gigantic face shifted, as if they were patches of coal smoke, and he trembled with terror when an amorphous mouth threatened to spread and utter horrible secrets on the wind. He reasoned with himself that it was not a face at all but rather the midnight moon suddenly revealing herself in this secret and secluded place; yet she had never been so pale, so near, so full of promise. Perhaps if he sang to her he could appease the lunar doom, and thus he opened his mouth, but the one sound that issued between his dry lips was a rattle that aped death, a noise that was grotesquely answered from some place underneath him. He saw, then, the other smaller face that rose through the rotting grass and winked at him; a familiar face, for he had recently seen its semblance on a spool of film that recorded an image behind glass, an oval face that had been fastened to the pitted stone of one ancient tomb. The face floated toward him in the growing wind, framed by the rotting hair that issued like dead grasses from the scalp. He watched, aghast, as the slit that was a mouth parted, and yellow vapor poured from between the lips, toward him, a vapor that filtered through his eyes, cradled his hot brain and made him dream.

XXII.

Uncle Silas was not a literary man, and when I realized that as I approached manhood I felt a distinct disappointment. There he was, surrounded by Elmer Harrod's magnificent library of weird fiction, and he let the books gather dust, except for the summers when I visited, at which times I was left alone in the mammoth library poring over the nameless fictive lore. I don't think that Uncle Silas recognized that I was having less to do with him during my visits, or that my youthful high opinion of how wonderful he was had been tarnished by his lack of interest in books. He did, after all, bequeath me his haunted house and its fabulous contents, and for that I was amazingly grateful and had his portrait painted and hung in the living room, which I rarely occupied. The spacious library became my happy little world, and I devoted myself to the genre in which I plotted to become an active and popular voice, working on my own book of supernatural fiction. I could not help, at times, to look around me and laugh out loud at the world I had inherited; for as a television horror host, Harrod had crammed his abode with props from films and nightmarish gifts from fans and friends, so that his home came to resemble something out of Charles Addams. Yet for all his outlandish behavior, I felt a kinship with Harrod, for he had loved weird literature. There were, on the walls, framed stills of Harrod with certain celebrities, many of them horror film players, but some few the actual authors of the books that the horror host had collected. I had discovered a large scrapbook in which Harrod had pasted some few newspaper articles or photos from the local media, who enjoyed writing about him around Halloween. I was charmed by a photo of him reading an edition of Machen in Old Dethshill Cemetery, and on a whim I decided to hunt for and peruse that very edition, which was easily found. As I opened the book, dry soil spilled onto my lap, and I suspected that the debris was graveyard dirt, which gave me a bit of a thrill. In the newspaper cutting, Harrod was reading the book with the aid of a large flashlight, but that seemed wrong to me, and thus I was happy to find, in the basement, an antique oil lamp; for I had determined to journey into the graveyard that very night, book in hand, and read a story from it with the aid of the lantern's glow.

I had turned a small room adjacent to the library into my bedroom and thus rarely visited the three upstairs bedrooms; but I was feeling a bit clownish and decided that I

wanted to dress up for my first night tide visit to Old
Dethshill Cemetery, and so I climbed the carpeted stairs and
went into Harrod's old room, where many of his outlandish
television outfits remained. He had been as lean as I and
about the same height, and so the tuxedo decorated with
synthetic spider webs fitted perfectly, and thus attired I
took the lantern and Machen and stepped into the night. The
night was very still, and I could not see the moon, although
the sky was dotted with sparkling stars. The cemetery was
very near to the old house I had inherited, and I paused before the low stone wall that encircled it and listened to the
graveyard's stillness—for there was a quality in its silence
that confused me, and I could not understand how quietude
could seem so unnaturally absolute. The few lights that I
had left on in the house illuminated the rotting yellow grass
that reached my knees in places, and as I passed the weed-
choked markers and tombstones I felt a kind of sorrow for
the neglected dead who had been interred here so long ago. I
did not like the encroaching darkness of the vast wooded
area that was Old Dethshill Cemetery, the squat old trees
that continued on the distant rising hills. There was no wind,
but the late August air was chilly, and so I stopped and lit
my lantern, which aided sight but gave no warmth.

And then I heard a cry from somewhere in the trees just
beyond me, and at their sound a night wind rose, cool and
smooth, that played with my length of hair; and as if in answer to the cry a dark cloud melted in the sky and thus was
revealed the moon that had been secreted behind it, and I
blinked as its dead light fell onto my eyes. Another sphere
arose, as if from buried earth, small and delicate, with black

243

pits where a human face would have worn eyes, and a scarlet mouth that parted.

"*Ses yeux profonds sont faits de vide et de ténèbres . . .*"

The figure stopped its recitation and cocked its head. I watched as it hopped from the tabletop slab on which it stood and walked a few steps nearer, and I noticed that this stranger also held a book.

"I suppose you don't know French, judging from your dumb expression. Let me translate and sing the verse again, thus:

> 'Her eyes, made of the void, are deep and black;
> Her skull, coiffured in flowers down the neck,
> Sways slackly on the column of her back,
> O charm of nothingness so madly decked!'

"Delicious, is it not? And how clever of Luna to show her form just now, so as to aid with ghastly light. One should always read poetry in moonlight, don't you agree?"

"Certainly, if the poet is Baudelaire."

"*Ah!* An educated soul." The voice was high and nasal, yet masculine. His eyes were concealed behind round black lens of what looked like antique wire spectacles. His fantastic mauve hair was piled high upon his dome in thick tube-like coils, and moonlight shimmered on the crimson gloss with which his simpering lips had been coated. "I've been looking for mine kindred dead, many of whom are planted here." He looked at me from behind his queer spectacles and did not smile as he spoke his name. "Randolph H. Carter, from Boston. And yes, I am ruefully related to the writer and man of mystery. Have you read his famous book?"

"I've inherited an edition, but haven't scanned it yet.

What was his mystery?"

"He had many, actually. There is the mystery of what happened to his friend and mentor, Harley Warren, who was last seen with Randy on the day of Warren's disappearance. I actually know a direct relative of Warren's here in town, a fabulous painter who has a studio on French Hill. It was she, actually, who told me of this place; she often paints it and its denizens. Just now she is conjuring a life-size doppelgänger of Obediah Carter, who was whispered to have been a wizard."

"That was his tomb you were standing on just now."

"I thought it might have been, although I couldn't quite make out its faded inscription."

"Perhaps," I ventured, "you should remove the shades . . ."

"Don't be absurd." He began to move away from me through the high dead grass, and so I held my lantern higher to light his way. We both saw the tree at the same time, and I could not suppress a shudder. "Some fool hanged himself on that tree last year." He turned and frowned at the expression on my face. "How sad you look; but then, who wouldn't dressed like that? You look like some Gothic hobo. Well, I should depart, morning classes come so early. What are you reading?" I told him. "Ah," and he winked, "be on guard for the little people. This is their kind of demesne, I imagine." I watched him saunter toward the trees and disappear into their darkness, and suddenly I felt alone and vulnerable. Turning, I found my way homeward, climbed over the stone wall and examined my house. It looked a grotesque thing in the sallow moonlight, with its cupola, widow's walk and many gables. Lunar light feasted on the face of the gargoyle that Elmer Harrod had added as Gothic touch, and which had been featured in the opening shots for many of his episodes where he was seen before the house in his outlandish outfits and ghoulish makeup, costumes that usually had some connection to the horror film that he would introduce and mock throughout. Standing as it did at the end of a dead end street on which most of the decaying houses had been abandoned and uninhabited, the Victorian pile seemed especially desolate, a classic haunted house; and so it was, haunted by myself and my strange imagination, my conjurations, my spectral dreams.

Entering the lonesome place, I went to the library and found the collection of horror stories by Randolph Carter, *The Attic Window and Others,* which had been published by private hands some few years after his strange vanishing act in 1928 had caused a sensation, resulting in his early and un-popular book being reprinted by a New York publisher. The new edition had been an enormous success. I was pleased to see that Harrod's copy was the original first edition. I began to read, oblivious of the subtle keening of windsong that emanated from the graveyard next door; but soon my eyes grew heavy, and my long day came to an end in the cozy armchair of my quiet room.

XXIII.

She climbed the winding wooden steps that led to the small door, pushed it open and coughed into the dry air that, issu-ing from the attic room, assailed her face. Her candle's feeble flame threw shadows into the room among the litter of an-tiques, the wooden crates, the shrouded figures. She was cu-rious to see that their dark sartorial camouflage resembled her own, and she wondered if they, too, had hoped to conceal themselves from the world of men when roaming the streets at night. Pressing her hand against the breast of one still thing, she felt its torso of twisted wire; and then she lifted her face to its sad mask, the expression of which filled her with such remorse that she drifted from the thing, to the attic window. Bending before the small panes of glass, she gazed into their latticework at her peculiar wavering reflection, upon which shadows frolicked. She watched one patch of shadow sink into one particular reflected eye, and her eye of flesh experienced a bothersome tugging sensation, as if some playful thing were pinching it. She did not like how dark that eye looked on the window's glass, and so she brought her candle very near it, until its lashes were lightly singed.

The contents of the attic room began to spin, like leaves caught in a dance of wind, inviting her to trip the light fantastic; and so she rose and pirouetted around the place, one hand holding her taper, the other at her breast, beneath which she could feel a latticework of dainty bone. She gazed again at the dark shrouded ones who watched her with their awful masks and saw that on each mask one eye-hole was larger than the other, giving each faux countenance a slight distortion of feature. Raising a dainty hand, she stroked the rough surface of one mask, and then she gasped as the thing loosened from its mannequin and slipped into her hand, which grasped it. Gently, she lifted the mask to her face and pressed its rough surface to her soft soft skin, against which it adhered. Gracefully, lifting her free arm in imitation of the figures that began to move about her, she joined in their danse as candlelit shadows on walls watched unmoving. She capered until exhausted, and then fell once more upon her knees near to the attic window, toward which she turned so as to behold the reflection of her mask; but it was not the stiff papier-mâché veil that appeared there, but rather a misty countenance that wore a beguiling and sinister smile. Setting her taper on the floor, she crept to the attic window and touched her finger to one of the small squares of glass, and she shivered as the image behind the window lifted its mouth so as to kiss her hand, which experienced sharp pain.

Falling away from the attic window, she lifted her hand and marveled at how the beads of blood that spilled from the slit thereon shimmered in the candlelight, like rarest gems. Beyond her hand she could espy the wavering of night's mist and the face within it, the face with a blemished eye and bloodstained mouth. It was a face that seeped through the reality of glass and wood and floated just before her, joined by spectral arms in antiquated dress that reached for her with hands that, taking hold of her mask, lifted it away.

XXIV.

I chuckled at myself when I awakened in the library arm-chair with Carter's book in my lap. That explained the snatches of fleeting dream about attic windows that had filled my imagination as I slept. The morning light seemed extremely muted, and so I got to my feet, stretched and went to open the front door. Thick fog covered Arkham, and nothing could be seen of Old Dethshill Cemetery; but I could *feel* it, that place, so very near my home, like some unholy presence; and I could certainly hear the sounds that seemed always to subtly emanate from it, the rustling and sighing, the whispering. I was becoming obsessed with the place, as had the other tenants of the old house; and yet I was oppressed by that queer tree on which my uncle had extinguished himself. The thickness of the fog inspired me, and I went into my basement and found the can of petrol that had been left there by my uncle. I put on some garden gloves and carried the can with me out of doors and over the shrouded wall of the burying ground. The atmosphere was thick with weird foreboding, and I almost felt that I had entered into another strange dream as I found my way through the damp dead grass, stumbling over shrubs and roots until the curious tree was before me. The mauve fog had a kind of luminosity about it, and up close I could make out every detail of the daemonic tree, its sickly hue, its moist trunk on which someone had carved anomalous symbols. I did not understand the unnatural looking vines that grew out of the outstretched branches, which in the creepily tinted fog looked like alien veins of something from the ocean's depths. Utterly repulsed, I opened the can of gasoline and splashed its contents all over the monstrous growth, and then I removed my glove, lit a long wooden match and tossed it to the tree, which instantly blossomed with roaring flame. The billowing smoke was concealed by the thickness of fog, but the stench that issued from the burning thing was so vile that I quickly fled the cursed spot.

I stayed away from the graveyard, slightly unnerved by my actions and not wanting to see their effect. To take my mind off the matter, I plunged into the writing of my book of short stories. A friend in New York who operates a small press devoted to weird fiction, and from whom I have purchased many titles, expressed an interest in looking over the few yarns that I had completed, and he was impressed enough to say that he would print a limited edition of my first book in hardcover, which greatly pleased me. Finally, one day when I was stretching my legs and walked out onto the front porch, I saw a familiar figure traipsing among the high grass and gravestones of Old Dethshill Cemetery. I watched him for a little while, and suddenly he turned and waved. I returned his salute, expecting that he might come to chat; when he didn't, I returned inside and lost myself in work. I had decided to write a story based on the graveyard and the mysterious fop, Randolph H. Carter, whom I had rechristened "Samuel." The ideas of the tale so stimulated my imagination that it turned into my book's lengthiest work, one in which I evoked much of the mysterious past of Arkham legend, folklore that fascinated me increasingly the more I studied it.

At last my book was published, in a limited edition of three hundred copies, fifty of which were bought by a shop in Arkham that specialized in horror and fantasy fiction, histories of witchcraft, and other such titles. Invited to the shop to sit and sign books for an evening, I went to Elmer Harrod's old bedroom and found the vampire cloak that he had often donned before the television camera, and I used some of the money that Uncle Silas had left me to purchase a fine tuxedo. On my way to the signing I stopped at a floral shop and bought a beautiful red rose to slip into my jacket's buttonhole, and it pleased me when the florist recognized me from the small feature about my book that had been published in a local newspaper. The evening was a success, many books were sold and signed, and I was happy. The event was coming to an end when Carter entered the shop and purchased a book, then slid to the table where I had been signing.

"Inscribe, please; but not to me—sign it to Julia Warren.

Are you done here? Let me take you out for a small meal, you must be famished." I signed my signature and rose to take my leave, thanking the shop owner and congratulating her on the night's success. Carter slipped the book into a shoulder bag and motioned for me to follow him. I was surprised when we stepped outside to find a cab waiting for us in front of the store, and followed Carter as he stepped inside it. He smiled at me strangely and took a long piece of cloth out of a coat pocket. "Indulge me, Hayward," he said as he smoothed the cloth over his knee, "but I have a little adventure planned. No, don't frown—this will be amusing. I'm going to tie this around your eyes, and I think you'll be pleasantly surprised. I read in that newspaper interview that you haven't seen much of the town, preferring to stay buried in your library writing your fantastic fiction. I'm going to show you a special Arkham haunt tonight. Okay? No peek-a-boo? Excellent, I knew you'd be a sport."

I had been aware, on entering the cab, of a peculiar odor, and as Carter leaned against me I ascertained that it emanated from his hair. I couldn't refrain from asking, "Is that your real hair, or is it a wig?"

"Don't be stupid. If it were a wig it would look more natural. Sit still, Hayward. There, I've tied it tight enough, I think. Such a soft fabric. Okay, cabbie." The car began to move, and I sat blindfolded and bemused. It was true, as I had mentioned in the newspaper interview, that I hadn't seen much of Arkham, preferring my solitary life in the comfortable home that I had inherited. It had never been in my nature to be social—I was a bookish introvert who relished his solitude and silence. I had written my book because I had a fondness for the genre of supernatural tales; that the sale

251

and small local popularity of the book may make me a figure sought by others was something I had not anticipated. I assured myself that I would be cautious, and then I smiled at the fact that I was sitting blindfolded in a cab next to someone I did not know, being taken to a place of secret rendezvous. So much for imaginary caution!

Carter, as we rode, was more talkative than usual, and I sensed that he was trying to distract my attention and thus disrupt any attempt of mine to determine our direction. Smiling and silent, I listened to his babble, until at last the car came to a halt and I was guided, still blindfolded, onto a lane of gravel. The cloth was loosened from my head and slipped from my eyes, but blackness was still my domain— for we stood in a slim alley between what looked like two antiquated warehouses, one of which had a steep and twisted flight of weathered wooden steps, to which I was led.

"It can't be safe, climbing those."

"As long as it's not raining there is no danger. Hang on to the railing if you're feeling cowardly. I climb them often and they are perfectly secure, despite their great age. The past is far more solid than this present plastic age, my dear." We climbed the many steps to a small landing and Carter pushed open the door before us, allowing a variety of smells, among which was the odor of turpentine, to assail our nostrils. Entering a spacious candlelit chamber, I soon recognized it to be an artist's studio, although looking like something from a distant era. Antique furniture stood here and there, as did many ancient brass candelabras, on some few of which a number of candles furnished the moving amber light. One wall was made of mirrors, and a curious and concealed electric light effect made it appear to be a wall of shimmering water, like some perpendicular pool in which I watched my wavering reflection. "This is one of my special haunts," my companion whispered.

I glanced at various large canvases that leaned against the walls or were propped on easels, and then I experienced a freezing of the blood as my eyes fell upon a life-size reproduction of the awful tree that had once stood in the neglected necropolis and on which my uncle had enabled his extinction. I could not resist the compulsion to go to the enormous canvas and touch it, to study the structure of the outré tree with its sinister pale vines that seemed like the writhing veins of some unfathomable chimera.

"It's no longer there," spoke a husky voice from one corner of the studio. "Someone has destroyed it, there's just a pile of white ashes where it used to stand." Turning to face the speaker, I saw the small form that moved through shadow toward me, a middle-aged woman with short gray hair who was dressed in black shirt and jeans that were spotted with paint and chemicals. "It was your relative who hanged himself from it, wasn't it?"

"It was," I whispered.

"And you who destroyed it?"

"Yes," I confessed, turning again to gaze at the painting.

"I'd have done the same myself," was her response as Carter, wearing an astonished expression, floated to where we stood.

"This is Julia Morgan Warren, grand-niece of Harley Warren, the friend of my ancestor. And this, dear Julia, is Hayward Phelps, author, haunter of graveyards and avenger of hanging trees." He reached into his shoulder bag and brought forth my book. "Otherwise known as Deth Carter

Hill, up and coming fantasist. Here is his premier collection, which he has signed for you, and for which I have served as minor Muse." I laughed at his conceit. "Your fictive portrayal was, of course, an exaggeration, but thankfully not a parody."

The artist nodded her thanks to me for the book, took up an old rag and wiped her hands. "You wrote the book in Elmer Harrod's haunted house?"

"Yes, which I inherited eighteen months ago. It still contains Harrod's amazing library, with which I've been acquainted since my late teens."

"Your uncle purchased the house—from whom?"

"I never knew. He never said." I studied some of her artistic tools and picked up a straight razor with its blade concealed inside a lovely ivory handle. Opening it, I found the blade to be remarkably sharp.

"Isn't that lethal tool amazing?" Carter said. "She got it when she purchased a Victorian mortuary kit. It helped who knows how many corpses to their last shave a century ago."

"This may interest you," spoke Miss Warren, motioning that I should follow her to a large canvas on which she had painted the house I had inherited. She had perfectly captured the Gothic atmosphere of the place, which was the reason that Harrod had bought it. Yet she had enhanced its curious quality, with clever touches, the way in which the trees she had painted contained a kind of sentience, the way in which shadows seemed to peer from places in the stormy sky. "The house has an aura of mystery, hasn't it? So did your uncle. We never got to know him."

I smiled. "Our clan tends to keep to themselves."

"You're a writer, and they work in solitude. So do I. I

painted that a long time ago. God, how the years melt into a blur. Now that I'm sixty, I feel as old as the hills." She squinted her eyes at Carter. "You smile, Randy, because you're young. Young folk think they're immortal."

"It's your art that is immortal, my dear. This newest piece is magnificent." I followed him to a life-size canvas on which wet paint glimmered in the light thrown on it by the two large candelabras. I recognized the face from the miniature I had seen on Obediah Carter's tomb, but I didn't understand the distortion of the right eye. I thought perhaps the paint there had somehow melted or run amok, but as I stepped closer to the canvas I saw that the disfigurement was deliberate. "Ah, yes—*the blemished eye.* There have been some few Arkham families that have suffered individuals born with such an eye, which links them to whispers of witchcraft. Family legend has it that dear Obediah owned such an orb, although he had the fault corrected in all portraits painted of him." I turned and studied Carter's pale face, the painted lips, the dark spectacles. Smiling, he removed the eyewear, revealing normal eyes of palest gray. "'Tis not a hereditary ailment, I'm happy to report." He frowned at candlelight and returned the spectacles to his face. "Anyway, Julia has restored nature and portrayed him with his imperfection. She's good, yes? You should have her paint you, Hayward. A painted portrait on the back of one of your books would be more individual than some dull photo-snap."

"I can see the family resemblance," I said softly, peering at the painting, "despite your ridiculous tresses. You're much younger than he is here depicted, far leaner; but it's there in his expression, a kind of superior cynicism. What is it that sets your brood above we low mortals, Carter? What have you personally accomplished in life?"

He seemed dumbfounded by my sudden criticism. "I appreciate art and literature."

"Is that all?"

"It's enough for now. I choose to live an existence that is exquisitely bohemian. I'm frightfully young, you see; and, like you, I've come into my little inheritance. Adulthood, from what I've seen of it, is hell. I shall stay a child for a little while longer."

"It's nice to have you venture out of that old house and brave the public. I suppose you did it to help promote the book, but at least that gives us a chance to get to know a little more about such an enigmatic creature."

"I beg your pardon."

"You've been a bit of a mystery ever since moving to Arkham and claiming Elmer Harrod's home," Julia continued. "Yes, we still call it that, and always will. That marvelous place has such a hold on our imaginations because of seeing it on television for so many years, and it gained an additional aura after Elmer's grotesque corpse was discovered in the graveyard. I used to attend some of his parties when I was a very young artist trying to persuade Elmer to let me paint his portrait. There was always a buzz of activity there, as if Elmer couldn't stand to be inside it alone. He was always having guests stay over, horror writers or film actors. He used to host an annual Halloween party for local kids, and they were a hoot. Non-stop partying, never-ended streams of guests—the place bubbled over with life."

"That will never happen as long as I am there. What I adore about the residence is its sense of solitude, the feeling when I am there that I have escaped not only the world but time itself. It's not a sense that comes over me just because of the antique furniture and quietude—it's something . . . other, that I cannot quite comprehend and thus cannot express. Living there is like living in a book, actually—I have the same feeling of escape there that reading gives me. I've not explored much of Arkham, that's not why I came here. My world before this—oh, it was small and unfulfilling. I was stifled by convention, damned by an existence that lacked imagination. My one escape, besides the books I devoured, was to visit my uncle in that house during the summers of my youth; and then I mostly lived in the library, curled up with one of Elmer Harrod's creepy books. All the rest of the year I yearned to be there again, in that wonderful realm that took me from the sordid reality of a mundane world. Now I have the freedom to dwell within that world always, and I want no other. I will confess to a new interest in this old witch town and some of its more colorful denizens, an interest that has partially blossomed from roaming that old burying ground that is my nearest neighbor, and also from reading the Randolph Carter collection of topical horror fiction, linked as it is to local legend." I turned to smile at the other fellow. "Your two ancestors begin to fascinate me, they and their legends. I know they both vanished under curious circumstances, right?" They looked momentarily at each other, and the small woman smiled.

"Oh, we know as little as anyone else. It was a long time ago. Legends, as you say." From the expression on her face, it seemed obvious that Julia seemed not to care that I knew she was lying. I returned her feeble smile.

"And yet you have unearthed the buried fact of Obediah

Carter and his blemished eye," I pointed out, motioning to the painting of the sorcerer. "There may be other secrets to expose, if one knew where to hunt." I winked at them and smiled again, and they tried to smile as well; yet I detected something, unspoken and secretive, underneath the curve of their lips and in the shadows of their eyes.

Young Carter blinked at me. "Well, I promised you dinner. Let us depart. Will you join us, Julia? No? My dear, I *never* see you eat. However do you nourish yourself?"

"My art sustains me, Randy," she whispered, winking; but when she turned to gaze at me, I imagined that her eyes contained a secret that I was somehow supposed to understand.

XXV.

We found you in the darkness wherein you might have been spawned, sitting on a stump beside a wall of reflective water. The crimson fabric in which your majestic flesh is sheathed smells of roses and thunder, and the towel that decorates your head writhes like a thing composed of one thousand silent maggots sewn together. We marvel at your flawless skin, as white and smooth as powdered bone, and feast upon the cold fire of your penetrating eyes as we set up our easels. We took our palettes in hand and dipped our brushes into pools of blackness and blood, of moonlight and madness; and as we studied you we could not comprehend your reflection on the wall of water, which rippled while you sat unmoving. We tried to paint the luster of your wide mouth, but the scarlet smear on our palette would not quite do, and so we pricked our thumbs and dipped our brush into the ruddy bead that blossomed from our flesh. You did not move, nor make any sound, even when the rain began to spill and spoil our art. We did not understand why you, too, began to blur and fall apart and scatter on the ground. And yet—the liquid phantom that is your reflected image on the wall of water watches us still, and when it opens its mouth your invocation washes to us. Thus beguiled, we push our easels from us and move as pack toward the wall, and through it, to your embrace.

XXVI.

"Would you care to come in?" Our taxi had taken me to my home, and the young man and I sat for a few silent minutes before I opened the door.

"That would be amazing!" Randolph enthused, taking out a billfold and paying the driver. We stood and watched the cab drive away, and then he turned to peer into the graveyard. The moon was very high above us, and the wooded area of the cemetery and the forested hills beyond it were entirely dark. From somewhere among the tombs something cried in eerie ululation.

"That's queer," I spoke. "I've never ever witnessed birds in that place, day or night."

"Was it a bird?" the lad whispered with a faraway voice.

"I suppose it might have been some other creature. It's strange, I never see any vermin roaming around in there, and yet one feels a constant presence, continual movement within the tall dead grass. It's as if the very ground were a kind of animal rustling in the sun or quivering in moonlight. I experience it night and day, at odd hours, in my home— the summoning from a thing that remains hidden and yet commands attention."

"'Summoning' is exactly right," Carter whispered. "It has drawn me to it time and again. Once I knelt on the ground and pushed my finger through the dirt, writing my name. The strangest sensation came over me straight away, something that got to me so violently that I rose and scraped my etched name away with my foot. But I came away with the feeling that my name is still there, never to be erased."

I could not refrain from laughing loudly. "It's such fun, the way we spook ourselves! Come on, I have some very good coffee." He followed me to the wide porch and up the steps, stopping momentarily to tilt back his head and study the gargoyle that Elmer Harrod had attached to the building's roof. We entered, and I led him to the library, motioning for him to either sit in one of the many comfortable chairs or prowl so as to study the titles on the shelves built into the walls. I moved away and went into the kitchen to brew coffee and select a variety of cookies. From a distant place outside, I heard again the creepy cry in the cemetery. As the water was brewing I went to open the kitchen door that led to the side of the house and stepped onto the stone walkway. I listened—and when the queer cry came again I parted my lips and uttered a replication of the sound. I felt the air turn chilly as the sky darkened and the earth faintly fumbled with some deeply buried hill noise that might have been nothing more than my imagination. Night's silence strangely transformed, becoming more quiet and yet seemingly attentive—waiting, waiting. The bubbling of percolation came from the kitchen, and I returned inside and shut the door of antique wood. But I could not shake off the sense of something brooding just outside the house, something that had awakened to my cry. I tried to grin and tell myself that this was just my horror writer's imagination doing its job, for the weird fantasist's brain never stops working, I have found; even after we have completed a new book, the imagination is working always, forming new ideas that may be used as fictive fodder. Picking up the tray, I went to the library and saw my guest return a book to a shelf and remove another. He turned to glance at me as I set the tray onto a small table and then he opened the book. We both watched the particles of debris that fell from it to the floor.

"That's the third book I've opened that has dirt between the pages. What the hell?"

I shrugged. "Both Elmer Harrod and my uncle were wont to take books into the graveyard." I pointed to a framed newspaper photo on one wall of the horror host in ghoulish makeup, posing with an edition of Blackwood as he sat upon a tombstone. "I think one or both of them had a habit of sprinkling cemetery sod into the books. It's certainly strange."

He returned the book to its place on the shelf and sauntered about the place. "This room has a nice ambiance, and I love the fragrance of old books; but all in all I find the house rather disappointing. I was expecting it to feel more haunted. I mean, the previous two tenants were both rather queer. No one really knew what Harrod did with his private time. He seems to have spent most of his time trying not to be alone in this place. Film crews, constant houseguests, visiting fans who came for tea and tall tales. And then your enigmatic uncle did quite the reverse and never had anyone over, except apparently yourself when you were a child."

"My uncle was a loner, certainly—and, yes, I'd say he was strange. He had made a fortune, under circumstances I never came to know. Not that I was interested. I certainly didn't expect him to leave everything to me, especially as I became rather distant during adulthood, not really having the time or desire to journey to weird antique Arkham and spend time with an old fellow who had no talent for conversation. His big love in life was watching horror films, and that was fine when I was a kid, but . . ." I looked at him and grinned. "How amusing, though, for you to speak of how queer *my* relative was. I've read your namesake's book, with its brief biographical essay. The original Randolph Carter was unique, I must say. A mystic, they call him, but what exactly does that mean? Was he some kind of occultist, as Obediah Carter is rumored to have been?"

His voice was very quiet as he said, "Obediah was much more than that." He stood regarding me with a peculiar expression on his face as the room's soft light glimmered on his dark spectacles. Reaching into his shoulder bag, he produced a small book that was bound in red cloth, and he gazed at the thing for some silent moments before handing it to me. "That's the diary of Randolph W. Carter, written before he became middle-aged and disillusioned, before the incident with Julia's ancestor, with whom Carter lived and studied until the night of intrigue and disappearance. You look lost, Hayward. I thought you said that you had studied this nefarious history."

"I know some of the legend, and I've read the introduction to his first book of weird tales. I've never bothered to read his novels, which are rumored to be poor and unimaginative."

"No, they're fascinating, and proved popular in his day. His current reputation is stupidly tied to the mystery of his disappearance and little else, although his books are still in print. I grew up in a family of staid Bostonians who were slightly embarrassed by family ties to Arkham and 'mystics.' The family legend is that no one paid much attention to Randy's estate, although there are doubts as to how vigorously the family was sought by the queer fellow in New Orleans who had been named in the will as literary and financial executor. Randy's early work was a shunned subject when I grew up because it's tied too intimately to his link with magick and this town. We don't like Arkham in Boston, and the family has never forgiven Randy for returning here to vanish in the hills, or under them, or in one of his beloved burying grounds. You've noticed that that diary is almost exclusively a record of time spent in cemeteries. You're looking for mention of Old Dethshill Cemetery, aren't you? You won't find it. It seems implausible that he never visited it, so many us our kindred dead have been dumped there. His story, 'Return of the Warlock,' is said to be inspired by Edmund Carter, a sensational sorcerer who barely escaped hanging and whose diary Randy had found—and the pages of which he sealed!"

I was only half-listening to his prattling as I scanned the equally interesting pages of the small personal diary in my hand. It was a history of Carter's seeking lost and forgotten ancestors in the graveyards of New England, but more interesting than his historical pursuit was the affection he obviously held for these fields of death. The combination of Carter's tale, told in his faint voice, and the imaginative lines of the diary, which were beautifully expressed, filled me with an overwhelming desire to dream and write. I sensed the beginning of my own first novel, one that would relate the history of the Carter family of witch-haunted Arkham. I would have to alter the name and much of that history, but locals would certainly guess the origin of the family whose dark history I would record. I looked up as Carter walked away from me, toward a window. "I suppose your family changed its tune once his novels began to sell again," I reflected

"That was part of it. We heard from some old writer in Providence, Rhode Island, who had saved a packet of letters Randy had written to him. The guy wanted to reprint some of Randy's early stories in a handsome limited edition hardcover and include the best of the letters as an appendix. He had sought out my grandfather for permission. Then someone wanted to write a biographical novel about Randy's weird vanishing into the Arkham hills or whatever, which Grandpa did not allow. But they must have sensed a growing interest and saw its financial allure. You know," he whispered as he pushed back a curtain and gazed into the outer darkness through his odd spectacles, "Randy wasn't the only Carter to vanish somewhere in the hills of Arkham. Another of the clan went missing under mysterious circumstances in 1781. Less than ten years later Obediah was born under what has been whispered to have been savage conditions linked to alchemy. God, what a heritage." I studied his slim feminine figure, the tight-fitting black apparel, the impossible hair piled in coils on his head. This was the first time I had studied that hair in decent light, and I marveled that human hair could look so artificial, more like vines or tubes than anything else. The more I stared at it the more I was certain that it was not his natural growth but some clever synthetic attachment.

I didn't know how to respond to his talk, and so I remained silent as he moved from the window and to another wall shelf lined with books. I watched as he removed a volume of Henry James's ghost stories and raised the old book to his nostrils, shutting his eyes as he took in its smell. He opened the book and allowed some particles of graveyard dirt to fall into one hand. His face seemed to darken as he stared at the rubble in his palm, and then he brought that palm to his mouth and touched the debris with his tongue, as from somewhere out of doors a thing cried to night tide.

XXVII.

I sat with one lamp on in the library, rereading *The Attic Window* and contemplating the novel that was bubbling in my brain. I must have dozed off because I started awake to the sound of something's shrill cry in the graveyard beyond my home. I thought of how the locals continued to call this place "Elmer Harrod's Haunted House," but it was the graveyard that was truly haunted, by phantoms of the past and their mysteries. One such phantom must have been the author of the book that had fallen into my lap. Looking around the room, I espied the antique lantern by which I had read books within the graveyard. It had been some time since I had ventured into the cemetery with a book, and the most appropriate book was in my lap at the moment. So I stood and picked up the lamp and walked out the front door. I hadn't stopped to check the time, but like Hamlet's Ghost I seemed to smell the approaching dawn. Setting the book and lamp on a porch chair, I found a match and lit the lantern's wick, and then I picked up both objects again and stepped off the porch, along the little lane that took me out of my yard. I crossed the dead end street and climbed over the low stone fence that surrounded Old Dethshill Cemetery.

Yes, it was *this place* that was truly haunted, not my

happy home. I could feel it all around me, hear it in the low moan of wind, in the rustling of tall dead grass. I saw it in the mournful swaying of thick growths of trees. I sensed it before I saw the spectre who stood so still among the weathered stone. This eidolon in white raised an arm and motioned me to her, and so I approached and took Julia's proffered hand. In her other arm she cradled a box of fragrant wood on which elder symbols had been carved, symbols that disturbed me for some reason I could not ascertain. Julia stood near to where Obediah Carter's weed-choked slab was located, and so I raised my lantern toward that slab and tried to understand the thing that rested thereon. My lantern's glow caught the movement of one slim hand that clawed into the earth and clutched a fistful of cemetery sod. I watched that pale hand move from the soil to the reclining creature's mouth, into which the dirt was packed.

The wind arose, as did the figure on the slab. And with him rose a cloud of mist that aped a human shape, like a shadow of mist conjoined to the youth who lived. Carter's face had never looked more blanched, all color having leaked from the texture of flesh. I couldn't help but begin to laugh, because he resembled too closely one of Elmer Harrod's ghoulish make-up concoctions. My laughter seemed contagious, for the young man smiled, which allowed a little earth to slip out of one corner of his mouth. As he chortled, the coils piled atop his dome fell to his petite shoulders and moved in the wind, although I thought they moved too vigorously for it to be an effect of the breeze that brushed us. I sensed Julia's small body lean into mine as she lifted herself so as to whisper in my ear.

"We are happy to have you here, to share the gift of nourishment. Oh, my Hayward, you'll never be alone again." She opened the aromatic wooden box and I saw the pile of white ashes within it, on top of which was her Victorian mortuary straight razor that I had fondled in her studio. Sensuously, she inhaled of the contents in the box, and then she place one hand within it and pinched a bit of ash. She walked toward Randolph Carter and rubbed the ashes onto his soiled mouth. His tongue took in the substance as his tubes of hair began to flail and lengthen. He shuddered spasmodically for some few moments as I held the lantern so as to study his face; and thus I saw as his spectacles tilted and slid partially down his nose, revealing his eyes; and I did not understand why the one eye looked so blemished.

Julia bent low and put the box onto the ground, taking from it the razor as she rose. I watched as she lifted her arms, allowing the sleeves of her gown to slip down and thus reveal her wounded arms. Some of the cuts were old scars but others were fresh and new. She went to embrace Carter's hair with her trembling hands, pushing his spectacles up so that they covered his eyes once more. Strands of his hair, the tresses of which were now to his waist, wound sensuously about the woman's arms. I watched, nauseated, as she sliced into one arm with razor's blade, and I sickened as a tube of hair slipped into the wound and beneath Julia's ruptured skin. Carter raised a hand, and I saw that it held a fistful of earth. Bending back his head, the creature opened his mouth and made the weird wailing sound that I had heard and imitated earlier, and then he lifted his hand so that the debris sifted through his fingers and fell into his mouth. I watched and shivered as the tubes that grew from Carter's head grew dark with the substance that filtered through them, through the extension that had planted itself into the artist's arm. Julia laughed and licked her lips. "More," she begged, "more. My arms hunger."

They turned to gaze at me, and I moved my eyes from them, wanting so to flee, yet transfixed. "Hayward," chanted the young man's choked voice. I could not resist and so looked at him, at his winding tube-like tresses, at the subtly altered face from which the spectacles had now been removed, revealing fully the blemished eye. "Hayward," he laughed, licking his mouth with a soiled tongue still littered with particles of graveyard dirt. I set my lantern and the book onto the ground from which morning's mist began to rise. I saw the other mist, that was conjoined with the young man's form, a ghostlike mist that resembled something old and cruel and ravenous.

I stumbled to them as dim light began to fill the morning sky. I removed my jacket and rolled up my sleeve as Julia's razor floated to my arm.

XXVIII.

Ah, Howard—my brother, my Muse. I close your commonplace book which has so stimulated my dreaming. Yet, though the book be shut, its pages are still before my enchanted eyes, and the penciled words whirl round and round my head. They have done for me as they did for you, as they will do for others yet unnamed and unknown. I have partaken of them, as equally as Augie did, and used them to pay tribute to you in language of my own. They have been an intoxication, your entries, and I have yet to drink my fill. I know that, sometime in haunted future, I will open your book again—and feast. Selah.

Acknowledgments

"An Identity in Dream": original to this collection.

"Artifice": original.

"Cesare": original.

"The Host of Haunted Air": originally appeared in *Sesqua Valley and Other Haunts* (Delirium Books, 2003).

"Hempen Rope": original.

"Cathedral of Death": originally appeared in *Grue* #14.

"House of Legend": original.

"Inhabitants of Wraithwood": originally appeared in *Black Wings*, ed. S. T. Joshi (P S Publishing, 2010).

"In Memoriam: Oscar Wilde": originally appeared in *The Tangled Muse* (Centipede Press, 2010).

"The Zanies of Sorrow": originally appeared in *Tales of Love and Death* (Delirium Books, 2001).

"In Remembrance: Edgar A. Poe" originally appeared in *The Tangled Muse*.

"Keepsake": original.

"Necronomicon": originally appeared in *Dreams of Lovecraftian Horror* (Mythos Books, 1999).

"Postcard from Prague": original.

"Sickness of Heart": original.

"The Tangled Muse": originally appeared in *The Tangled Muse*.

"Chamber of Dreams": original.

"Some Distant Baying Sound": originally appeared in *Weird Inhabitants of Sesqua Valley* (Terradan Works, 2009).

"Some Buried Memory": originally appeared in *The Tangled Muse*.

"Your Ghost on Glass": original.

"Letters from an Old Gent": original.

"Uncommon Places": sections I–XVIII originally appeared in *The Tangled Muse*; the remaining sections are original to this collection.

WILUM HOPFROG PUGMIRE
is an eccentric recluse who dreams in Seattle, Washington.
He is obsessed with H. P. Lovecraft,
a madness he hopes never to outgrow.
His goal as an author is to dwell forevermore
beneath Lovecraft's titan elbow, and the only readers
he strives to please are his fellow Lovecraftians.
His most recent books include *The Tangled Muse*
(Centipede Press, 2011), *Some Unknown Gulf of Night*
(Arcane Wisdom Press, 2011),
Depths of Dreams and Madness (Dark Regions Press, 2011),
and *The Strange Dark One—Tales of Nyarlathotep*
(Miskatonic River Press, forthcoming). He is currently
writing books with Maryanne K. Snyder
and Jeffrey Thomas.
He is the Queen of Eldritch Horror.